THE BIG FIFTY

THE BIG FIFTY

A Western Story

Johnny D. Boggs

Five Star • Waterville, Maine

Copyright © 2003 by Johnny D. Boggs

First Edition, Second Printing.

Published in 2003 in conjunction with
Golden West Literary Agency.

Set in 11 pt. Plantin by Minnie B. Raven.

Printed in the United States on permanent paper.

Library of Congress Cataloging-in-Publication Data

Boggs, Johnny D.
    The Big Fifty : a western story / by Johnny D. Boggs.
        p. cm.
    ISBN 0-7862-3782-1 (hc : alk. paper)
    I. Title.
PS3552.O4375 B54 2003
    813'.54—dc21   2002068964

For Mike Goldman, an old pal;
and Jack Smith Boggs, my son,
born while I was finishing this novel

Chapter One

Rifle in hand, he bellied up the collapsed side of an arroyo and stared at the swaying brown ocean before him. The scene took Coady McIlvain's breath away. Hundreds, no thousands, of buffalo had cut through the tall-grass prairie with the efficiency of one of those mechanized reapers produced by the McCormick Harvesting Machine Company he had heard about—not that he ever cared much for farmers or their equipment. No, as a scout and a hunter, in fact one of the best ever to fork a horse or pull a trigger, James Coady McIlvain had little use for farmers.

He had some hunting to do this fine spring morning.

The great shaggy beasts mulled about, chewing their cuds, grazing, bawling like a herd of Jersey cows. Well, maybe not a bunch of milch cows. Coady McIlvain had never heard tell of a herd of cattle this big, not in Kansas anyway. As far as he could see, buffalo blotted out the prairie. In his years on the border, he had seen some big herds, but nothing like this. He lay still, barely breathing, and studied the horizon for any signs of Indians, although the thought of running into any Kiowas or Cheyennes didn't scare him—least ways, not as long as he had his Sharps rifle and a bandoleer of true-shooting cartridges—but it paid to be careful. He hadn't lived as long as he had acting foolishly.

Nothing but buffalo.

He smiled then, breathing easier, and drew his .50-caliber Sharps closer, checked the breech, pulled off his leather gauntlet, wet the tip of his pointer finger, and rubbed it on the sight at the top of the long barrel. He did that with the practice of a veteran

7

to cut down on glare, and for luck. By nature, buffalo runners were a superstitious lot, and he was no exception. He removed his weather-beaten Boss of the Plains, placed it crown down by his side, and brushed the long, sandy bangs out of his eyes.

For the next ten minutes, the steely-eyed hunter studied the herd. Find the leader, he told himself, drop him first and the buffalo won't stampede. He'd have himself a stand, one of the best ever, maybe even top that record he set a few years back when he killed two hundred and seventy-nine in one sitting, a feat that had even impressed his good friend and fellow border man, William F. Cody. Yeah, Buffalo Bill would be jealous when he heard about this day, the young hunter thought, smiling in satisfaction.

He spotted the leader a second later, a big cuss still shedding his winter coat, birds dancing on his back, pecking away at ticks and fleas. The old bull's beard almost dragged the ground as he snorted and pawed the earth. High-humped, standing six feet at the shoulders, weighing probably a ton, the leviathan sported battle-scarred horns and flesh. His hide wouldn't fetch top price, but he needed to be eliminated first to thwart a run. Yes, this was the leader. Drop him, and the rest of the herd would stand around dumbly and get slaughtered.

It almost seemed a shame, he thought, to kill an animal this magnificent, a herd this stunning, but the vultures and wolves would appreciate the meat he would leave behind, and he would enjoy eating rump and tongue tonight. Besides, buffalo hides were fetching ten bits per over in Dodge City, so after today's slaughter Coady McIlvain would have himself a right smart of money.

He brought the stock of the Sharps Big Fifty to his shoulder, thumbed back the hammer, and pressed his finger against the trigger. Right between the eyes, he told himself, let out a breath, and started to squeeze.

★ ★ ★ ★ ★

"Coady, what the Sam Hill are you doin'?"

Twelve-year-old Coady McIlvain dropped the tobacco stick and jerked to his feet, brushing off his trousers and looking sheepish in his mother's garden as he found his watching father. He felt the rushing blood, knew he was blushing from embarrassment, as his pa just shook his head and said: "Beans ain't gonna get planted that way, Son. Best hurry up and finish, 'cause I got another chore to saddle on you once you're done here."

Coady mumbled a—"Yes, sir."—and dropped his head as his father strode away. Caught daydreaming again, confound the luck, playing buffalo hunter rather than dropping seeds in Kansas earth. At best, this evening his sisters would bedevil him till bedtime after hearing Pa tell Mama about the incident. At worst, Pa would tan his hide in the barn before washing up for supper and scold Coady for slacking off with his chores. Come to think of it, a whipping might be better than hearing those demonic snickers from his sisters.

He grabbed the sack of bean seeds in his left hand, the tobacco stick in his right, and started walking, head still down, between the recently plowed rows. Methodically he used one end of the well-cured stick to poke holes in the fresh sod, into which he dropped a few seeds, then covered them with his dusty brogans. As far back as he could remember, the tobacco stick had been both tool and toy. He could recall the hot days in Scotland County, North Carolina, when his father, uncles, and older nephews would work the fields. A handful of workers chopped down the stalks, split them with a small knife to a few inches above the base, and tossed them to the side. Others loaded seven or eight stalks onto each stick, securing them with twine, before hauling the load to the barn to be hung and flue-cured. Hard, sweaty, messy work, but Coady, too young to participate in the fields and barn, certainly admired those tobacco sticks, four feet long or more, hard as iron from years in the fields and hot curing barns.

He grabbed a stick when he was four years old, used it to beat down weeds, make noise, dig holes. Once he even clobbered a bobcat that got into a little row with the family dog, Fletcher.

That had been after the war—the "recent unpleasant-ness", his mother called it. Coady was too young to re-member anything about the War Between the States. Brent McIlvain had worn the gray, serving with the Pee Dee Ri-fles, and Coady never met his father until after Robert E. Lee surrendered to now President Ulysses S. Grant. Back home, McIlvain hung up his rifle, except for hunting, and started with the plow again as if nothing had happened. Cotton remained the king cash crop in the South, but the McIlvains couldn't do much on thirty-two acres—about half of that piney woods—so they grew tobacco, cured it in the barn, and hauled it across the border to Cheraw to sell, keeping just enough for the men folk to turn into plugs to be chewed, or stuffed in their pipes, or, later, once ciga-rettes became fashionable, rolled in store-bought papers or thin cornhusks.

Brent McIlvain never spoke of the war, but, like many former Confederates, he brooded, watching carpetbaggers and the Reconstruction government make things tight for Southerners. The soil was playing out, and, after two con-secutive failed crops, McIlvain looked West. The late Mr. Lincoln's Homestead Act of 1862 allowed citizens, or in-tended citizens, to lay claim to any unclaimed, surveyed public land up to one hundred and sixty acres. All they had to do was pay a pittance upon registering, and work and improve the land for five years.

A quarter section must have seemed like half the world to a poor Carolina sodbuster trying to make a living on thirty-two acres of worn-out sand, so in the spring of 1868 Brent McIlvain sold his farm to his brother-in-law, Silas Coady, loaded up a rickety old farm wagon, and lit a shuck for Kansas. They settled about fifteen miles northeast of Fort Dodge, the new post that had been established at the end of the war on the Arkansas River to guard the Santa Fé Trail.

Western Kansas—a gently rolling expanse of prairie with nary a tree to block that bitter winter wind or blistering summer sun—felt, looked, and acted nothing like southern North Carolina. It took a while for the McIlvains to adjust, except Brent McIlvain, who, with tobacco farming out of the question in this climate, immediately began clearing fields and learning all he could about growing hay and wheat. The rest of the family clung to their Southern ties. Coady's mother brought the family Bible, pretty much keeping it clutched against her chest during the fourteen hundred mile trek. His sisters, Lois, two years older, and Faye, five years older, brought their favorite dolls. James Coady McIlvain, then only seven, grabbed a tobacco stick.

Imagination could transform that rough-hewn piece of timber into anything, saber or stallion, fishing pole or spyglass, banjo or rifle. As the years passed, the family grew to like their new surroundings—most of them, that is. His mother, Liz, still read the Bible daily, but no longer called Scotland County home. Home had become a sod house and hardscrabble barn in Ford County. Lois and Faye had new dolls, and Brent McIlvain sold hay and grain to the Army at Fort Dodge and did a mite of trading in the bawdy town that had sprung up nearby.

Coady had also forgotten much about North Carolina, but he kept his tobacco stick. Today, it had been a .50-caliber Sharps rifle, now demoted to a hoe. He sighed. Coady always dreaded farm work.

Twelve-year-olds wanted adventure, not the drudgery to be found milking cows, planting gardens, reaping hay, or pounding his stick against his father's hay rake. Lately his appetite had been whetted by a handful of thin novels published by Beadle's Half-Dime Library. Earlier that spring, a traveler on the Santa Fé Trail had dropped by the McIlvain homestead looking for a contrary mule that had run off. Coady and his father helped the man find the jenny, and, as payment—although Coady's father said there was no need—the stranger left behind a handful of five-penny dreadfuls.

His father didn't hold much truck with fiction, especially the muck churned out by Beadle's hacks, and frowned upon the gift, especially when Coady started devouring them. According to the law of Brent McIlvain, the boy should bury his nose in a MCGUFFEY'S READER, but Coady's mother thought it good that her son read so eagerly. As long as he did his chores and read a passage from the Bible each night—along with the MCGUFFEY'S schoolbooks—Coady could read all about Buffalo Bill Cody's adventures.

THE HAUNTED VALLEY; OR, A LEAF FROM A HUNTER'S LIFE . . . KANSAS KING; OR, THE RED RIGHT HAND . . . THE PEARL OF THE PRAIRIES; OR, THE SCOUT AND THE RENEGADE—all of them managed to take Coady far from the McIlvain farm. He would finish one and light into another, rereading them till he knew plots and dialogue by heart. His favorite was DEADLY EYE; OR, THE UNKNOWN SCOUT, in which William F. "Buffalo Bill" Cody detailed various hunting expeditions in Kansas, killing buffalo after buffalo with a .50-

caliber Springfield rifle he named "Lucretia Borgia", and his shooting match in Omaha against "The Unknown Scout", a legendary buffalo runner who never missed with his Sharps Big Fifty.

Now Coady McIlvain loved Buffalo Bill Cody. After all, they carried the same name although spelled differently (Coady had been christened with his mother's maiden name), and he absolutely believed everything Buffalo Bill wrote to be the gospel truth. "The Unknown Scout", however, and his Sharps rifle simply mesmerized the young boy.

His dad had carried a Sharps in the war, even said—in one of his rare stories about the "unpleasantness"—he plucked it off a dead Yankee, and hung it over the front door of their home, but plow handles fit his hands better than a long-barreled rifle, and the weapon had been left behind with Coady's Uncle Silas.

By that spring of 1873, Dodge City had started to boom with buffalo hunters, called runners out on the Kansas plains, and the Sharps rifle was fast becoming their weapon of choice. Indians said the gun could shoot today and kill tomorrow, and it definitely packed a wallop. In DEADLY EYE; OR, THE UNKNOWN SCOUT, after tying the scout in the shooting match in Omaha, Buffalo Bill takes to the border with "The Unknown Scout", and they go after buffalo. After each sharpshooter has dropped two hundred and seventy-six buffalo without a miss, the great border man kills number two hundred seventy-seven. He stands up, stares at "The Unknown Scout", and watches him aim.

POW! roared The Unknown Scout's Big Fifty, but, to my astonishment, no buffalo fell, and the herd stampeded, churning up dust so thick we no longer could see the rising Rocky Mountains in the distance. I offered my gauntleted hand, and helped the man with the deadly eye to his feet. As he reloaded, I ejaculated: "Sir, I have bested you at last! But know this, my good man, that you are a fine competitor and one of the greatest shots I have ever witnessed."

He said nothing, simply shoved his killing instrument into a scabbard, mounted his trusty steed, and galloped into the dust without a word. Not wishing our friendship to end over some silly hunting match, I leaped into the saddle, Lucretia Borgia at the ready, and loped after this strange *hombre*.

I located him three quarters of a mile distant, sitting in the saddle, but staring at a body in the tall Kansas grass. When I rode to his side, I almost gasped. Lying below was the noted red devil, Iron Heart, a ghastly hole in his forehead, long rifle still clutched in his evil hands.

" 'Twas not a buffalo I was aiming at, my friend," The Unknown Scout told me, "but this butcher. And I am glad to have lost our match in order to save you."

"By jingo," roared I, "not half as glad as I! I propose that your last shot struck its mark, as your aim was true as proved by the body of this cowardly fiend who has wreaked havoc on good people near and far."

"No," replied the strange man, "our bet was to see who could kill the most buffalo without a miss or second shot, and today that was you, Buffalo Bill." There was a glitter in his eye, however, as he concluded: "But perhaps one day we shall meet again."

Hunting buffalo, now that was the calling of adventurers—not farming. The last time Coady had been in Dodge City, he had seen hides stacked taller than his father beside the railroad tracks, waiting to be shipped back East. He remembered sitting transfixed in the back of his father's wagon, staring at those long-haired men with big hats, greasy buckskins, and rifles always at the ready: Springfields, Remingtons, Enfields, but mostly Sharpses.

"Coady!" he heard his father calling. "You finished yet?"

He kicked dirt over the last hole of bean seeds, and sprinted to the barn, answering his father as he ran, clutching the old tobacco stick in both hands. He entered the barn with apprehension, because Pa could wield a razor strop that bit like blazes, and Coady probably deserved a whipping after playing in the garden when he should have been working.

"Got the beans planted?" his father asked without looking up, inspecting some harness.

"Yes, sir."

"You filled up the box?"

"Yes," he answered. He had done that, too—filled up the box with dried buffalo dung—about the only thing that would burn out here. It made him a little sad that the closest he'd ever get to hunting buffalo would be picking up their droppings so his mother could cook.

"And you milked Jessie?"

Jessie was their Jersey cow. He had done that, too. Maybe he wasn't about to get a whipping.

"All right," his father said. "I'm goin' to town to pick up that cultivator. Figured you might wanna tag along and help me out some." Brent McIlvain's blue eyes glimmered, and Coady knew his father was in a good mood, after all. "You can bring your rifle with us," he said, pointing at the tobacco stick.

"Oh, Pa," Coady moaned.

Chapter Two

To a devout Methodist like Liz McIlvain, Dodge City seemed ten times worse than Gomorrah. Lots of folks shared her views. Before the arrival of the Atchison, Topeka, and Santa Fé in 1872, the wicked little town had been called Buffalo City. The post office rejected the name, and the collection of huts, *jacales,* and flimsily built wooden buildings became Dodge City. It had a population of five hundred in 1872. A year later, that had ballooned to four thousand, although two-thirds of those had to be transient buffalo men. Saloons, gambling dens, and cribs began occupying the lots, and owlhoots, drunks, and tinhorns began filling the cemetery locals took to calling Boothill.

Liz McIlvain never wanted her son to go to town, but her husband assured her they would head straight to Zimmermann's Hardware Store on Front Street, load the cultivator in the wagon, and come home. It might be night before they reached home, Brent told her, but the moon would be full. They'd be all right.

"Keep your britches on," Coady heard his father tell him before tossing a sack of sandwiches underneath the seat and crawling aboard the wagon. "We'll get there directly." He blew a kiss to Liz and Coady's sisters, flicked the reins, and grinned at his eager son.

Frederick C. Zimmermann didn't just operate a hardware store; he sold guns. Born in Prussia, he apprenticed under a gunsmith in Paris before immigrating to New York in 1863. A few years later, he was working in Kit Carson,

Colorado, before setting up shop in Dodge City in June of 1872. Sure, Zimmermann's Hardware Store stocked cultivators, plows, shovels, and hammers, but the Prussian also had scores of Winchesters, Springfields, Colts, and Remingtons. Zimmermann and J. C. Lindley of Hays City became the two most popular men in Kansas among buffalo hunters because they also did business with the Sharps Rifle Manufacturing Company of Hartford, Connecticut and kept a steady supply of those choice longarms on hand.

Philadelphian Christian Sharps invented his single-shot, breech-loading rifle in 1848, and the high-powered weapon quickly gained high marks among hunters, soldiers, and riflemen. John Brown and his raiders carried Sharps carbines when they attacked the arsenal at Harpers Ferry, Virginia in 1859, and the rifle became synonymous with Union sharpshooters during the Civil War after Colonel Hiram Berdan's marksmen used scope-fitted Sharps with deadly effect. The weapon was easy to operate, and three times as fast as any muzzleloader. You just pulled down the lever to open the breech, shoved in a cartridge, pushed up the lever to close the breech, cocked, aimed, and fired.

The New Model 1863, in .52-caliber, was introduced for the Army during the war, and the Sporting Rifle, in .40-50, .40-70, .44-77 and .50-70 Government, came out in 1868. There were other calibers as well. When buffalo hides became a profitable venture around 1871, hunters soon came to trust the old reliable rifle, making .50-calibers the first choice of runners because of range and knockdown power. That's what "The Unknown Scout" had used to save Buffalo Bill's life. Coady McIlvain couldn't wait to see the weapons Zimmermann had in stock. He knew his father wouldn't let him hold one, but maybe, if Zimmermann and Pa weren't looking, he could touch one.

Anyone living in western Kansas before 1873 had likely seen buffalo, and Coady was no exception. His father had stampeded a herd out of the hayfield their first summer in Kansas, and had forced a drunken hunter and skinner off their property in early March. Coady had seen a few bulls, cows, and calves, but nothing like the great herds he heard and read about. Anyone living in western Kansas after 1873, however, might only see pictures of the huge, slow animals or listen to big windies from out-of-work hunters and skinners. In a few short years, the Kansas herd had been all but exterminated.

Sun-bleached bones sprouted among the wildflowers like something his father might have planted, littering the old slaughtering grounds near the bumpy road that stretched from the McIlvain farm to the Santa Fé Trail. Buffalo skulls resembled marble tombstones; rib cages rose like aspen saplings in winter. Fields of white, like this one, had become common across the state. Butchery, white leaders like General Philip Sheridan and Dodge City entrepreneur Charles Rath called it, in the name of progress. Kill off the buffalo, kill off the Plains Indians who depended on the animals for just about everything in their culture—food, tools, shelter, clothing. The sight of the bones made Coady's heart sink, but his father nodded in satisfaction when they came across a group of sunburned men filling two mule-pulled wagons with bones.

In his last trip to Dodge City, sometime in October, Coady had heard one buffalo runner remark that "the lowest sort of man is one of 'em bone pilgrims." His father didn't agree, so he greeted the bone gatherers with a friendly—"Good mornin'."—while Coady refused to make eye contact with any of that sorry-looking lot. "They turn the bones into fertilizer," his father had said. "Farmers need fertilizer." About the only thing Coady could say to that was that maybe buffalo fertilizer wouldn't smell as bad as what he usually had to pile on the Kemp's manure spreader back home.

Coady gripped his tobacco stick harder, staring ahead at the emptiness. The herds would be all gone by the time he grew up. He let out a sigh and tried to take his mind off the disappointment, tapping out a mental tune with his stick on the floor of the wagon until his father told him to quit that racket.

A second later, Coady's life changed.

The Indians, a mixed raiding party of Comanches and Kiowas, simply appeared on the plains. One second, the McIlvains had been staring into Kansas emptiness, and the next they saw a bunch of screaming, painted warriors. They had been hiding in a shallow ravine, a patrol of cavalry troopers from Fort Dodge would later deduce, probably waiting for the right moment to kill and scalp the bone hunters—which they did—when one of them became eager to steal the McIlvain mules, bolted up the ravine, and started the ball.

"Jump!" Brent McIlvain roared, but never gave his son the chance. Pulling back the reins with one hand, he pushed Coady over the side of the wagon with his other giant, calloused hand, set the brake, and reached for the shotgun he kept under the seat beside the sack of sandwiches Liz McIlvain had fixed. Coady, still clutching his toy stick, landed with a *thud*. "Run!" his father shouted. "Run, Coady, and don't look back!" He started to yell something else, but the words were lost among the whooping Comanches and Kiowas, thundering hoofs, and gunfire.

Not that Coady heard or understood anything anyway. He was struck dumb, shocked, but the sight of the Indians loping right at him got his feet working, and he sprinted through the tall grass, biting his lip, crying, too scared to pray, absently gripping the tobacco stick harder and harder as he ran.

Brent McIlvain had charged one barrel of his shotgun with birdshot, the other with buck and ball, and he let loose with both loads simultaneously, but his lead struck only air. With a determined grimace, he flipped the shotgun, caught the hot barrels, and prepared to swing it like some medieval battle axe at the closest brave, only an arrow sliced through his left calf, and he dropped the weapon and screamed, limping across the driver's box. Another Indian raced by and struck him across the face with his bow, and McIlvain flipped over the wagon's side to land where his son had fallen just seconds earlier.

Being so close to what passed for civilization in that part of the country—near Fort Dodge and the United States Army, in spitting distance of the bustling Santa Fé Trail and Atchison, Topeka, and Santa Fé tracks, and only ten miles from Dodge City and its horde of gunmen and sharpshooters—no one expected any Indian trouble. Brent McIlvain had carried only a muzzle-loading shotgun, likely figuring to use it only if he came across a covey of quail or maybe an antelope. The gents loading bones into wagons left Dodge armed with a few cap-and-ball pistols and one .52-caliber Hall Model carbine with a busted stock. Most of the Indians carried bows and arrows, but could turn a body into a pincushion in the time a skilled marksman could get off a couple of rounds with a muzzleloader, or empty a revolver. The fight was over almost before it started. The whites were outnumbered and sorely mismatched.

Coady heard the popping of weapons as most of the warriors swarmed the bone collectors. The sounds snapped him from his panic, and he spun around, gasping at his father on the ground. "Pa!" he shouted, and ran back to help.

The Comanche who had taken first coup by slapping Brent McIlvain with his bow reined up his pinto, spun around, and galloped back to finish the job. A wiry man of maybe thirty, with a face scarred by the white man's smallpox and two fingers missing on his left hand, he wore breechcloth, bone breastplate, moccasins, beaded sheath and cougar-skin quiver, with his long, black braids wrapped in otter skins. Coady saw the Indian smile a broken-toothed grin as he halted beside the wagon and casually fetch an arrow from the quiver and position it, draw the bowstring tight, and send the arrow into his father's back with such force that the feathered shaft vibrated.

"No!" Coady screamed as his father sank into the grass, but his shrieks and tears again were lost. If the Comanche brave heard, he paid no attention, simply slid off the back of the pinto, slipped a curved buffalo bone knife from the fancy sheath, and squatted beside the prone body of Brent McIlvain. Coady tried to find extra energy to reach his father in time. No longer did he dream about hunting buffalo and adventure, no longer did he dread the humdrum but hard life on the McIlvains' quarter section of prime Kansas farmland. The only thing the boy wanted was to save his father from an ugly, brutal death. With practiced skill, the grinning Comanche sliced with the knife across the top of Brent McIlvain's head, sheathed the weapon, gripped McIlvain's sandy hair, and jerked, ripping off a section of scalp with a sickening sucking sound. Brent McIlvain neither moved nor groaned. Yelling some guttural chant, the warrior raised the bloody trophy over his head, maybe to show it off to his comrades committing their own depredations a few rods away.

That's when Coady McIlvain struck him a blow that broke the tobacco stick and the warrior's nose.

The Indian fell back against the right front wheel of the wagon, blood spurting, tears welling in his eyes. Coady dropped the busted stick and looked at his still father, then at the Indian, whose screams caused the mules to bray. With a look of hatred, the Comanche reached for his knife, and Coady, too late to save his father, turned to run again.

Gunfire had ceased. The only sounds Coady now heard were the Indians' whoops, the mules' wails, and the pounding of unshod hoofs behind him. While many warriors continued mutilating the bodies of the seven dead men from Dodge City, others collected the livestock, and a few set the bone wagons on fire. This battle was over, except for the ugly Comanche who had just gotten his nose broken by a twelve-year-old swinging a tobacco stick.

Running, the boy cried—not for himself, mind you, but for his father, and his mother and sisters. Liz, Lois, and Faye McIlvain would never see him and Pa again, at least not alive. And if they saw them in death . . . ? He couldn't imagine how heart-broken that would leave his family, for he had just seen his father scalped and couldn't believe it himself. The rapidly approaching Comanche made Coady's legs churn harder. He was fast for his size, but twelve-year-olds can't outrun any Comanche on horseback, and the angry, hurting, bleeding brave caught up with his attacker quickly.

Coady screamed as the pinto raced beside him, tried to run harder, but the Indian lifted the boy by his collar and dashed him against the stallion's side. The move should have broken Coady's back or neck, but the pinto stumbled at the last second, and the Comanche, trying not to be thrown, couldn't apply the deadly force needed, not that it mattered.

The boy lay spread-eagled, lungs trying to remember how to work again, his own nose bleeding, staring blankly, finally recalling how to pray. Through vision blurred from tears and pain, he made out the ugly Comanche, who dropped from the lathered horse, knelt, whipped out the ugly knife, and placed the bloody blade against Coady's throat.

Chapter Three

That's pretty much the story as it was related to me, Dylan Griffith, quite a spell later. I can't exactly tell you where I was at the time of what became known as The McIlvain Massacre (although there were only two McIlvains involved and seven buffalo bone haulers). To be truthful, Cheyennes, Kiowas, and some Arapahoes and Comanches were becoming quite active in their attacks against buffalo men and settlers, and The McIlvain Massacre simply blended in with the Warren scalping and a slew of other bloody affairs. I can tell you what I was doing that spring of '73, but first should provide some background about your narrator.

I arrived in Dodge City during the last bite of winter, a tramp printer looking for a new place to dirty my fingernails with ink. In a badly beaten carpetbag, I carried the tools of my trade—assorted pieces of lead type, souvenirs mostly, and one National Typographical Union traveling card— along with extra long johns, socks, two shirts, handkerchiefs, case for my wire spectacles, pewter flask, toilet kit, Navy Colt converted to take brass cartridges, a copy of THE CELEBRATED JUMPING FROG OF CALA-VERAS COUNTY, AND OTHER SKETCHES, and one deck of Lawrence and Cohen playing cards, so new the edges of those paste cards felt sharp as needles.

From the depot, I wandered in a miserable February wind toward the collection of tents south of the railroad tracks but north of the Santa Fé Trail for the purpose of warming my tonsils and refilling my empty flask, thinking that refreshments in the tents and dug-outs would come a mite cheaper than in the frame buildings with silly façades popping up along Front Street. At Hoover & McDonald's canvas watering hole, I topped my flask with what some might say passed for whisky, had a couple of shots of forty-rod rotgut, and, while wiping dust off my eyeglasses with a handkerchief, asked a chipper man with rheumy eyes for directions to a print shop or newspaper. With a snort, he suggested I catch the next eastbound to Topeka.

There you have it. Four thousand souls in Dodge, but nary a newspaper. I had arrived a year or two early to set type, but that didn't bother me in the least. I had many other skills that could add to my poke, which sometimes paid better than a dollar per thousand ems of set type. Those rheumy eyes belonging to my first source brightened when I broke out my deck of cards, and I invited him to join me in a game, but seven dollars and forty-three cents later, the man retired for the night with one final snort.

My luck held over the next few months, and by spring I resided in George Cox's and F. W. Boyd's Dodge House on Front Street, taking my meals at the adjoining restaurant and watering hole, and earning my rent at James Hanrahan's saloon a few lots west.

When winter broke, the hide men started venturing out in search of buffalo as they did each spring, but this year many returned all too soon, expressing concern that there just weren't any buffalo to be found north of the Arkansas River, at least not enough for a man to make a living. Some took their chances south of the Arkansas but north of the Cimarron, although this had once been designated Indian country, but other less brave souls stayed in Dodge and gambled. More often than not, when they matched cards against me, they lost.

Such was the case in early April at Hanrahan's when I dealt a friendly game of five-card draw around a table where sat a drummer from St. Louis, a wheezing Southerner with a big mustache and potbelly, a soft-spoken, mustached man in a gray derby, James Hanrahan himself, and two men in dire need of baths. The latter two called themselves Pattison and Wheatley, buffalo runners who did their own hunting and skinning, a comment that caused Derby to chuckle heartily. By mid-afternoon, Derby was up a considerable sum, much more than me although I had held my own, but while Pattison and Wheatley overlooked Derby's wins, they shot chilling looks each time I raked in a pot.

Hanrahan had called it quits for the day, Wheatley had just gone bust, and Drummer had folded after a series of raises before the draw, and I dealt two cards to Pattison, three to Derby, three to Big Mustache, and one to myself. The first bet belonged to Pattison, who checked. Derby bet two dollars, Big Mustache folded, and I called. Pattison tossed in a couple of coins, then pushed in a stack of greenbacks.

"Raise you fifty," he said, and Wheatley joined his coyote laugh.

"I've seen men shot for checking and raising," Derby said, but called the bet anyway.

"It's not the way gentlemen play," I added, bet fifty and raised fifty, just on principle.

Neither Pattison nor Wheatley cared much for that, but they raised their last twenty, and Derby folded with a sigh. Poker is business, nothing more, so I called Pattison, and raised him fifty more.

He almost vomited. "I ain't got no more," Pattison said with an oath.

Derby chuckled again, and said to me: "If I had more confidence in a pair of treys, I might have done the same thing." After pushing back his hat, he told the stinking buffalo man: "Table stakes, gent. Call him, or get out of the game."

"But I got a full house, queens over kings. Ain't no way he's got me beat."

"Then put fifty dollars in the pot, or it's his," Big Mustache said while rolling himself a smoke.

"I ain't got fifty dollars."

"Then you have to fold," Drummer told him.

Me? I kept quiet, knowing Pattison and Wheatley didn't care much for me. That's when Wheatley suggested his partner bet the rifle he kept cradled across his lap.

"No," Pattison snapped back. "It's mine, and I ain't bettin' it."

I had noticed the rifle before the reeking gents joined our game. "It's a Sharps, isn't it?" I said.

They eyed me suspiciously, but both nodded. I asked respectfully if I could look at it. Pattison licked his lips, but, after a nudge from Wheatley, hefted the long rifle over the table and passed it to me. When I almost dropped it, both men laughed. "Must weigh twelve to fourteen pounds," I said, and the two men nodded in silence.

Big Mustache whistled and said: "That's a right handsome piece. Fifty caliber?"

The hide men's heads bobbed in rhythm. "Set trigger, too," Derby commented, now really wishing he hadn't folded, and I let him examine the weapon while I cleaned the lenses on my spectacles. He flipped up the tang sight affixed between the hammer and stock. "What's the barrel length, thirty, thirty-two inches?"

The men nodded once more, although they didn't answer Derby's question. He didn't mind. "Octagonal barrel, case-hardened frame, silver front sight. Yes, sir, this is a fine rifle. Bet you could kill many a buffalo with this masterpiece."

"If there were any more buffalo," Wheatley said dryly.

"You know yer weapons," Big Mustache, unlit quirly dangling in his lips, told Derby, who didn't have the look of a marksman, but then neither did I, and definitely not Wheatley and Pattison.

"I've been around them," Derby said before handing me the weapon, which I returned to its owners.

Big Mustache lit his smoke, and drawled: "Rifle like that's worth fifty dollars, I warrant. Them double triggers alone cost four extra dollars, special order. Yup, that's some gun." He knew his weapons, too.

I had to agree. "I'll price it at sixty dollars," I told the gamblers. "That's more than fair. Put your Sharps in the pot, and I'll add ten dollars."

Pattison wet his lips. Wheatley nudged him, but the rifle disappeared underneath the table, resting on his thighs once again.

"Take that bet," Wheatley said. "Put the rifle in the pot. You got him beat. He ain't got your full house beat. He's bluffin'."

"I ain't sure," Pattison said sheepishly.

"Bet him!" Wheatley roared.

"No," his partner screamed, and tossed his cards onto the deadwood. "It's yourn."

His partner swore again, and, as I pulled in the collection of greenbacks, coins, and chips, Wheatley reached across the table and grabbed my winning hand before I could stop him.

He let go with a litany of curses when he saw my two

pair, tens over fives, and almost slapped his partner for folding the winning hand. I didn't say anything as I passed the deal to Drummer, stacked my money in silence, waiting for the pair to take their Big Fifty and wander to another saloon to lift their spirits, if they could find enough change between them for the price of two whiskies. When they hadn't left by the time Drummer passed the cards for me to cut, I said I'd stand them to a drink before they took their leave.

Insulted, Pattison leaped up, almost overturning the table. I barely moved, but the Colt I held underneath the table was now cocked and pointed at Pattison's gut.

"You think you're pretty slick with them cards, Mister Four Eyes," Pattison said. "Well, how 'bouts we try another game?"

"Such as?" Derby asked.

That stopped them, but I glanced at the beautiful Sharps rifle, lowered the hammer on my Colt, and suggested: "A shooting match . . . for the Sharps?"

Looking at my eyeglasses, Wheatley and Pattison couldn't hide their grins. "Right," Pattison said. "You beat me, you keep this here Sharps. If I win, I take that pot you just won." Fifteen minutes later, we stood on the outskirts south of town with quite a crowd of followers, including Derby, Hanrahan, and Big Mustache. Hanrahan gave Big Mustache two empty whisky bottles, but Big Mustache saw maybe a taste left in one of them so he sucked it dry before wobbling a hundred yards to an abandoned wagon. He set both bottles on the rotting seat and came back to the crowd, out of breath from the afternoon jaunt. Hanrahan handed him a mug of beer, which he downed in three gulps and mumbled a thank you.

"First one who misses, loses," Hanrahan said.

I didn't take part in the betting going on behind me. Derby flipped a coin for first shot, and Pattison won. When Wheatley pulled a pair of rest sticks from a canvas bag, however, Big Mustache, refreshed by his beer, shook his head and jerked the sticks out of Wheatley's hands. "No shootin' sticks," he said.

I felt like asking Big Mustache who put him in charge, but the way he glared at Pattison and Wheatley made me accept his authority. Pattison pulled a two-and-a-half-inch brass cartridge from his vest pocket, chambered the round in the Sharps, and aimed. Onlookers fell silent until the Big Fifty boomed, and the bottle on the left shattered. Smug and satisfied, Pattison passed the rifle to me, and Wheatley handed me another .50-90 cartridge.

"Good luck, Four Eyes," he said, without meaning it.

Time for a confession. The .50-caliber Sharps rifle Brent McIlvain had brought home from the War of the Rebellion and sold to his brother-in-law before lighting out West could very well have belonged to a friend of mine. I had served in Colonel Hiram Berdan's U.S. Sharpshooters at Seven Pines . . . Gettysburg . . . all through the war. "Snakes in the grass", Johnny Rebs called us. To join that Federal unit, I put ten consecutive balls within three inches of the bull's eye at two hundred yards. Of course, that had been twelve years earlier, and my now forty-year-old eyes had been failing me for some time, common for any type-setter.

I hit my mark, though, which caused a ripple of curses and chuckles from the crowd, and blank looks from Pattison and Wheatley. "Scratch shot," Pattison said as I put the Sharps back in his hands. Money exchanged hands between the bettors while Hanrahan told Big Mustache: "Well, Cuthbert, guess I'd better fetch two more empties for you to take out yonder."

Big Mustache sighed, but perked up when I said: "Why bother?"

"What do you mean?" Derby asked.

I gestured toward the bottle I had hit. The base had vanished, but the neck miraculously dropped onto the seat and stood straight up, glistening in the sun, which was about all we could make out from a hundred yards. It wasn't much of a target, but would definitely make things interesting.

"You couldn't hit that," said a fat woman with unkempt red hair and unkempt face. "Nobody could shoot that good."

"If we both miss, Cuthbert can take out two more bottles," I offered.

I could tell Pattison didn't like it—knew he was outclassed—but he was game and not about to back down. When he missed, no one could blame him, and he handed me the rifle knowing he had lost. He had more confidence than I really had in myself, but my shot proved true and the bottleneck disintegrated.

That prompted a celebration, but Wheatley started fussing, saying that I had tricked them, that my glasses weren't real, that I was nothing more than a confidence man. Derby fetched my glasses and looked through them, laughed, and handed them back to me as he pinched the bridge of his nose.

"Those lenses are mighty strong," he said, so Wheatley started complaining that my glasses gave me an unfair advantage. No one listened to him.

"Drinks on the house!" Hanrahan roared, and we made our way back to Front Street. The thought of a free drink eased Pattison's and Wheatley's pain, and they disappeared. I wouldn't see the two again for another year.

I hefted my new Sharps and followed the dust to Dodge City proper, but Derby stopped me and asked: "Reckon you don't want to sell that Sharps, do you?"

"Afraid not," I answered.

"Well, good shooting," he said, and offered his hand. "Bat Masterson."

"Dylan Griffith."

He turned to catch up with the whisky stampede, and I joined in only to be stopped by Big Mustache.

"Name's Cuthbert Jenkins," he said, "and I gots a proposition for you, son."

I gave him my name, and waited for this silver-headed, bowlegged man in buckskins with the molasses drawl to make his pitch. "A man who shoots as good as you," he said, "ought to be runnin' buffler. That's me trade," he went on. "And I'm of mind to take on a partner."

"I might have considered it," I told him, "but it looks like the buffalo business has gone bust. The herd's played out."

"Not south of the Arkansas . . . at least, not yet."

We walked while we talked, although I admit my gait had slowed considerably. Tramp printers are vagabonds, and I had the itch to travel and experience new things. At least, that's what I had been telling myself for years. My journeys as a tramp printer carried me across the frontier, and my itch to see the elephant prevented me from becoming attached to any newspaper, any town, anyone—or so I thought at the time. I had lived many fine adventures, like the heroes in those silly novels Coady McIlvain had read.

In truth, however, I was a coward, running to forget, and often I could block out my past by trying new things. I didn't just set type and deal paste cards. Since the war, I had been a reporter, herded cattle, worked as a jehu on some stage line, tended store, swamped saloons, sold farm implements, taught school, served Taos Lightning, hunted, trapped, panned for gold. . . . Buffalo running caught my fancy.

Jenkins wanted a partner and a shooter, and I filled the bill. I wanted to light out again, and hides remained in demand back East. We shook hands before we entered Hanrahan's saloon, partners.

That explains why at the time of The McIlvain Massacre, I found myself south of the Arkansas River with a couple of wagons, four skinners, a cook, and my new partner and friend, Cuthbert Jenkins. So, while I was on the watch for Indian sign, Coady McIlvain was feeling a Comanche's knife against his throat.

Chapter Four

The Indian, you've probably already guessed, didn't kill Coady McIlvain, but only because another Comanche rode up and barked something. Ugly Face shouted back, waving his knife at the mounted warrior before gesturing at the petrified Coady and the Indian's own misshapen mess of a nose. Unmoved by Ugly Face's argument for revenge, Mounted Comanche spoke harsher, pointed one end of his bow at the raiding party and rising smoke, and waited.

Unable to understand the caustic exchanges, Coady still felt death lurking. All Ugly Face had to do was bring the blade down in one lethal swipe. Mounted Comanche could do nothing to prevent Coady's murder, but Ugly Face seemed to respect, or perhaps fear, the tall warrior on the paint horse. Ugly Face rose quickly, forgetting his tormentor, and Coady's head sank into the spring grass. The argument continued as the remaining warriors gathered with their plunder and scalps. When two braves laughed hysterically at Ugly Face's injury, Coady thought for sure he would be killed.

Mounted Comanche belted out a final phrase of harsh syllables, and Ugly Face angrily sheathed his knife, kicked at Coady's head, and stormed away in a huff, mounting his pinto to the heckles and laughs of his comrades. Coady knew his life had been spared, for the moment, by Mounted Comanche, yet he also felt keenly aware that he had made an enemy for life in Ugly Face, who clenched the hackamore with one hand and wiped blood from his face with the other.

Five years in Kansas had educated Coady on the ways of the frontier. He knew Indian raiding parties often took children captive, although a twelve-year-old boy was more likely to be killed and scalped. Briefly he thought he might be saved again, prayed the Indians would leave him behind—hadn't they inflicted enough grief on him by murdering his father? The stories he had heard and read about white captives forced into a life of hardship, indeed slavery, chilled him. He pulled himself to his feet and stood uneasily, like a spinning top on its last seconds upright. Mounted Comanche spoke to him urgently, a tone reminiscent of one his father used back on the farm, and Coady considered making a final break for freedom, although his legs might not co-operate.

Something must have flashed in his face, because the Indian leader grunted and the paint horse lunged in front of Coady, so close the boy lost his balance and landed on his backside. Mounted Comanche snapped at Coady, who scrambled to his feet and stood nervously, eyes darting every which way as he tried to pick and choose a plan. Too late, though, because the Comanche warrior leaned over, jerked Coady off his feet, dropped him belly-down between rider and withers, and kicked the horse into a trot, the other warriors following, all laughing except Ugly Face.

Coady started to squirm and kick, but Mounted Comanche stopped that by slapping the back of his prisoner's head. The Indian wore a ring, its large face facing the palm, and the impact of gold on bone had its desired effect. Coady yelped in pain and stopped moving. Instead, he cried silently as the horse moved into a canter, then a full lope, carrying Coady McIlvain south, away from the burning wagons and dead bodies, away from the life he had loathed but now terribly missed.

Only when the raiding party stopped to rest the horses after hours of hard traveling did Mounted Comanche allow Coady a more comfortable position. Sitting in front of his captor, Coady looked back, hoping to spot dust trails of his deliverers, but saw only ominous black clouds gathering from whence they had come. Rain, usually a farmer's blessing, would wash away the Indian trail. Coady would not be rescued.

They halted that night and butchered one of the McIlvain mules. The Indians sang, chanted, and enjoyed a familiar banter among one another, although Ugly Face sat by himself in the shadows, morose. The Kiowas spoke in a singsong, caustic melody that gave Coady a headache. He didn't see how anyone could understand their language. The Comanche dialect, although equally throaty, fell softer on Coady's ears, and he had already picked up a few words: *Kwahadi* and *puha*—he had no idea what either meant— *tuinéhpua,* which is what they called him, and what he assumed was the name of Mounted Comanche, Quanah.

Quanah stood taller than the others, glistening, black hair wrapped in long braids, his face painted black, his skin a hard copper, darker than any of his companions. He wore heavily beaded, long-fringed buckskins, bone earrings, and looked as menacing as any redskin villain ever to appear on the cover of a half-dime novel, yet many of his features seemed more white than Indian. The ring, Coady determined upon closer inspection, heralded the United States Military Academy Class of 1867, and likely came off some unfortunate young officer. A war trophy. Quanah's penetrating eyes, however, shone blue-gray, and Coady suspected the Comanche leader had some white blood coursing through his veins. Maybe that's why he had spared his life.

Pretty smart for a kid. Coady had no way of knowing this, but Quanah's mother had been a white girl abducted down in Texas in 1836. The Comanche war chief, later to be called Quanah Parker, was the half-breed son of Cynthia Ann Parker and Chief Peta Nocona. Quanah was only twenty-three or so at the time of The McIlvain Massacre but, among his people, had quickly become one of the most respected leaders of the Kwahadi band of Comanches, and, among settlers, one of the most feared warriors on the Southern Plains.

They didn't offer Coady any mule meat, not even water, that first night. Before going to sleep, one of the Kiowas tied Coady's hands and feet with rawhide strips that bit into his skin and almost cut off all circulation. For good measure, the Indian spit in the boy's face and popped his head before muttering something unintelligible and urinating beside the prisoner's bed. Coady bit his trembling lip to keep from crying, closed his eyes, and hoped, when he woke up the next morning, this would all have been a dream, his father would be alive and practically dragging him out of bed, yelling to get a move on and milk Jessie before breakfast.

At dawn, Quanah sliced through the ankle bindings with a knife and, leaving his hands tied, tossed Coady on the back of one of the stolen mules. They still gave him nothing to eat or drink, and pushed hard all that day. Storm clouds overtook the war party early that afternoon, and the party rode in a chilling rain. Coady shivered in the fierce wind, but lifted his sunburned face to catch raindrops with his tongue. He thought he saw Quanah smile at his actions, only he couldn't be certain.

That night they made camp in a blackjack grove, and Quanah at last let his prisoner eat. The Comanche opened a yellow parfleche, brilliantly painted with red circles and blue stars, and grunted, gesturing at the rawhide box's contents. When Coady gave him a blank look, Quanah pretended to be eating. Still Coady did not move, so the Indian reached into the parfleche, scooped out a handful of mush, and ate. Coady hesitated, but the smell overpowered him, and he crawled toward his captor and reached inside the smelly square box. He thought of his mother, how she would scold him for eating with his fingers, but what could he do? He sniffed a pinch of the strange substance first, then dropped some on his tongue. Meat of some kind, he guessed, mixed with fat and dried berries. Old-timers back in Dodge City said Indians ate all sorts of things, including dog but never fish, and Coady had seen with his own eyes that they had no qualms over mule meat.

He hoped this wasn't dog. Whatever it was, pounded fine, it tasted great, and he pulled out a handful and ate the pemmican hungrily. Quanah left him with a smile, returning moments later with a hollowed-out gourd filled with water. He took away the parfleche of pemmican and left Coady alone. The Indians did not bind him again this night, knowing he was too tired to attempt escape.

Besides, where would he go?

They had been traveling south and a little west, and the country began to change, harsher, broken, drier, inhospitable. On the third day, the Kiowas sang their good byes, took their share of booty and mules, and rode east. Quanah, Ugly Face, and two other Comanches angled farther southwest, heading into the *Llano Estacado,* the Staked Plains of Texas.

Days melded together. The sun fried the top of his head—he had lost his hat fleeing Ugly Face—and his muscles ached, but his thighs no longer felt so chaffed, and his sunburned skin seemed to toughen and harden. Ugly

Face, whose name Coady determined was Ecabapi, kept his distance, but the other two Indians began giving Coady orders, slapping his back with their bows when he couldn't understand what they meant. Coady gathered buffalo chips for fuel, fed and watered the livestock, prepared supper. He had become nothing more than a Comanche slave. Was this why Quanah had spared his life? If so, the boy wished the Indians had killed him and left his body beside his dead father.

Quanah did take time to try to communicate with Coady when they rode. He would point out things and speak slowly, and Coady would try to repeat the word or phrase, although the tough grunts weighed down his tongue.

"*Anicútz,*" Quanah said, pointing at a red ant picking at a dead beetle.

"*Anicútz,*" Coady repeated, and the Comanche beamed, although Coady didn't know if *anicútz* meant ant or beetle.

Horse was *puc,* horsefly was *pihpitz,* centipede was *soomó,* prickly pear was *ocuebocopi,* ring was *motzinica,* and rifle was *piaet.* Yet the language proved too difficult for a scared twelve-year-old to master with only one lesson, and by the next morning Coady, who the Comanches now called Soyáque, had forgotten everything but *puc.* Quanah remained patient, much to Coady's surprise, and continued the lessons for the remainder of the journey.

A sea of sage stretched endlessly across the stark, flat country, broken up only by an occasional coyote or wolf and a great herd of buffalo, which, to Coady's astonishment, the Comanches ignored. The table top appeared to stretch on forever, but the *Llano Estacado* held many wonders, and a great chasm suddenly appeared in the plains, a deep cañon of sandstone monuments and red, orange, yellow, brown, and white walls, pockmarked with juniper and mesquite. They rode along the rim of the cañon for a couple of miles, then followed Quanah as his paint horse slowly picked a way down a narrow trail of switchbacks that hugged the wall.

Coady held his breath as his mule followed Quanah and Ecabapi, half expecting the ugly Comanche to try something, to scare Coady's mount into rearing, throwing Coady to his death below, but maneuvering his own horse down the path, slippery from the rain, commanded all of Ecabapi's attention, not treachery, and everyone reached the bottom without incident.

The other two Comanches broke into laughter and song as Quanah continued to lead the way, gliding with ease through a maze of rocks and woods until reaching a red stream, which they followed another mile or two. The Indians picked up their pace, and Coady smelled wood smoke, food, and other odors repugnant to his sensibilities. Still, his stomach groaned, and he licked his cracked, bleeding lips. He saw the first teepee, then another, most of them hidden by giant cottonwoods.

Dogs began to bark, and Comanche men, women, and children rode or ran out of the village, shouting. Quanah and his comrades began singing louder, lifting scalps high over their heads, gesturing toward the captured mules. Coady cringed as Ecabapi pointed at his grisly trophy with a whoop. It was his father's scalp.

Memories flooded his brain, and he see-sawed, fought back nausea, somehow kept his seat aboard the mule's back. Quanah spoke to him, nodded toward a teepee at the edge of camp, and Coady followed. A white-haired, hump-backed woman, her face wrinkled with deep crevasses, emerged from the teepee, followed by a young, raven-headed girl maybe Coady's age.

Coady listened to the exchange between Quanah and the hag, but the words flowed too quickly for him to grasp anything. The woman moved slowly toward Coady and touched his filthy pants, asked Quanah something, and waited for his quick reply and nod, then grasped Coady's wrist. He yelped, for the ancient witch had a vise-like grip, and jerked him off the mule. He landed with a *thud,* and felt the woman kicking his stomach, yelling orders, pointing at the cook fire.

Coady rose quickly to escape the woman's rock-like moccasins, grasping that he now belonged to this hideous, foul-smelling creature, and she wanted him to bring more firewood. He told her—"Yes'm."—barely audible, and ran to a thicket, but not before she broke a branch over his back. He glanced over his shoulder to see the hag talking to the young girl. He looked for Quanah, but he was gone.

Coady couldn't fathom how deep the cañon cut into the *Llano,* or how far back it went, but he felt as if he had fallen off the edge of the earth. No one could find him here. No white man even knew of this place. Buffalo runners and skinners back in Dodge City spoke of the *Llano Estacado* with reverence and fear. Comanche country, where only Indians knew how to find water. No one traveled there, even after buffalo, unless they wanted to lose their hair. Coady tried to accept this. He must live with the Comanches.

For now.

Chapter Five

Life in a Comanche camp bore no resemblance to any half-dime novel.

The hag, Piarabo, raised welts on Coady's back and legs, and fed him barely enough to sustain him through another hard day. Comanche dogs nipped at his heels, and boys and women hurled insults, sometimes even stones, at him as he performed his chores. Coady, however, did have two benefactors: Quanah, who occasionally sat with him outside the lodge and refreshed his Comanche lessons, and the girl—Piarabo's granddaughter, Coady assumed—who applied salve over his wounds and, after his clothes became threadbare, made him a pair of deerskin britches and moccasins, and gave him a muslin shirt about three sizes too big.

He thought the girl might be a captive, too—maybe a Mexican; he had heard Comanches often raided farther south—and decided, if such be the case, that the two of them might escape together. Sitting by a fire one evening, chewing on antelope gristle, he watched her approach tentatively. She looked over her shoulder, saw no one lurking, pulled two persimmons from beneath her blanket, and dropped them in Coady's lap.

When Coady reached for her, she retreated and started to run.

"No," Coady said frantically. "Please stay!"

She turned, licked her lips, slightly trembling, but another backward glance revealed no Comanche snoops. Coady admitted to himself that she looked prettier than his sisters despite the grease and dirt covering her face. Tall and bony, she had mesmerizing black eyes and a round face, thin lips, her long hair plaited. She wore a dress of lemon buckskin, laced with leather thongs, with a ratty wool blanket draped over her like a poncho to fight off the chill of the spring night, and beaded moccasins.

Coady had seen a handful of Mexicans in Dodge City. If she were a captive, maybe he could communicate with her in Spanish, but he only knew one Spanish word.

"Adiós," he said tentatively.

"¿Adiós?" She stared at him, and his heartbeat quickened.

Did she understand? Coady nodded eagerly and repeated the word.

"Adiós," she said again, and smiled. *"Soyáque . . . adiós."* She pointed to her heart and said—*"Tunequi."*—repeating both gesture and word.

He sighed, heart-broken. "No," he said, "my name's not *adiós.* It's Coady. James Coady McIlvain." He looked up again, eyes filled with despair, and she smiled.

"Soyáque?" she said.

"Yeah, my name's Soyáque, whatever that means."

"Tunequi."

"Yeah, I know. Thanks, Tunequi." He looked at the persimmons she had given him, and began peeling the fruit. Hearing Piarabo returning, Tunequi hurried into the teepee. Coady stuck the persimmons underneath his shirt, and pretended to sleep. The ancient witch snorted at him and spit before going inside.

In late summer, Coady gave up all hope of being rescued. For the first months, he would stare at the cañon wall, looking for a cavalry guidon, maybe The Unknown

Scout or Buffalo Bill picking a path down the rim. No one came except other Comanches. After six weeks, he stopped crying himself to sleep. Indians respected toughness, and Coady understood that he must harden himself, mentally as well as physically, to survive the Comanche camp and eventually escape. Never would he forget the image of his father's scalped body lying on the Kansas plains, but it could not continue to haunt him. He had to move forward.

He had struck up a friendship with Tunequi, although language remained a barrier, and continued his lessons with Quanah. Ecabapi kept his distance, and Piarabo cut down on the beatings. The other Indian children picked on him sometimes, but not as often as they had done upon his arrival, and the ravenous curs had grown accustomed to Coady's smell because they didn't growl, bite, and bark at him much any more.

"Patience," he told himself repeatedly. "Be patient."

Once, he found a long stick in the cottonwoods, and picked it up. Visions of the old tobacco stick flooded his memories, and tears welled in his eyes. He heard the *clop* of hoofs and ducked behind a giant tree, and carefully spied down the trail to see Ecabapi riding toward camp. Coady brought up the stick as if it were a rifle, steadied it against the cottonwood, and aimed. A Sharps would have done the job just fine. He could send a bullet through the Comanche's heart, splash across the stream, grab the hackamore to the startled horse, and perform one of those Pony Express flying mounts. He'd be galloping out of the cañon before the Indians realized what had happened. He would have avenged Pa's death and escaped.

Coady dropped the stick and slid down, sobbing. He didn't hold a Sharps rifle, just a whittled stick, likely some Comanche boy's faulty attempt at making his first bow. An escape attempt would be nothing but pure folly right now. Not a skilled rider, he would never even make it halfway up the cañon, and, once captured, the beatings would return, harder, more frequent, or maybe the savages would just kill him, burn him alive, or perform some other gruesome torture.

When the tears ran their course, Coady spotted Tunequi standing on the far bank of the little stream, staring at him. He caught his breath and wiped his eyes and nose, started to stand, but his legs wouldn't work for him that moment, so he simply looked back at her. He couldn't think of anything to say.

Sadly, maybe grasping Coady's pain, Tunequi lowered her gaze and walked along the creek, head down, saying nothing as she returned to the encampment.

Piarabo kicked him awake, bellowing orders he couldn't understand. Coady rolled over to escape her stone-hard moccasins and leaped to his feet, trying to comprehend the excitement around him. Methuselah's grandmother pointed at the teepee, and, when Coady blinked, she raised a stick menacingly over her head. He wiped sleep from his eyes. The whole camp seemed alive. Men tied the tails of their horses, while women and children began striking camp. Dogs scurried about, trying to escape the stampede of feet. The Comanches were moving, Coady understood, and instinctively ducked the hag's swinging stick that sliced just above Coady's head.

"All right, all right!" he yelled. "You want the teepee taken down."

He moved to the smelly lodge, uncertain how one went about the task but pretending to be tugging at a stake so Piarabo wouldn't smack him any more. Tunequi knelt beside him, to help him, he realized, and another teen-age boy joined the chore. Lodge poles came down quickly, and by the time their teepee fell, Piarabo was barking out new orders. The speed at which the Comanches worked amazed Coady. Dogs were turned into pack mules, loaded down with parfleches, or harnessed to a travois. By mid-morning, the entire village headed up the switchbacks, leaving the cañon behind.

All of the men rode ahead, while the children and women walked along, eating dust. After climbing out of the cañon, Quanah led his people southwest, across the parched *Llano*. Autumn had arrived on the Staked Plains; the days remained warm, but the nights had become much cooler. They camped that night, and started early the following morning. Prickly pear mangled Coady's feet, despite his moccasins, but he knew better than to complain or stop longer than it took to pull out the spines.

"Where are we going?" he asked in broken Comanche, and was shocked to hear an answer.

"Cuhtz."

Tunequi walked beside him, smiled, and pointed her chin at the head of the column. *"Cuhtz,"* she repeated. *"Cuhtz."*

He remembered that word from his lessons with Quanah. "Buffalo," he said, and for the first time since his abduction he felt excited. He tried to fight off the emotion, yet couldn't. Certainly he hated Ecabapi and loathed Piarabo, but, after five months, he had grown to like Tunequi, Quanah, and a couple other Comanches, although he had tried not to. The mood of the Comanches magnified his feelings as the Indians sang and laughed despite an intense wind that stirred up biting sand and blinding dust.

On this day, they stopped around noon, and Coady had to dodge several of Piarabo's blows. He helped raise the lodge while Tunequi prepared a meal. After they had eaten, Quanah and two other riders returned to camp, shouting, pointing, singing. Men, wearing nothing more than breechclouts and carrying bows, quivers, and lances, leaped onto their horses. Coady groaned as Piarabo's stick smacked the small of his back, and he stumbled into the dust. His tormentor pointed the stick at the teepee, and Coady scrambled to start taking it down yet again. He had barely finished the task when Quanah, who had just ridden up, spoke to him.

Coady stared disbelievingly at the gray mare the chief pulled behind his own horse. The Comanche spoke again, nodding first at Coady, then at the mare, and Piarabo muttered something under her breath and walked away in a huff to find some other poor lad to torture. Coady pointed at himself. "Me?"

The tall Indian replied with a smile.

"Miar," said Tunequi, pointing at the mare. When Coady still couldn't budge, she took his hand in hers and led him to the awaiting horse.

Raised on North Carolina and Kansas farms, Coady had often ridden without a saddle, although almost always on a mule and not a horse. The gray had been saddled with some sort of pad, and Coady looked at how Quanah sat aboard his Comanche saddle before grabbing a fistful of mane and the hackamore and pulling himself onto the mare's back. A hemp rope had been loosely coiled around the horse's belly just behind the front legs, and Coady, following Quanah's example, stuck his knees under the rope. Quanah grunted in approval and rode out of camp. Coady glanced back only once, saw Tunequi beaming at him, and he rode a little taller.

Men, and a handful of teens, waited just outside of camp. A silver-headed man grunted at Quanah and smiled, but Ecabapi surged forward on his pinto, thrust the point of a red lance at Coady's chest, and yelped at Quanah. The white boy's presence so upset Ugly Face, he had trouble controlling his horse. Coady didn't have to speak Comanche to understand the words. Ecabapi had not forgotten who had broken his nose, who had embarrassed him in front of his companions. His hatred for the captive whose life Quanah spared had not diminished at all.

Quanah shook his head, spoke in a low tone, and rode ahead, ignoring the irate Ecabapi, who let loose with an ear-splitting—*Aiiiyeeeeeeee!*—kicked his pony into a gallop, and vanished in the dust ahead of the Comanche hunters.

Quanah wouldn't let Coady take part in the hunt. He gestured at him to dismount and wait, and Coady obeyed, holding the hackamore tightly but letting the mare graze. The herd of buffalo before him looked magnificent, just the way he had pictured back in Kansas while pretending to be the great buffalo runner. Dust from the approaching Comanche women rose behind as the men, faces masked with determination, prepared to begin the harvest.

Obviously the Comanches had not read Buffalo Bill's novels. They didn't even use rifles, mostly bows and arrows, and chased the buffalo on horseback, yipping, singing, slinging arrows through the air. Naturally the herd stampeded, and the ground shook with such force that the gray mare reared and screamed, dragging Coady several yards before he could get a better hold on the hackamore and calm his mount.

Coady turned back to watch the hunt, and, despite dust stinging his eyes, he could make out Quanah chasing a cow far to his left. An arrow sailed low and vanished in the animal's coat—maybe even went all the way through the beast, although he couldn't tell for sure. Then another, which sank halfway into the cow's back, just above the tail. Coady found himself holding his breath as Quanah rode closer to the buffalo, shifted bow and hackamore into his left hand, leaned over, grasped the shaft of the errant arrow with his right, and jerked it free. Without even slowing down, Quanah straightened, notched the arrow, drew back the string, and sent the arrow into the running cow, which collapsed and lay still. Quanah's victory yell rose above the deafening noise, and Coady's heart pounded as the Comanche found another arrow before resuming the chase, bolting into the thick, brown cloud, and disappearing.

He would have tolerated numerous beatings from the rotten-toothed witch to be with the men in the hunt, even if they didn't do it correctly. Coady had a horse, had been left alone, but for some reason he didn't even think about trying to escape. He wouldn't have known which way to ride, anyway.

The hunt had ended by the time the women and children arrived. Quanah motioned Tunequi and Piarabo over to the first cow he had killed, and Coady watched as the two women went to work skinning the buffalo. The hag took a knife, cut into the dead animal's belly, and withdrew the bloody liver, which, to Coady's astonishment, the three of them ate raw. They butchered the animals, skinned them, and used almost everything but left behind the hearts. Some kind of Comanche superstition, he guessed. Maybe he'd learn why later.

That night they danced and feasted on buffalo. Piarabo even let Coady have plenty of supper. Everyone looked happy—the Comanches accepted Coady now—and Coady, who would never let himself feel contented here, realized he could learn from the Comanches, and not just their language. Sleepy, he wandered back to Piarabo's teepee, when a forearm connected against his throat, and he fell, trying to breathe.

Through blurred vision, he spotted Ecabapi standing over him, one hand gripping the handle of his scalping knife. Old Ugly Face's horse had been gored and killed by a buffalo bull during the hunt, and the Comanches had teased him without mercy that afternoon. Surely Ecabapi didn't blame Coady for his horse's death, too. The pockmarked Comanche whipped out his knife and started to kneel. Coady tried to scream for help, but his voice wouldn't work. He could barely breathe.

The Indian straightened, looked to his left, grunted, spit at Coady's face, and jumped into the shadows. Coady closed his eyes and mumbled a prayer. His throat still hurt, but he could breathe now. Footsteps sounded, and Coady realized someone had scared Ecabapi, saving his life. Quanah, maybe, or Tunequi.

A hard foot slammed just beneath his ribs, and Coady groaned, sat up weakly, and ducked another blow from Piarabo. He scrambled to his feet and ran to the lodge, felt a buffalo bone sail over his head, thrown by the witch. He was laughing by the time he reached the teepee, laughing for the first time since his abduction. The hag had saved his life! He fell on his blanket, and giggled till his ribs hurt.

Piarabo stared at him, mumbled something underneath her breath, and left him alone.

Chapter Six

Only tenderfeet called themselves buffalo hunters. Hunting had nary a thing to do with what we did in southwestern Kansas in 1873. Cuthbert Jenkins made it plain and clear to me early during our venture that we were buffalo runners, although we didn't run after them, either. No . . . one word describes what we did better than any: slaughter.

When I left Dodge City with my new partner and crew, several runners still felt antsy about venturing south of the Arkansas River, and only a lunatic would have hunted beyond the Cimarron. For a few weeks, we had the grounds to ourselves, but with hides fetching $3.50 back East, by late summer it seemed that every fool with a rifle, skinning knife, and wagon had taken to the plains. Indians killed a handful of runners. Competition drove some back to Dodge or points east. Others simply couldn't find a herd, and a plague of locust devoured most of the grass to make buffalo even more scarce. Yet I think the smell drove away most of the greenhorns.

We left most of the meat behind, although Cuthbert Jenkins insisted we save the tongues to sell back in Dodge. Buffalo didn't smell like lilacs—that's for certain—and I gave thanks that I didn't have to skin them, just shoot them. Our four skinners reeked of dried blood and old guts, but the sickening stink I recall the most came from putrid carcasses left behind to draw wolves, vultures, and swarms of flies. Carrion picked away at the rotting meat, stripping bones to bleach in the sun, later to be hauled away by pilgrims and farmers.

Bone hunting wasn't as profitable as it would become a few years later when the herds had been all but destroyed and companies back East sought buffalo bones to be used, in addition to fertilizer, as combs, utensils, or in sugar refining. Eventually bones would fetch six or eight dollars a ton, but in the early years mostly farmers and a few fertilizer entrepreneurs sought them, such as those men killed in The McIlvain Massacre.

The sounds of single-shot rifles echoed across the Kansas prairie that summer and fall. I'd guess some two thousand runners took part in the . . . yes, *slaughter* is the right word.

I am as much to blame as anyone who shot a buffalo. Greed is a common vice, and for me the money came easy.

During my first stand, I dropped eighty-four animals in one morning before the herd stampeded. I expected Jenkins to praise my marksmanship, but he cursed me up and down, and the skinners we had hired joined him. Don't kill more than the crew can skin, I learned, and afterward limited my stands to no more than fifty kills. Seldom did I reach that total, however, averaging twenty-eight before the herd ran, plenty of work for the two skinners following me.

The skinners, whose names I have now forgotten, cut away with a surgeon's skill, pulling off the hides and carrying them to camp, where they would be doused with poison to kill fleas, ticks, and buffalo mange, then pegged, flesh side up, to the ground to dry. We also dried the tongues, and ate roasted buffalo rump and sourdough biscuits, washing the grub down with bitter coffee.

Every morning my partner and I rode out of camp in opposite directions, followed by two skinners in each wagon. Our cook, J. C. Claybrooke, stayed behind in camp. I can't say he was much of a cook, but he could handle a team of mules, shovel, and Spencer carbine, and didn't mind the stench of buffalo or, after a few weeks, of us. Claybrooke had been a belly-cheater on a cattle drive from South Texas, but the Texicans didn't much fancy his past service in the Union Army and cheated him out of his pay after they reached Ellsworth, so he stole the chuck wagon and lit a shuck for Dodge.

A sandy-haired gent with mustache and goatee, Claybrooke carried with him a fiddle, which he played every other evening. On the nights when he didn't fiddle, he borrowed my copy of THE CELEBRATED JUMPING FROG OF CALAVERAS COUNTY, AND OTHER SKETCHES and read aloud a story. His fiddling made up for the poor coffee and burned biscuits, and perhaps had he sawed a few tunes of "Lorena" during the trail drive, the waddies might have taken a shine to him and he would have found himself back in Uvalde County instead of in Indian country. His recitations of Samuel Clemens were enjoyable as well.

He had fought with the 52nd Illinois, took a Miníe ball in the shoulder at Pittsburg Landing, and knew his way around weapons—another reason we tolerated his grub. He handled the Spencer as well as he fiddled, and offered to reload our empties when we left camp. Ever superstitious, I declined his generous offer, loading my cartridges after supper, but my partner accepted. Big-mustached Cuthbert Jenkins might have been the laziest man I ever met, but he knew plenty about running buffalo.

The old Texican favored an old 1859 model Sharps in .52-caliber linen with a thirty-inch barrel and brass telescopic sight, similar to the one I used during my Federal service with Colonel Berdan. Naturally I carried the rifle I won off Pattison and Wheatley, and bought an open-top Colt .44

with a seven-and-a-half-inch barrel, at Jenkins's suggestion, which I used to shoot any wounded buff in the head. This I wore in a holster on my hip while keeping my smaller-caliber revolver in the carpetbag.

Our supplies also consisted of lead, powder, and bullet molds. Ammunition didn't come cheap on the Kansas frontier, so we loaded our own cartridges, and I soon learned to put an extra ten grains of powder in my loads. The Sharps barrel was strong enough to handle repeated use of .50-100 rounds, but cleaning that rifle after a stand proved quite a chore.

We also equipped ourselves with Winchester repeating carbines, the 1866 models in .44 rimfire called Yellow Boys because of their brass frames. They didn't have the power of the Sharps, and weighed only seven and a half pounds, but the carbines held twelve cartridges, which could come in handy if we got waylaid by Indians. We grew accustomed to the well-spaced heavy booms of the Sharps and understood that quick pops from a Winchester meant trouble.

My partner taught me to tear small strips of cotton and stick them into my pocket before lighting out after breakfast in search of buffalo. Once I found a herd, I would hobble my horse and approach the buffalo, keeping the wind in front of me, as close as I dared, no closer than two hundred yards and sometimes as far away as four hundred. It didn't matter. I could hit a target as big as a buffalo as far away as six hundred yards without a problem. I carried two bandoleers of Big Fifty cartridges, a pair of shooting rest sticks, canteen, Winchester, and the cotton strips, which I wadded up and stuffed into my ears. Muffling the reports of the Sharps definitely helped my hearing, although my ears would still ring long after a successful stand.

Cuthbert Jenkins also gave me something else to use in

case of an Indian attack. I prayed I would never have need of it.

"Keep this with you when you're out yonder," he drawled, handing me a cartridge from my Big Fifty. "I mean always. You stick to this like a preacher sticks to his Bible. You don't want to get yerself captured alive by some Cheyenne buck, Dylan. This is quick, painless. And Injuns won't butcher a dead body. If things get hopeless, you make sure you bite the bite."

He had emptied the powder from the cartridge and filled it with cyanide.

I rolled the cold piece of brass in my fingers, my stomach dancing a jig, before forcing a smile and sliding the bite into my vest pocket. "You didn't mention this back in Dodge," I said lightly, although I felt anything but easy.

"God willin', you won't never have to bite the bite, pard," he said. "I'm just lookin' after your well-bein', alive or dead."

I didn't have to bite into that cartridge for I saw not one Indian, friendly or fighter. Toward the end of our venture, we found few buffalo, either, and decided to haul our fortune back to Dodge City. We returned with just under six thousand hides, and sold them for $2 each. After paying off the four skinners we had hired at $50 a month, and J. C. Claybrooke, who signed on for $75 a month, Cuthbert Jenkins handed me $5,290.50.

"We never signed no papers, but I reckon fifty-fifty is fair," he said.

"It's more than generous," I agreed. "You're out the wagons and livestock."

"Maybe so, but you shoot straighter than me. I'm satisfied if you are."

I nodded my satisfaction, and began stuffing the greenbacks and coin into a money belt.

"You gonna winter here?" he asked as he began rolling a smoke.

"No," I said. "First I'll take two or three baths to get the stink off me. Next, I'm going to eat the biggest steak . . . beefsteak, not buffler." After five months on the prairie, I found myself talking like my partner, calling buffalo "buffler" or "buffs" more often than not. "Then I'm going to get drunk and sleep for a week. After that, I'll sit in on a few hands of poker, and then I'm heading south. Denison City, Texas."

"Newspaper job?"

"That's right, if they need a printer."

I had worked six months in Denison before journeying north, but my reasons for traveling back to Texas had more to do with a woman I had met there than the job. Cuthbert Jenkins didn't need to know that part, however, and I assumed he would never learn that Denison, like Dodge City, supported no newspaper. The Denison *Herald* wouldn't start publication until 1889, and I had worked as a barkeep at some canvas watering hole which had gone out of business just before I rode the rails to Kansas. My trip south might turn out to be pure folly because for all I knew Sarah Elizabeth Cabell had moved on to parts unknown or had gotten out of the business. The roots of soiled doves ran about as deep as those of tramp printers.

"Well, I was hopin' you'd head back up this way come spring," Jenkins said. "We could run buffs ag'in."

"I don't think they'll be any buffs to run," I answered honestly. "Not in Kansas, anyway. You know that as well as I do, and this is about as north as I care to travel." I pretended to shiver. "My blood has thinned out over these years since leaving Wisconsin and I can't stand the cold."

Jenkins's eyes glittered. "Well, pard, let's you and me mosey over to Hanrahan's. I reckon he's got something that'll warm us both up a mite."

I had my bath and my steaks, took a room at the Dodge House, and proceeded to lose about six hundred dollars playing poker. Such is the way of cards. With November on the horizon, I decided to buy a horse and ride south to Denison and Sarah Elizabeth Cabell. If I couldn't find her, I'd try Fort Worth or Dallas, two burgs which I knew had newspapers.

I made it to Texas that winter, but not Denison, or Fort Worth, or Dallas.

Cuthbert Jenkins caught up with me one blustery afternoon at the depot, where I watched another outfit of runners unloading thousands of buffalo hides, including a white one that the leader of the outfit, a tall, peg-legged fellow with a Remington Rolling Block rifle, sold for ten dollars.

"That's Capt'n Grover Barr," said Jenkins, out of breath as usual. "Says he's headin' back out after he and his boys drink Hanrahan's dry."

I laughed at the notion of running buffalo when we had practically wiped out the great herd.

"I might see if he wants a pard," Jenkins said.

"You're serious?"

Jenkins replied with a nod. "That's why I come to see you. Thirsty?"

"I could be persuaded," I answered, and we left the depot, crossed Front Street, and headed toward Dog Kelley's saloon. Two ryes later, Jenkins asked if I had the itch.

"What itch?"

"Buffler itch."

"My plans haven't changed," I told him. "I'm bound for Denison." Still, I did have a desire to run buffalo again. Five thousand dollars for five months' work held a lure stronger than gold, or some fallen angel who might or might not have been plying her trade in North Texas. For five thousand dollars, a man could tolerate a sore right shoulder, ringing ears, bad coffee, and the horrible odor.

"I talked to J. C. Claybrooke, and he'll hire on as cook, and I can find us four skinners," Jenkins said as he refilled our glasses. "If you join us . . . and I'm offerin' you the same deal as before, fifty-fifty, less expenses . . . we'll light a shuck out of here quicker than you can yell keno. If you ain't comin', I'll join up with Capt'n Barr."

I shook my head, removed my glasses, and wiped the lenses with a handkerchief. "Cuthbert," I said, "where do you plan on finding any buffalo?" Jenkins's influence on me had lessened, as I now pronounced the word correctly.

"Texas," he said quietly.

That caused me to roll my eyes with a chuckle. From what I had garnered, the Medicine Lodge Treaty of 1867 gave Plains Indians exclusive rights to hunting south of the Cimarron River, and I told Jenkins as much. He was talking about carrying the hunt into the *Llano Estacado,* Comanche country, and I didn't fancy dodging warring Indians as well as the Army trying to chase us down and kick us off Indian land.

"Dylan," Jenkins said, "I've read a mite myself, and the treaty don't reserve that land for Injuns. Heck, till this season, we all considered the Arkansas River the deadline for runnin' buffler. And we don't have nothin' to fear from the Yanks."

"How's that?"

"You know J. Wright Mooar?"

I told him I knew of the big-outfit hunter who worked out of Dodge but hadn't made his acquaintance.

"Well, Mooar, Steele Frazier, another runner hereabouts, and me rode over to the fort three days back and had us a little parlay with Colonel Dodge, picked his brain, you might say, about what the Army would do if white men started runnin' buffler south of the Cimarron."

"And?"

"Well, he didn't say nothin' contrary to Army policy, mind you, but right before he bid us good day, he told us . . . 'Boys, if I were huntin' buffler, I would go where the buffler are.' "

I sipped my rye. "I thought you planned on waiting till spring," I said.

He laughed, caught his breath, downed his whisky, and answered: "And let Mooar and Capt'n Barr take all them hides for themselves? I don't think so, pardner."

Ol' Cuthbert Jenkins had me hooked. We shook hands again, and I bought a winter coat at Rath and Company's General Store, along with plenty of powder and lead. We hired Claybrooke and four skinners: a wiry cuss in a porkpie hat named Lillard Butler; a soft-spoken Mexican who called himself Ignacio; a greenhorn from Iowa named Chet McDonough who knew how to handle a skinning knife; and Trabue, a Texican with a mustache even bigger than Cuthbert Jenkins's.

During the second week of November, we left Dodge City, heading southwest to the Texas Panhandle, moving closer, although we didn't know it at the time, toward a Comanche captive named Coady McIlvain.

Chapter Seven

Vultures circled against a cobalt sky directly in front of the moving village of Kwahadi Comanches, and Coady knew they would soon discover the dead or dying that had attracted the carrion on this late winter or early spring afternoon. He had lost track of time wintering with his captors. His thirteenth birthday had come and gone without notice, his skin had darkened, his hair lightened, his muscles hardened, and he had grown a few inches and added a few pounds.

Her whippings had scarred his back, but Piarabo no longer beat the boy the Comanches called Soyáque, or Mockingbird. He was too big for that, and could have easily thrashed the hag. Coady did his chores, though, and could speak rudimentary Comanche, limiting most of his conversations to Tunequi. Otherwise, he kept to himself. He was a white boy, and the Comanches his age wouldn't let him forget that, nor would Coady forget it. He didn't plan on spending the rest of his life a slave. Tunequi probably understood this, but she didn't tell Piarabo or Quanah. Oddly Coady actually missed his time with Quanah. He owed the young Comanche chief his life, had learned much from him, but now Quanah kept busy. He had more important things on his mind, and Coady sensed a mix of restlessness, sadness, confusion, and hatred among the Indians.

Long before they reached the blood-soaked ground, Coady knew what had brought the vultures to the *Llano Estacado*. So did Quanah.

60

A pack of coyotes bolted at the sight of the Indians, and vultures and ravens, which had been resting on the ground a few rods away, took flight. A woman began wailing, and Coady was surprised to see it was Piarabo. Ecabapi clenched his bow tightly and barked out war cries; others simply turned their heads at the malodorous carnage, and a lone tear rolled down Tunequi's cheek. Quanah and another warrior rode forward.

Before he stopped counting, Coady tallied eighty-nine buffalo carcasses—calves, cows, and bulls. No meat had been taken, only the hides, and several of those, ruined during the skinning process, had been left to rot.

The Comanche with Quanah, a man called Esihabiiti, dismounted near the remains of a cow, dropped to his knees, and began chanting a prayer while Ecabapi loped around the field, looking for sign. Comanches used just about every part of the buffalo—skin and sinew, bones and paunch, dung and marrow, meat and entrails—but the men who had done this sought only the hides. They didn't even offer buffalo hearts to the gods.

Ecabapi jerked his pony to a halt and yelled at Quanah, pointing his bow at wagon tracks headed east. Esihabiiti mounted his roan and began talking to Quanah. They spoke in hushed voices, but kept glancing at the tracks Ecabapi had discovered. After Quanah's head bobbed slightly, Esihabiiti rode back to the group, called out half a dozen names, and galloped toward Ecabapi. The men followed him. Ecabapi cut loose with a shrill yell, and the Indians thundered after the white hunters.

Coady's heart sank. He felt torn, saddened, knowing how the Comanches depended on buffalo, yet also afraid for the white hunters who had no idea that they had just become the hunted. Since leaving their winter camp, the Indians had come across four other killing grounds such as this one, but here the blood remained sticky, and Coady understood the Comanches would find the hunters soon. Recalling that terrible day in Kansas last spring, he shuddered at what would happen.

With a signal from Quanah, the Comanches followed, leaving the dead buffalo behind for the watching coyotes, ravens, and vultures. No one spoke.

At first, Coady thought the main party of Comanches had found the buffalo runners, who stood near a *playa* waving their big hats, gesturing for the Indians to join them. *Inviting the Comanches to their camp?* Coady squinted his eyes for a better look. No white man welcomed Comanches—an invitation to death. Quanah had trouble holding back some of the younger braves, and at last relented. Yipping excitedly, four warriors raced ahead, and Quanah frowned. A man with a big hat tossed something in the air, and the first brave leaped off his bay and caught it, shouted, lifted it over his head, then held it to his lips and drank greedily.

These men weren't buffalo runners. They drove giant carts, with wheels taller than men, pulled by oxen, and Coady recognized a word—Comanchero. Indian traders, poured forty-rod whisky down the throats of the young braves, held out bolts of cotton and silk for the women, speaking in Spanish and butchered Comanche. He counted six carts, ten covered wagons, and hundreds of horses, maybe thirty Mexicans, all bearded, all dirty, all armed with braces of pistols, bandoleers across their coats, and rifles handy.

Piarabo told Coady and Tunequi to begin setting up their lodge, and ran to the traders. Coady expected her to join the women fighting over cloth and beads, but, instead, she knocked down a young brave, jerked the brown clay jug from his hands, and drank. Comanches, even the one she had tackled, joined the Comancheros in laughing.

Quanah did not laugh.

Nor did Coady.

Briefly he considered asking the Mexican traders to help him escape, but he knew little Spanish and he could not trust these vile, belligerent men. He remembered a few lines from one of his Buffalo Bill novels back home:

Drawing and quartering any white man who dares trade with savage Indians is not just punishment. Their bodies should be buried in the burning sand, their eyelids cut off to bake in the blistering sun, and then honey poured over their heads to attract ants. Even that is too humane for these treacherous fiends.

He kept close to the lodge that night. Piarabo had passed out, and he and Tunequi had dragged her inside the teepee. He wondered how Tunequi would be able to sleep in there with that snoring old hag who stank of vomit and whisky. Outside, Coady closed his eyes but knew he wouldn't sleep, either, couldn't sleep, and not only because of the boisterous singing, cursing, and dancing, or Piarabo's muffled snores. Despite Ecabapi's absence, he feared that some drunken Comanche or Comanchero would slit his throat in the night. Already he had heard three or four fights among the Comanches.

Why did Quanah allow such disgrace among his own people, or tolerate the foul-mouthed, foul-smelling Comancheros?

Guns.

He learned that the following afternoon, when the leader of the Comancheros, a burly man with a thick beard, more salt than pepper, and long greasy hair, used a crowbar to open a long crate, and dumped a dozen or more weapons on the ground in front of Quanah, a silver-haired warrior named Naséca, and two relatively sober Indians.

After moving closer, Coady knelt so he could peer between the legs of a dozen or so men and women who had gathered around to watch. Naséca picked up a battered old percussion shotgun with a broken stock, tossed it aside with a grunt, and rifled among the collection, shaking his head, muttering his opinions of the arsenal under his breath before lifting an old Sharps rifle, its barrel weathered with age, stock chipped and worn, action stiff, definitely not one of the newer models Coady had seen on the streets of Dodge City and in Zimmermann's store. Still, Naséca seemed to think it the best of the lot, and said something to Quanah.

"Piaet!" Quanah demanded, and Coady remembered the Comanche word for rifle or carbine. Quanah made the action of cranking a lever, firing rapidly, and spoke again. Coady interpreted the phrase as meaning "shoots a heap".

"No repeaters," the Comanchero chief answered, causing Coady's mouth to hang open. He had spoken in English. The Mexican shifted to Spanish, pointing to the weapon Naséca held and saying: *"Carabina. Muy bien."*

Quanah folded his arms, spit, turned his back on the traders, and walked away. Naséca tossed the Sharps relic on the pile and followed his chief, and Coady stood quickly to avoid being trampled by the Comanches. The Comanchero leader yelled something, but the Indians refused to listen until he reached into the cart and brought something shiny to his lips. At first, the bugle tooted horribly off key, but the Mexican drew in a deep breath and managed to play something that bore some resemblance to one of the calls Coady had heard at Fort Dodge.

Naséca stopped and turned. A few others stared at the Comanchero, but Quanah never wavered.

One of the traders said something in Spanish to the leader, who smiled and tossed the old Army bugle to Naséca. He brought it to his lips and blew out a horrible noise that made Coady's skin crawl. The Comancheros laughed, and Naséca tried again, a little better.

"Piaguoin," a middle-aged Comanche woman said, covering her ears.

The Comanchero leader made several signs with his hands, speaking in Spanish, and Naséca's head bobbed. He smiled slightly, drew his knife and sheath, and tossed them at the cart. A slim Mexican wearing a cavalry kepi walked over and picked them up. Naséca, still practicing his bugle, hurried back to the village.

The bartering reconvened later that afternoon, and the Comancheros finally wore down Quanah. They refused to sell any repeating rifles, so the Indians took the available weapons, trading horses, gold, and, to Coady's amazement and horror, a young girl captive. The burly Mexican offered Quanah a drink of whisky, but again the tall warrior spit at the Comanchero, who simply laughed. Quanah left in disgust, and Coady followed.

For the second night, he couldn't sleep. The drums and laughter echoed through his head. Both Mexicans and Indians were so drunk, he doubted if they could see straight.

Coady shot straight up. Piarabo, drunk again, had passed out for the second time and snored in her teepee. Fires blazed in both Comanche and Comanchero camps, but no one seemed to be watching the Indian pony herd.

He'd never get a chance like this. Steal a horse and ride . . . which way? No matter. Just ride!

He glanced toward the teepee, threw off his blanket, and scrambled to his feet. He moved quietly, barely breathing, until he tripped and fell with a groan. Sitting up, Coady spotted the figure of a man lying in the middle of the path, and realized it was a Comanche brave, passed out, snoring louder than Piarabo and sleeping in his own vomit. The man didn't stir once, and Coady started to rise, thought better of it, and sat back down, inched closer toward the drunken Indian, reached out tentatively, grasped the bone handle of the knife sheathed at the Comanche's waist, and gently withdrew the weapon. Then he jumped to his feet and ran several yards, stopping near the horses to catch his breath.

A quarter moon appeared beneath the clouds, and Coady moved again, sweating despite the chill of the wind. Something cracked behind him, and he froze, waiting, hearing his heart pounding against his chest. He didn't move for five minutes; life with the Indians had taught him patience. At last, convinced the sound had been his imagination, he took a step forward.

"It would be a mistake, *gringo*."

That wasn't his imagination. Coady sighed, his shoulders sagged, and he waited.

Laughing, the burly Mexican leader stepped into the faint light. "You are white, no? ¿*Tejano*? Texas?" His breath reeked of whisky and tobacco smoke.

"Kansas," Coady said at last.

The Comanchero nodded. He wore embroidered, open-sided black pants stuffed inside scuffed brown boots, yellow silk shirt, short jacket, and an arsenal strapped to his waist: knife, machete, and at least three revolvers. His graying beard hid a vicious scar on his left cheek while his hair glistened like a raven and fell to his shoulders. "Kansas, is good. If you were *Tejano,* I would have killed you on principle. I am José Piedad Tafoya." He bowed slightly. "At your service, *señor.*"

"I am. . . ." He saw no reason this treacherous swine should know his real name. "They call me Soyáque."

"Soyáque, I have men, sober men, on guard. Quanah has braves hidden with the horses. He is no fool. Nor is José Piedad Tafoya. My men would have mistaken you for a Comanche and would have killed you. Quanah's bucks would have mistaken you for a Comanchero and would have killed you." He laughed. "You see, we do not trust one another. We simply tolerate the existence of each other. Our trade does have its benefits. You desire escape, no?"

He shrugged in reply. When Tafoya reached over and gripped his upper arm, Coady clenched the stolen Comanche knife tighter. The Comanchero must have seen the weapon, but he didn't worry about it. "You are strong, Soyáque, stronger than you look. José Piedad Tafoya might have a spot for you, if Quanah will trade you."

"No thanks," he said, feeling his stomach flutter. "I don't want to be a Comanchero."

Laughter and spit exploded from the Mexican's mouth, and Coady staggered back, wiping saliva off his face, thoroughly disgusted.

"Comanchero? No, little *gringo,* I thought to sell you to the silver mines in Zacatecas." The laughter and beam in the bandit's eyes died. "Back to your lodge, boy."

He hid the knife in his left moccasin. The Comancheros left the following afternoon, which pleased Coady—and Quanah. With most of the Indians sick with hang-overs, the Comanches stayed at the *playa* another day before continuing their journey to the next camp.

The next morning, Piarabo coughed herself awake at last and told Coady to get to work. Why wasn't food prepared? she yelled at Tunequi, sporting a bruise underneath her left eye that Coady had not noticed till now. He cursed Tafoya and his fiends although, for all Coady knew, Tunequi had gotten the shiner from a drunken Comanche. This he tried to block out of his mind. The Mexican traders had gone, and the village would be on the move soon.

They pushed hard, set up camp, and turned in early. Coady hadn't slept much the past few days, and exhaustion enveloped him. He didn't move until a savage scream jerked him awake well after dawn. Piarabo might have stopped beating him, but she never let him sleep in. Maybe she was dead. No, he heard her chants on the far side of camp. The screams made his skin crawl. After wiping sleep from his eyes, he walked cautiously toward the horrible cries. The old hag and several other women had gathered around something, some animal they must be torturing.

Then he saw Ecabapi, smiling his broken smile, watching the women raise bloody knives, pointed sticks, and Coady moaned. Ecabapi and the war party had returned with a buffalo runner, wounded but alive, letting the women do what they did best.

"Kill me!" a voice shrieked piteously. "For the love of God, kill me!"

Bile and supper exploded from Coady's mouth, and he fell to his knees, gagging. Two Comanche warriors laughed and pointed their bows at him, but he didn't care. As the women laughed, sliced, and jabbed, the screams intensified. Crying, Coady pulled himself to his feet, and ran back to the lodge, covering his ears with both hands, but nothing could silence the morbid sounds.

Chapter Eight

Arms loaded down with firewood, Coady stared at the entrance to the old Comanche trail hidden in the colorful rocks and junipers along the steep cañon wall. With the Kwahadis back at the encampment where he had first been taken, Coady decided he would have to make a run sometime this spring, summer at the latest. He had been prisoner for close to a year, but didn't know if he would live much longer. Piarabo's beatings had resumed, the boys hurled stones at him again, and men and women stared at him with malevolent eyes.

Anxiety and hatred ran high among the Comanches, and buffalo runners were to blame. White men committed slaughter in Indian country, and Ecabapi, among others, lumped a white captive—although he was a *tetzóteuei,* or plowman, not a runner—with the hunters wiping out buffalo for only the skins. Riders from other Comanche bands—Penatekas, or Wasps; Noconis, or Wanderers; Yamparikas, or Root Eaters; and Kotsatekas, or Buffalo Eaters—frequented the Kwahadi camp, as well as Kiowas, Cheyennes, and Arapahoes. They talked of war, and something else.

His Comanche remained roughshod, but he picked enough scraps to understand some prophet had appeared with strong words, and the Indians listened eagerly.

Isa-tai claimed to have raised the dead and could vomit up thousands of cartridges for use against the white men. Bullets fired by white men could not harm him. Coady found a correlation between the medicine man's claims and his name, which meant Coyote Droppings. The prophet preached that Comanches and their allies must rise up against the runners, wipe them out, take back the buffalo country. If not, they would wind up like the Caddos and Wichitas, puny, weak, more white than Indian, not even worth scalping. Isa-tai had called for a sun dance, and, as best as Coady could tell, Comanches had never held a sun dance, although they had attended a few Kiowa ceremonies.

To Coady's surprise, Quanah believed Isa-tai, spoke highly of the medicine man, and planned to attend the dance. War talk grew hotter. The kettle would soon boil over.

"Soyáque?"

He turned, almost dropping his load, to find Tunequi. Coady forced a smile, crossed the stream bed, and followed her back to Piarabo's lodge, where he dropped the wood on the ground. Tunequi cracked a joke, and he laughed. She had remained his protector, along with Quanah, but how long could they keep him safe? As he stacked a few pieces of wood that had spilled, he glanced again toward the cañon, trying to devise a plan that wouldn't get him killed.

José Piedad Tafoya and his Comancheros had returned, bringing with them whisky, trinkets, and a few repeating rifles. They had hauled their merchandise down the cañon trail on pack mules, probably unable to negotiate the switchbacks and narrow widths with wagons and the giant carts. The Comanches drank, shouted, built bigger fires, and Coady clenched his fists and bit his lower lip. He wished Quanah were here, but the chief had led several braves to join Isa-tai's sun dance.

Unfortunately Ecabapi had stayed behind.

70

Ecabapi's drunken, ribald laughter echoed down the cañon as Coady threw a blanket on the ground in front of Piarabo's teepee. He didn't know where the hag had wandered, didn't care, just wanted to pretend to be asleep, then sneak away. He would escape tonight, or die.

The scream came from inside the teepee just as he lay on the blanket, and he immediately recognized Tunequi's voice. Coady shot upright and bolted inside Piarabo's lodge, smelling the strong scent of trade whisky. Eyes wide in fright, Tunequi pressed her back against the far end of the teepee while a massive figure crouched in front of her, laughing, slurring his words, speaking in a mixture of bad Comanche and Spanish.

"Leave her alone!" Coady shouted, and leaped at the intruder.

José Piedad Tafoya's backhand caught Coady hard across his forehead, and he dropped like a shot-dead buffalo, falling on top of something cold, unmoving. His mouth fell open as he recognized Piarabo, eyes open but not seeing, a lake of warm, sticky blood pooling underneath her body. The Comanchero had slit her throat.

"Little *gringo*," the Mexican said with a mirthless laugh. "Find a pony and run. Turkey Vulture looks for a reason to kill you. He will say you did this." He glanced at Piarabo, dismissed the boy, and turned back to Tunequi. "And this."

Turkey Vulture was Ecabapi, and Coady knew the Comanchero was right. He couldn't count on Quanah—a hundred miles away for all Coady knew—to help him, and many Indians looked for any reason to kill the white boy called Soyáque, or trade him to Tafoya. Run. His only chance.

Tafoya laughed and closed in on Tunequi, whose eyes

71

now blazed with hatred, not fear, but she would be no match for this *muviporo*.

He stood quickly, sailing into the Comanchero leader again. When the killer's right arm shot out to thwart the attack, Coady lashed out with the knife he had stolen a few months earlier.

Tafoya screamed in pain and staggered back, holding his bleeding right arm. He cut loose with a barrage of Spanish curses and lunged forward, reaching for his machete but tripping over Piarabo's body. Inexperienced and more than a little stunned, Coady retreated too slowly. He spun around and dashed out of the lodge, hoping to lure the Comanchero away from Tunequi, but Tafoya managed to trip Coady and send him sprawling on his blanket outside.

He rolled over, tried to find his knife, couldn't, and shouted a warning in Comanche as the Mexican exploded from the lodge. Coady screamed louder, but no one heard, not with the drums, singing, laughter, and music. He rolled to his side just as the machete thudded into the ground, crawled a few yards, trying to find his feet, then felt the air leave his lungs with a sudden *whoosh*.

Coady landed on his back, blinked away tears and pain, tried to breathe. Leaving the machete buried in the blanket and dirt, Tafoya kicked the boy again, straddled him with his crushing weight, and drew a sharp skinning knife with his right hand. Coady stared at the ripped shirt sleeve and the blood running in rivulets down Tafoya's fist. The Comanchero cursed again in Spanish, and Coady closed his eyes and prepared to die.

A violent *crack* jerked his eyelids open. Coady couldn't believe it as Tafoya's eyes rolled in the back of his head, the knife slipped from his fingers, and the Comanchero dropped to his side. Lungs working again, Coady sat up.

Tunequi stood in front of him, holding a stout piece of firewood in both hands, her chest heaving, determination chiseled in her small face. Coady tested his legs, found they could support his weight, and located the knife, trying to formulate a plan. If only Quanah were here. . . .

He never heard Ecabapi. Ugly Face was soft on his feet—Coady would have to give him that—and the Comanche warrior gripped Coady's hand tightly, twisting it until the knife toppled into the dust, and tossing him beside the unconscious José Piedad Tafoya.

Tunequi dropped the wood and began pleading with the warrior, gesturing at the Comanchero and inside Piarabo's lodge, saying how Coady had saved her life, how the *tabebo* had killed her grandmother, but Ecabapi didn't care. His broken smile flashed once, and he pulled his knife, stepping toward Coady. Filled with whisky and hate, the Comanche remembered his broken nose, his embarrassment, all because of this white boy. Coady didn't move, just watched Ecabapi come closer, watched Tunequi pick up the piece of wood again and swing.

This time they ran, leaving Ecabapi sprawled beside Tafoya, picking up Coady's knife plus a hackamore and Comanche saddle, moving quickly to the Indian pony herd. He spotted a good strong stallion, and Tunequi nodded in approval.

"Niatz," Coady said suddenly, grabbed Tunequi's hand, and jerked her into the shadows. She stared at him in bewilderment, but said nothing. Something didn't seem right. He pursed his lips, and remembered. Back in Piarabo's lodge, Tafoya had told him to steal a horse and run. Why would he have done that? Coady sighed suddenly, understanding. Months ago at the *playa*, when the Comanchero had caught Coady, had warned him off, what was it he had

said? *Quanah has braves hidden with the horses. He is no fool. Nor am I. My men would have mistaken you for a Comanche and would have killed you. Quanah's bucks would have mistaken you for a Comanchero and would have killed you.*

Quanah wasn't here, but Ecabapi was far from stupid. With Comancheros so close, he'd surely have braves, sober ones, guarding the herd. Tafoya would also have left men at his camp. Still, Tafoya and Ecabapi would wake up soon and sound the alarm. Even with Tunequi, Coady didn't think the Comanches would believe him—if he lived long enough to tell his side of the story.

He explained this as best as he could in a whisper, and Tunequi's head bobbed slightly. She surveyed the herd and moved closer to a horse, a smaller pinto mare, not the stallion they had first spotted, slipped on a hackamore, and led the horse to a cottonwood. Coady said nothing as the girl saddled the animal, and handed him the hackamore.

"What are you doing?" he asked urgently as she approached the stallion. He glanced over his shoulder, lowered his voice, and asked her again in Comanche. She turned briefly, smiled, and moved closer to the stallion, humming a tune, gripping a handful of mane and pulling herself on the horse's bare back.

"You will know what to do," she said in Comanche. "Be safe, Soyáque." Her knees tightened, she screamed a war cry, and guided the loping stallion across the creek and toward the cañon wall.

"No!" Coady yelled in English, then in Comanche: *"Niatz, Tunequi, niatz!"*

The pinto mare reared, but Coady kept his grip on the hackamore. A rifle boomed, followed by another. The last he saw of Tunequi, she had hung her body over the side of the stallion—"à la Comanche," Buffalo Bill had written in

THE UNKNOWN SCOUT. Voices echoed behind him, and Coady pulled the mare deeper into the cottonwoods.

Comanches and Comancheros galloped after Tunequi, and Coady at last understood. No one would recognize him in the darkness. They'd think he had joined the pursuers. He struggled onto the horse's back, took a deep breath, and kicked the pinto into a walk . . . trot . . . finally a full gallop, holding on tightly, trying to keep his balance, hoping the horse knew its way up that path.

The wind blasted him when he reached the top of the cañon. Hoofs thundered across the *Llano,* toward the rising moon, while other riders galloped up the steep trail. Coady turned his horse north, walked her softly, prayed no one would see him. The riders behind him paused briefly before taking off after the sound of the hoofs. Only then did Coady let out a breath.

He kicked the mare into a canter, and rode till dawn.

Water. Coady hadn't thought to bring any, hadn't had time really to think about it. The sun baked his head and the wind blistered his face, but he moved toward the circling vultures, hoping he had guessed right about what they had found. He wondered what had happened to Tunequi, worried that Tafoya and Ecabapi might be leading a group of angry men after him at this very moment, but tried to block these from his mind. He had enough problems. The mare faltered, Coady's body begged for water, and he was lost somewhere in the merciless *Llano Estacado.*

He took to calling the mare Fletcher, after the dog he had had back in North Carolina, but tried not to speak much. The horse snorted and pawed the earth once they neared the killing grounds, and no matter how hard Coady coaxed, she refused to budge, so he reluctantly dismounted, wrapped the hackamore around a clump of sage, and walked—more like stumbled—toward the bloating buffalo carcasses.

Nearly a year with the Kwahadi Comanches had taught him a few things, and he thanked Quanah for letting him observe that buffalo hunt last year. Coady dropped to his knees beside a slaughtered cow, gripped his knife, and, choking down bile, reached inside, and sliced. The buffalo's paunch held water, not much but some, and Coady drank and rested before moving to another dead buffalo. He saved the paunch's inner lining from a dead bull to use as a water bag, walked back to the tired pinto mare, and let her drink.

Mounting proved difficult. His muscles ached, and his knees didn't want to bend, so he led the horse and positioned it so he could mount from higher ground. It still wasn't easy, but Coady lowered his backside onto the Comanche saddle pad and led the mare away from the dead buffalo.

He woke up the following morning, and cursed his own stupidity. "Fletcher!" he yelled, but the pinto mare had wandered off. He should have figured out a way to hobble the animal, but had been too exhausted.

"Fletcher!"

Nothing, only an endless expanse of prairie and an already broiling sun. With no landmarks to guide his way, he had to rely on the sun to tell direction. The water bag held water, and he drank before staggering north.

A nightmare woke him late that night, and he sat up screaming. Coyotes, or perhaps wolves, answered his cries, and his heart pounded. With his water almost gone, he knew he would die here, alone, on this god-forsaken prairie.

He felt the knife in his right hand and thought about ending his misery, just slicing his throat. He had heard of people doing that. Frowning, he stuck the knife into his moccasin and stood. A half moon and a million stars gave enough light, and he decided it would be better to walk in the night, take advantage of the cooler temperatures, than cook to death during the day.

Which way? Find the North Star, but the sky danced with tiny lights, and Coady had no idea which one was the right star. Something flickered in the lower horizon—too low for a star—and Coady blinked, saw it again a moment later.

Campfire? But whose? And how far away? Distances, he had learned, deceived you out here, and, for all he knew, the men around that campfire—if it indeed proved to be a campfire—could be Comanches or Comancheros. Not that it mattered, he decided at last. He would die anyway. He drained the buffalo gut of water and walked toward the winking light.

A horse snorted, and Coady froze. The sinking moon disappeared behind a cloud, and the firelight had vanished an hour earlier. Maybe there had been no light. Maybe it had been an illusion, a mirage. Buffalo Bill had written about those things, too. Another horse answered, and Coady realized this was not his mind toying with him. Someone was here . . . but who? He drew his knife and crept forward, toward the sound of the horses, wanting to call out but keeping his mouth tightly clamped.

Holding the knife in front of him, he poked through the darkness, wet his lips, listened carefully. Another animal stamped a hoof and whinnied. Closer. Coady stepped forward, the moon reappeared, and hard metal slammed against his wrist, sending the knife flying to the dirt as he screamed in pain. A rough hand grabbed him from behind and threw him to the ground.

Chapter Nine

The hand belonged to me.

Crouching while thumbing back the .44's hammer, I lined up my barrel with the buckskin-clad figure writhing on the ground and started to squeeze the trigger. Why didn't I? I'm not altogether certain. Divine intervention? Fear that some Indian would mark my position by gunshot or muzzle flash and fill me with arrows? Perhaps in the dim moonlight, I recognized that our invader, although in Indian clothes, sported hair and skin too fair for a Comanche, or the fact that, when I slammed the Colt's barrel against his wrist, his yelp sounded much like a barnyard epithet not found in any Comanche warrior's vocabulary.

No matter the reason or combination of reasons, I relaxed my trigger finger and lunged toward him, dropping to both knees and clamping my left hand against his mouth. "Quiet," I commanded, and he stopped squirming, eyes filled with tears and fear. His blue-gray eyes told me for certain that he wasn't an Indian. "You alone?"

He nodded, and I lifted my hand.

"Are you . . . The Unknown Scout?" he asked.

I blinked, uncomprehending, and lowered the Colt's hammer but didn't put the revolver away. As a printer, journalist, and traveler, I had read a lot, but Buffalo Bill's half-dime novels remained foreign to me. It took a moment to gather myself, and at last I shook my head slightly and told him my name, then asked for his.

"My name's . . . Coady," he said. "Coady McIlvain . . .

Comanches killed . . . my pa . . . last spring . . . took me prisoner. Escaped a few days back . . . lost my horse."

At that moment, Lillard Butler stepped forward, holding a Yellow Boy loosely, and asked: "What's going on here?"

Among our skinners, Butler was one sorry excuse for a man but a fair hand with a knife. No one could blame him for hating his job, but he knew it would be grueling, stinking, and pitiful when he signed on, and the way I figured things, $50 a month paid him for a full day's skinning, not bellyaching. Butler bragged about his days fighting to preserve the union with VI Corps' 138th Pennsylvania, even claimed to have shot and killed Confederate General A. P. Hill at Petersburg in April of '65. I had no reason to doubt his marksmanship as we had let him go hunting a few times while moving camp, and he consistently brought back cleanly shot game. His Civil War stories, however, I suspected as pure braggadocio, and it didn't matter. We paid him to skin buffalo.

We also paid him to stand guard during his watch, so I lashed out as I rose: "If this boy had been a Comanch', we'd all be dead. You fell asleep, you stupid oaf."

"No, I didn't." A thin man with a deeply pockmarked face and nasal whine, Butler straightened. The pitch of his whine tuned higher when he argued or complained. "I never slept once."

"Then how'd he get this close to our bedrolls?" I fired back, pointing the revolver barrel at the boy still on the ground. "He could have killed us or stolen our horses, leaving us afoot. If I hadn't heard the horses. . . ." I shook my head. "Fall asleep again on your watch, Butler, and you'll rue the day."

"I wasn't asleep," he whined. "I heard the horses, too." The Winchester rattled in his hands, and he blinked repeatedly as I pulled Coady McIlvain to his feet. Butler shifted the rifle, ran rough fingers through his thinning brown hair, licked his lips, and asked: "Well, who is he?"

"We'll find out." I led the boy to where the rest of our crew stirred, stoked the fire, and began cleaning my spectacles. Jenkins and the other skinners had been struck senseless; they simply stared at the boy kneeling by the flames, but Claybrooke warmed up the coffee and gave Coady a canteen and piece of jerky. A few minutes later, Coady told us his story.

Dawn was approaching when he finished, and we digested the tale. Butler shook his head and snickered, saying that story seemed as believable as a five-penny dreadful.

Or you shooting A. P. Hill, I thought.

"I recollect hearin' somethin' 'bout that when we was in Dodge. Called it The McIlvain Massacre, they did," commented Cuthbert Jenkins, head cocked, squinting at the graying sky.

I set down my coffee cup and tried digging deeper into my memories about The McIlvain Massacre, but my shot went wide. We had been on the plains too long, had been running buffalo when the Indian attack occurred, and, with the exception of Jenkins and his faulty memory, had been privy to no barbershop gossip or saloon chatter about the incident during our brief respite in Dodge City the previous fall.

Skinner Chet McDonough cut short our pondering by putting forth a fairly important question: "What are we to do with him?"

When no one spoke immediately, J. C. Claybrooke gave us all a fiery glare. "We need to take this boy home," he said, "to his ma and sisters. Buffalo camp ain't no place for a youngster."

Coady just stared at the fire.

Home probably meant his father's grave. He'd have to face this eventually, I thought, then stopped myself. Who was I trying to fool? Myself?

"Buffler ain't migrated yet," Cuthbert Jenkins said. "We head back to Kansas now, we'll be losin' a right smart of money."

Summer was slow to come to the Texas Panhandle that year. Sure it felt hot, and we and other runners had killed more than a few buffalo, but we remained greedy. The great Texas herd still ate grass deeper south, so, if we left now, we would miss the slaughter. If we left with the hides we had so far, Jenkins and I wouldn't break even.

"One of you could take him," Butler told Jenkins and me. "I'll take your place shooting buffs."

"Who'd skin 'em?" Jenkins said with a snort. He had as little use for Butler as I did, but we had both hired him and so had only ourselves to blame.

"You ain't about to send this boy all the way to Dodge with just Dylan or Cuthbert," Trabue argued. "Seen too much Injun sign for such tomfoolery. You'd get that boy kilt, and yourselves."

"Trabue is right," Ignacio said. "There is strength in numbers."

The two skinners had a point, so Claybrooke suggested: "Leave him at Adobe Walls. Someone'll take him back to Dodge from there."

One of the Bent brothers' unsuccessful trading posts back in the 1840s, Adobe Walls had been reborn on the north side of the Canadian River that spring because of the buffalo trade. Charlie Myers, Fred Leonard, Charles Rath, even James Hanrahan had left Dodge City to set up businesses at Adobe Walls, turning the ruins into a settlement where buffalo runners could sell hides and buy supplies rather than risking a journey to Dodge City or heading southeast to some Texas town like Fort Griffin, Fort Worth, or Denison.

"I'm thirsty," Butler said. "Adobe Walls it is."

"That's a right fer piece," Jenkins said, "but I guess we could use some supplies. We'll drift north, pick up any buffler we see on the way."

Claybrooke started breakfast while we broke camp, loading the skins we had drying onto our wagons.

The kid earned his keep. I expected him to retreat into his shell after all that had happened to him, and after months running buffalo, none of our lot resembled or smelled like gentlemen, nor did we have any idea how to act around a skinny thirteen-year-old who had spent the past year living with Comanches. Coady McIlvain, however, proved to be a top soldier. He gathered buffalo chips, washed dishes, helped Claybrooke with other chores around camp, smiled when Claybrooke read Mark Twain stories, and tapped his feet when Claybrooke fiddled. Ever the businessman, Cuthbert Jenkins felt no rush to get Coady to Adobe Walls, so when we found a small herd of buffalo, we made our stands, put the skinners to work, and waited. The boy didn't seem to mind, and I soon realized he enjoyed being in a camp full of buffalo men.

He was curious, too.

"What are you doing?" he asked one night after Claybrooke had entertained us by reading "Curing a Cold".

"Reloading my cartridges," I said, while carefully pouring powder from a flask into the brass casing. Once I had finished seating the bullet, I tossed the cartridge to him. He rolled it in his fingers. "It's a Fifty-Ninety casing, but I add ten more grains. Kicks like a mule, but it drops buffs."

"A Big Fifty," he said in awe. "I thought so, but wasn't sure. Is that what Mister Jenkins shoots, too?"

"Fifty-two caliber linen. His is an older model than mine, but both are Old Reliables. You like Sharps, huh?"

His head bobbed enthusiastically. "The Unknown Scout used a Big Fifty when he shot against Buffalo Bill."

Fighting back a smile, I said: "You'll have to tell me about this Unknown Scout."

"You never heard of him?" He looked at me as if I were some freak of nature.

I shrugged in reply, and, over the next twenty minutes, he filled me in about The Unknown Scout, the mysterious man who had saved Buffalo Bill Cody's life and tamed the savage border. When he finished, I suggested we might see about buying that half-dime novel because it sounded more interesting and exciting than anything Samuel Langhorne Clemens had penned.

"I bet Mister Claybrooke could read it good, too," he said.

"I bet he could."

My .50-caliber Sharps leaned against the hide wagon on the other side of the wheel where I sat resting my back. I reached over and picked up the heavy rifle, checked the breech, and offered it to Coady. His eyes widened.

"It's not loaded," I told him. "Go ahead, Coady, take it."

Coady probably weighed in at no more than eighty-five pounds, and the fourteen-pound Big Fifty proved quite a handful. As the barrel roamed around in a wild circle, I rose to my knees and steadied it by resting the barrel against the wagon wheel rim. Holding his breath, he pressed his cheek against the stock, closed his left eye, and sighted down the barrel. He couldn't work the hammer or lever, so I cocked the rifle for him.

"They're two triggers," he said in surprise.

"One's the set trigger. You pull it first, and the rifle's ready to fire." He smiled at the *click* the set trigger made, moved his finger, and froze like a young hunter with buck fever. I could recall that look on myself during my first deer hunt nigh thirty years earlier.

"It's empty," I repeated, and he pulled the trigger.

"That's good."

I took the Sharps from his sagging arms. "Most young 'uns jerk the trigger, but you squeezed it. That's how you do it. Now, what were you aiming at?"

"Prickly pear."

"No, what did you see out there?"

"Buffler," he said in his best Cuthbert Jenkins impression.

"You want to be a buffalo runner when you grow up?" I asked.

He started to nod, then said: "I don't know if I can wait that long. I used to dream I was running buffalo. I had this . . . well, you'll think it's dumb . . . but I had a tobacco stick I played with back on the farm. I pretended it was a Big Fifty, just like the one The Unknown Scout had. My pa. . . ." His eyes dropped for a moment, but he soon looked up, which I found healthy. "Anyway, Pa, Lois, but mostly Faye . . . she's my oldest sister . . . would tease me about it, but I liked it. I killed many a buffalo with that tobacco stick."

A native of Wisconsin, I had no idea what a tobacco stick was, but I smiled and said: "Imagination is a good thing."

"What did you want to be when you grew up?"

His question took me a little off guard, and I had to think long and hard before answering. "A logger, I guess. That's what my father did. We were Welshmen in a land full of Norwegians, and I didn't have many friends. Guess I was a lot like you. I made up my own games and stories. Logger. Miner. My grandfather worked the mines in Wales, and he had some stories to tell. Riverboat pilot. We didn't live far from the Saint Croix River. Then I wanted to be a newspaperman, a writer like Mark Twain. Then a soldier. I've wanted to be just about everything, and I've been just about everything in my life."

"You married? Kids?"

My stomach knotted, but I tried to smile. "Just a National Typographical Union traveling card." He wouldn't understand that, and I wanted to steer this conversation back to him as I found it to be getting more and more uncomfortable. "Where did you hit that buffalo?"

"Right between the eyes . . . just like Buffalo Bill and The Unknown Scout done."

"Well, that's not exactly how I do it, but I'm not saying it doesn't work. I mean, Buffalo Bill is Buffalo Bill." I leaned the Sharps against the wagon and went back to my bullet loading.

"How do you do it?" he asked.

"Well, I see which way the wind's blowing, don't want the buffalo to catch my scent, and sneak in maybe a couple hundred yards." I pointed to the tang sight. "That helps me with long-range shooting, and with my eyesight I need plenty of help. Anyway, I study the herd, find the leader. . . ."

"I know," he interrupted. "Buffalo Bill explained all that, too. And some runners I heard in town. You shoot the leader first, drop him so the buffalo won't run. Then you can kill hundreds, thousands of them." His words ran together in excitement.

I spoke as I reloaded. "Bill Cody made his name shooting buffalo for the railroad, the Army," I said. "So he might kill a couple hundred, but I won't shoot more than fifty, if I can get that many. Any more than that, and Ignacio and Trabue would be skinning me."

"Oh. What else?"

"Well, now I haven't been at this as long as Mister Jenkins, Coady, but in my experience most of the leaders I've found have been cows, hers, not hims."

"Honest?"

"Honest."

"Why do you keep that cartridge in your pocket?" he blurted out, and my eyes dropped to the piece of brass poking out of my vest. Seeing the bite of cyanide made me frown.

"For luck?" Coady asked.

"You might say that," I answered, pushing the poison deeper into the pocket and quickly changing the subject. "Say, Coady, you want to ride out with me after breakfast? Might see a buffalo."

"Really?" His pleasant beam made me forget all about the bite in my pocket. "I thought y'all planned on moving out."

"You in some particular hurry?" I asked in mock rebuke, and immediately regretted my words. He most certainly wanted to be back on his Ford County farm with his mother and siblings, but his smile spread.

"No, sir," he answered, and scurried off to his bedroll. "I'll be ready."

Chapter Ten

I didn't expect to find any buffalo that morning but, a mile out of camp, came across an old bull. We loped to the rising dust and spotted the ancient buffalo slowly rising from a wallow. Coady, riding behind me, slipped off first, and I dismounted, hobbled the horse, and grabbed my hunting possibles. After circling around, using a dry wash for cover, we moved up the side and lay flat beside the scattered bleached bones of a wolf and a badger that must have killed each other.

"This is close enough," I whispered, and began setting up the shooting sticks.

"Think he's alone?" Coady asked.

"Yeah. See how he favors that hind leg? Got in a little row with some wolves, I warrant, made out only slightly better than these two." I cocked my head at the bones, placed the barrel inside the triangle made by the crossed rest sticks, adjusted the tang sight for distance, and smiled at Coady. "He's old, too, probably came out here to die. This'll be more merciful than leaving him for the wolves."

"So, if there was a whole herd of buffalo, you'd spot the leader first?" he asked.

"Right." I started to explain how I determined the leader, but Coady fired another question at me.

"What happens when the herd runs?"

"I go after them, leave the ones I've killed behind for the skinners."

"Comanches, they run after the whole herd," he said.

"Stampede them and chase them down, shooting them with arrows mostly. Quanah, he once told me there was no honor in the way white folks kill buffalo."

"Definitely not much sport in it," I agreed, and pulled away from the rifle. "Take aim, Coady," I heard myself saying. "Let's see what you can do."

He didn't budge at first, but I told him I meant it, and he crawled over. While he stretched one of his long arms and rested the stock against his right shoulder, I withdrew another long cartridge from the bandoleer. The boy would miss—of that I felt certain—and the bull would hobble away, and I'd likely let him go, but he could also charge us if the wind shifted directions and he caught our scent. That bum leg would slow him down a lot, though, and I could take the Sharps, reload, and drop him before he got too close. "You have a side shot, Coady," I coached him, "so aim just behind the shoulder blade."

He hesitated, and I watched him wipe sweat from his brow, although it wasn't hot at all. After repositioning himself, he shut his left eye tightly, took a deep breath, and started shaking. I said nothing, but turned my attention to the old bull, while Coady fought off his nerves, calmed himself, took a final breath, and held it.

A second after the set trigger clicked, the Big Fifty roared, and I realized I hadn't stuffed my ears, or Coady's, with balled cotton. Coady groaned from the rifle's kick, and I reached down, ears ringing, grabbed the rifle, reloaded it, and stepped aside of the pungent, thick smoke. The old bull took a half step forward and dropped.

What I said is not fit for Christian ears.

"I got him?" said Coady, rubbing his shoulder while staring at me for confirmation, although the dead buffalo told the story perfectly.

"You got him," I said dumbly.

We picked up our gear and walked back to the horse to ride to the bull. "You'll send the skinners . . . ," he said as we circled the old beast.

"No," I said, too stunned to notice the eagerness in his voice. "A bull's hide is usually too tough, not worth that much, especially one this old."

"Then why did you let me shoot him?"

When I looked away from the buffalo and at the boy, his sad eyes stared up at me in confusion. I didn't want to tell him that, at two hundred yards, I didn't think he'd even hit the buffalo.

"You'll just leave it here?" Tears began to well, and I felt ashamed. "To rot?"

I had to look away. Buyers in Dodge City preferred cow hides, but we shot plenty of bulls for nothing more than their tongues. Coady had told me about the Comanches, how they used practically everything the buffalo offered, how they left the hearts on the ground so the Great Spirit, or whatever the Comanches believed in, could recreate the immense herds. No wonder Indians despised us. How many buffalo bulls had I left decaying on the plains?

"Well," I said, defeated, "I guess we can't leave your first buffalo behind. We'll fetch Ignacio and Trabue, and we'll let you keep this. Keep you warm when you get home."

Not that I'd want that piece of mangy, scarred hide any-where near me—even after treatment from the skinners. The smile returned, and I asked about the shoulder he kept rubbing.

"I'll be all right," he told me.

I had no doubt about that. "Think you could shoot that Sharps fifty times a day?"

"The shooting sticks help a lot, and I'd get used to the kick."

"You pace yourself," I told him. "Get into a rhythm, so to speak. I bring a canteen with me when I find a stand and run a wet rag down the barrel after three or four shots. Cools things off. I wouldn't recommend that on every rifle, but the Sharps can handle it."

"The Sharps can handle anything. What's the longest shot you ever made?"

"On a buffalo?"

"Yes, sir."

"About six hundred yards."

"Golly, I'm not even sure The Unknown Scout could do that, Mister Griffith."

"Call me Dylan." I tousled his hair. "We ought to see about buying you a hat when we get to Adobe Walls."

The skinners didn't say much when I asked them to skin the old bull. Ignacio cut out the bull's tongue and tossed it nonchalantly into the back of the wagon while Trabue hooked a chain to the rear axle and the buffalo's front leg. I had seen them do this many times, but Coady looked awestruck. Every aspect of the buffalo trade fascinated the boy, which made me happy. Anything that took his mind off his father, off his year with the Comanches . . . well, that had to be a good thing. Once the two skinners had finished working on the upper side of the bull, Ignacio climbed into the wagon, released the brake, and flicked the reins. The wagon moved just a bit, pulling the buffalo up a little, before Ignacio stopped, set the brake, jumped down from the wagon, and went back to work with his knife.

"What's that for?" Coady asked me, pointing to a forked piece of wood the skinners had secured to the rear axle near the chain. It angled down and dragged the ground.

"Extra brake," I said. "It keeps the wagon from backing up."

"Oh."

After more skinning, Ignacio returned to the wagon and pulled the buffalo carcass completely over so they could work on the other side. While they worked, I unfolded my pocket knife and went to work on the Sharps. Now, a rifle purist would have chastised me for carving the cross-grain walnut stock on such a beautiful gun, but I wanted to commemorate this day. Coady eyed me curiously but said nothing until I hefted the rifle and showed him the stock.

Coady M.
Killed His First Buffalo
With This Rifle
Texas, 1874

"But that's your Big Fifty," he said when he recovered his voice.

For now, I thought. "Yeah." I smiled. "And that's your buffalo." He fingered the carving gingerly, shook his head, and looked up, his face alight with delight, and turned back to watch the skinners. At last, they stripped off the smelly hide and loaded it unceremoniously in the wagon. Blood and grime caked Ignacio's and Trabue's hands, staining their already filthy shirt sleeves up to their elbows. Vultures had begun circling overhead, and the carcass began to stink, but Coady didn't seem to mind the smell or the swarming flies.

"Flies, Dan'l, flies!" he said, laughing at his own joke while jumping around and waving his hands. He had become a big fan of J. C. Claybrooke's readings of "The Celebrated Jumping Frog of Calaveras County".

Smiling, I swung into the saddle. "They'll treat the hide with poison to kill the ticks, fleas, and buffalo mange," I explained.

"Buffalo mange?"

"Lice." I offered my hand and pulled Coady up behind me. "We'll peg the hide down for three days, maybe four, and after that turn it over flesh-side up for a day, then alternate, flesh-up, flesh-down, till the hide's dry."

We rode back to camp, leaving the skinners to finish up. The sight of visitors left me surprised, almost as amazed as seeing a thirteen-year-old plow boy drop a buffalo at two hundred yards with one shot.

We competed for the same herds, stands, ranges, and buyers, but hospitality ran strong in any buffalo runner's camp. Peg-legged Captain Grover Barr, his three skinners, and cook stopped their wagons to swap buffalo stories and trade coffee for tobacco. His wagon beds sagged under the weight of the thousands of hides he had shot, and Cuthbert Jenkins turned pale at the thought of how rich he might have been had he joined Barr, instead of sticking with me.

"Who'd you kill to steal all them hides?" Jenkins asked in jest. The great Texas herd still hadn't migrated, and Barr had more hides than we had seen buffalo.

One of Barr's skinners, a half-breed in buckskins and a bell crown hat, took exception and stepped forward with a scowl, but Barr's laughter calmed him down. "Didn't see no need to wait for 'em," Barr said, resting his Remington Rolling Block against his outstretched wooden right leg. Dirty strips of canvas had been wrapped tightly around his left ankle, and, although he used his rifle as a crutch, he still needed his skinners' help to get around. He told us he had sprained his ankle—his cook said it was broken—in a prairie dog hole. "I went where the buffs were. Now I'm on my way back to Dodge to pay off the boys and have me some turns with Squirrel Tooth Alice if she ain't too busy."

"Now Capt'n," Jenkins said, "you got one leg shot off and tuther one busted."

"Them ain't the legs that matter with Alice, Cuthbert," he said wickedly.

"What's he mean?" Coady asked.

"Nothing," I shot back.

"Dancing?"

"Yeah, dancing. Do me a favor, Coady. Run open my carpetbag and fetch my bottle of whisky." I raised my voice. "I suspect Captain Barr is thirsty."

"You suspect right, my friend. Y'all had much luck?"

"Fair to middling. Shooting some stragglers."

"Well, the buffs are movin' north, boys, so they'll be thick as flies before long. Y'all seen Injun sign?"

"Nope," Jenkins said. "Not in a spell. Where you reckon they've run off to?"

"Sun dance," Coady answered, having returned with the half full bottle. I took the bottle, uncorked it, and passed it to Captain Barr, but his eyes remained trained on Coady.

"How's that?"

"Isa-tai," Coady answered. "He's been talking about war, invited a lot of Comanche leaders to a sun dance."

"Comanch' don't have no sun dance, sonny," the half-breed said, took a pull from the bottle, and passed the whisky to J. C. Claybrooke.

"This will be their first," Coady said. "I reckon they've had it by now. Cheyennes, Arapahoes, Kiowas . . . they were all thinking about following Isa-tai into battle."

Said Barr: "I ain't never heard of no Isa-tai."

Coady simply shrugged, and I broke in, telling the visitors that Coady had been abducted in Kansas and had been a Comanche prisoner for a year. With help from my crew, our guests had emptied the bottle by the time it got back to me, but Barr gestured toward his wagon and a black skinner ambled over and returned with a jug of corn liquor. We drank while Coady, prodded by Captain Barr, told all about Isa-tai's vision.

"Balderdash," Barr said after Coady finished. "Injuns ain't about to run us offen this buffler range, and I don't think for one minute Comanch' and Kioways would ride with Cheyennes and Arapahoes. No, sir. No need in tryin' to scare us, Jenkins. I'm done with runnin' buffler."

"Ain't got a notion to scare you, Capt'n," Jenkins said as he searched his vest for the makings. "Boy told us the same story. I suspect it's true, but we ain't leavin' till we got us a load of quality hides."

Barr wiped his mouth after a pull from the jug, which he passed to the black skinner. "Where'd you find this boy?" he asked.

"Fell out of the sky," Claybrooke answered, "a couple of weeks back. Pretty handy to have around camp."

"And a mighty fine shot," I answered. "He dropped a bull this morning at two hundred yards. One shot."

"With what?" Barr demanded.

"My Sharps."

Rye whisky topped with corn whisky had left us all in our cups, and I knew what would come next, but didn't do anything to stop it. Once Coady swore that neither he nor I had lied about the buffalo shot, Barr pulled out a wad of greenbacks, and the betting began. I sent Coady for my carpetbag, and, after he returned, I opened it, found my money belt, and matched Barr's $100. As side bets sprung up, I went to grab my Big Fifty while the skinners lifted the crippled old buffalo hunter and carried him to the edge of camp where Jenkins, carrying the empty rye bottle and clay jug, was counting off two hundred paces—just as he had done back in Dodge City when I won the Sharps. Coady had followed me, and, when I slid a cartridge into the Sharps, he cleared his throat.

"I can't outshoot that man," he said. "It was probably just dumb luck that I hit that buffalo."

"Nonsense," I said.

"But he's got a telescope on his rifle."

"Yeah," I said, "and he's full of John Barleycorn. Whisky and rifles don't mix, Coady. You remember that. Besides, he'll be shooting at his jug. That's brown clay, and it'll be hard to see sitting on the ground. You'll be able to see the bottle from the glare." That had helped me during my sharpshooting contest back in Dodge City.

"But that bottle's a lot smaller than a buffalo."

"Not the target," I lied. "The kill shot for a buffalo is about the same as that whisky bottle." Actually, the target on a buffalo was about the size of my hat. "Just do your best, Coady."

"But you'll lose your money if. . . ."

"I've lost more than that playing cards. This is for bragging rights, not money, and mostly it's for fun. Might even be better than J.C. fiddling for us or reading Mark Twain."

Crippled, tired, hurting, and pretty much roostered, Captain Grover Barr still took his shooting seriously. He had lost his leg at Antietam, fighting alongside John Bell Hood, and I figured the proof of his marksmanship lay with the thousands of buffalo hides strapped in his wagons. Sober, he'd be tough to beat, but he was three sheets to the wind. The Remington barrel circled like a magic wand, and he belched once before firing. The bullet didn't come close to either bottle or jug, and he muttered an oath before handing the Rolling Block to the black skinner for reloading.

Coady rested the barrel inside the shooting sticks I had set up and lay prone, pulling the stock against shoulder, stretching his arms, concentrating.

"Just do your best," Claybrooke said.

"Yeah," Butler added with a snort. "Pretend it's the buck who kilt your pa."

I turned savagely toward the Pennsylvanian, but Coady must not have heard—too busy sighting down the barrel of the Sharps. Everyone gave Butler hard looks, and Claybrooke, standing closest to the skinner, swatted him upside the head with his hat, called him a fool, and told him to shut up. Still, Coady McIlvain concentrated on the target.

"Just take yer time," said Jenkins, slurring his words. "You can hit that jug, boy."

I grimaced. Jug! I had told Coady to fire at the bottle, and we had named our targets while laying down ground rules. Perhaps he hadn't heard Jenkins. At least, that's what I hoped because I didn't have time to correct my partner before Coady fired. The rye bottle exploded, Claybrooke and Jenkins locked arms and started a jig, Ignacio, McDonough, and Trabue sent their hats sailing, Butler's mouth went agape, the black skinner laughed, another skinner groaned, and the half-breed cursed.

"Ain't I a suck-egg mule?" said Captain Barr, tossing money at my feet. "Anybody got some tonsil paint? Need to wash down some crow."

Slapping his recovered hat against his pants leg, J. C. Claybrooke fetched his fiddle.

"Well, that's jim dandy," Barr said with a smile. "My feet ain't up to dancin', but I got me a jaw harp. Glenn, you and Moses fetch a hide to use as a dance floor."

"But . . . ," Coady began, then Trabue and Ignacio lifted the boy over their heads and carried him around camp as we showered him with Yankee hurrahs and Rebel yells. Even Barr and his crew cheered the protesting boy's marksmanship. The sun began to sink, someone discovered another jug of corn liquor, and we forgot all about supper. We danced on the stiff buffalo hide till midnight, Claybrooke sawing his fiddle, Barr pounding the jaw harp, and me singing Welsh ballads as well as "Lorena", "Jeanie With the Light Brown Hair", "Buffalo Gals", and any other song I could halfway remember.

Barr's crew tied bandanas around their arms, designating them as women, for the first couple of hours, then our boys played the part. Coady ran up to me as I tied a bandanna on Jenkins's arm, but I told him to quit complaining, that he had to be a girl like everyone else. "No," he said, "that's not. . . ." Claybrooke silenced his protest by starting "Old Dan Tucker", and Glenn, Barr's six-foot-two, two-hundred-pound cook, grabbed the boy and carried him, squealing at first but finally laughing to the hide floor.

The dance ended when Captain Barr passed out. Moses and the half-breed stuck the jaw harp in Barr's vest pocket and carted him off to his wagon, and we called it a night.

And what a night it had been. Lightheaded from the whisky and dancing, I managed to unroll my bedroll and crawl in for some shut-eye, not even noticing Coady standing there until he started talking.

"Mister Griffith I been trying to tell you all night."

"It's Dylan. Remember? Go to sleep, Coady."

"But that shot I made. . . ."

"Heck of a shot, Coady." I pried my eyelids open. "We'll talk about it in the morning."

"But . . . Dylan. I wasn't aiming at the bottle. I know you told me to, but I heard Mister Jenkins say shoot the jug. That's what I was trying to hit."

I laughed so hard my ribs hurt.

"Shouldn't you . . . ," Coady began once my guffaws had made way for occasional snickers, "give Captain Barr his money back?"

Chapter Eleven

In spite of red-lined eyes and throbbing head, I made out the figure of Barr's half-breed skinner, Paria, standing over me. "Good morning," I said, although I couldn't detect anything positive about it just yet, and sat up, resting my back against a wagon wheel. J. C. Claybrooke's snores droned a few yards to my right, and I shook my head after pulling my eyeglasses from the case. "I hope your belly-cheater's got coffee brewing," I said lightly, jutting my chin toward our cook. "Don't think ours has recovered from all that dancing."

Paria didn't even crack a smile, and I noticed a Henry rifle, the barrel in the crook of his left arm, right hand in the lever, finger in the trigger guard—not what I would call a friendly gesture this early in the morning. Barr's other two skinners, the black man Moses and a Texican called Hunter, both carrying rifles, had also wandered into our sleeping camp. Not a one of them looked hospitable, and I didn't think it was because of the whisky we drank last night. The half-breed was the hardest of the lot, dressed in buckskins and moccasins like the rest of Barr's crew, with his thumb scratching the Henry's hammer. My Sharps rested, unloaded and out of reach, against the wagon, but the Colt .44 remained hidden under my bedroll, and my spare Navy lay tucked inside my carpetbag atop my copy of Mark Twain stories.

My first thoughts were of Coady McIlvain, that the boy had told Grover Barr this morning how he hadn't intended to hit the empty rye bottle, and Barr had sent in his crew to collect the money rightfully his. Well, I had planned on returning the old Johnny Reb's hundred bucks over breakfast. Coady lay tucked underneath his blankets, however, dead to the world, so Barr's men had come for some other purpose.

"Hallo the camp!"

Hoof beats sounded behind the mesquites, and I made out a couple of figures on bay horses. Paria stepped away from me and started to bring up his rifle while I fetched and cocked my open-top Colt. A few weeks back, I had come close to pistol-whipping Lillard Butler for falling asleep on guard duty. Well, what had I done? I had been too drunk to make sure someone took watch. I shuddered, relieved Barr's skinners remained alert. They must have heard the horses and gotten ready in case our visitors weren't friendly. At least, that was my assumption.

One rider wore a derby; both carried rifles at the ready. " 'Morning!" I called out, and stood, finally relaxing. Paria shot a cold glance at me, then at my Colt, and frowned, the first expression he had shown all morning.

"We're coming in," the voice called out, "unless you have any objections!"

By now, I recognized both the voice and derby. "Come ahead, Bat. It's Dylan Griffith."

Our crew began to stir as Bat Masterson and a tall, young man with flowing hair and a neatly trimmed mustache dismounted. Masterson slid his .45-70 Springfield into the saddle boot, but his friend kept his Sharps rifle for security. I doubted if he went anywhere without the custom rifle, and I couldn't blame him. The caliber was smaller than mine, but one glance told me that rifle was worth a fortune to any buffalo runner.

Masterson and I shook hands, and we made introductions all the way around while Jenkins, cranky because he hadn't had his morning cigarette yet, kicked our sleepy heads awake. Bat Masterson gestured at his companion. "This is Billy Dixon."

"Don't tell me y'all's runnin' a cold camp," Dixon drawled. "I ain't had a cup of coffee since we left Adobe Walls."

"Getting a late start," I said. "We had a bit of a fandango last night. Got good and drunk."

"Good and drunk . . . that's redundant," Masterson said with a smirk.

I enjoyed the young man's wit, thought he should be working at a big-city newspaper instead of chasing buffalo.

Dixon didn't smile at all. Buffalo runners generally had a devil-may-care attitude, quick with a joke like Masterson, but Billy Dixon looked as serious as a pious circuit rider eager to spout fire and brimstone. "Dangerous," he said. "Bat and me found Stuart Bowen and his outfit yesterday. Gutted like fish, scalped, wagons burned and the hides along with 'em, or stole. They ain't the first, neither. Shorty Shadler said he come across a bunch of pilgrims butchered on the Prairie Dog Fork of the Red. Looks like there's a war a-comin', boys."

I knew of Billy Dixon. Only twenty-three years old, he already had a reputation as one of the best shots on the buffalo ranges, and I wouldn't bet against him and the .44-caliber Sharps he toted. Dixon had partnered up with Jim Hanrahan at Adobe Walls; Hanrahan would supply whisky and skinners, and Dixon would do the shooting. Masterson had left Dodge to try his hand at running buffalo as well, but like many of the runners had stayed at the Walls waiting for the herd to return north. After Shorty Shadler's grisly discovery, Masterson volunteered to ride a wide loop in search of buffalo, or Comanche sign. Dixon decided to ride along with Masterson, and they had discovered the remains of Bowen and his two skinners.

"Reckon the boy was right," Jenkins commented after hearing Dixon's report.

"How's that?" Masterson asked.

I told him I'd explain over breakfast, which prompted Billy Dixon to ask about the coffee again.

"Glenn just put a pot on, fellas!" Grover Barr called out, leaning on his Remington rifle as a crutch. "Come on over."

Glenn Marcus made mighty stout coffee, thick and heavy enough to weigh down the liquor and keep last night's rotgut in my stomach. We sipped his brew while the cook fried up thick slices of bacon that had our crew salivating and forgetting all about our queasy stomachs and miserable headaches. We hadn't tasted bacon in months.

While Marcus cooked, the rest of us traded news. Coady gave Dixon and Masterson a shorter version of his capture, and Dixon explained in more detail the discoveries of the dead buffalo runners. Even the morbid topic failed to spoil our appetites as Marcus also heated up sourdough biscuits.

"You trail them Injuns that did it?" Barr asked.

"Tried," Dixon said, "but they didn't leave no sign. You said you went pretty far south running the buffler?"

"Past Double Mountain and clear down to the Colorado. That's how we got them hides. The early bird gets the buffs."

"Did you run into Stuart Bowen's crew?"

"Dixon, we ain't seen a white man since leavin' Dodge till we run across Cuthbert here." He passed his tin cup over to Marcus for a refill.

"I'm gonna need some more plates to feed this crew," Marcus complained after passing his boss's cup back, so I sent Coady to Claybrooke's stolen chuck wagon, the envy of many a buffalo outfit.

Masterson pulled off his derby, and ran fingers through his hair. "Bowen and his boys had been dead for a week, maybe two," he said. "Shot up close, pinned to the ground with arrows. Cut to pieces. Even pulled half a dozen arrows out of his dogs."

Jenkins cursed the Comanche nation, and Barr added a few oaths.

"That doesn't sound like Comanches."

Every face turned to Coady McIlvain, who stood beside me with his hands full of tin plates. I took them and passed them toward Marcus.

"What do you know, boy?" Paria asked testily. "My mother was Kiowa."

But you never lived with them, I thought.

"Then you should know Comanches wouldn't leave arrows in a dog," Coady said as he sat cross-legged beside me. "In a dead man, yes, but not in a dog or animal. They'd take them to use later. And they wouldn't hide their tracks. They'd dare you to come after them."

Shaking his head, Lillard Butler emptied the dregs on the ground and swore. "Boy, I'm getting sick of you defending them red butchers. You forget what them bucks did to your pa?"

"Shut up," Claybrooke snapped. "Nurse your hang-over in silence. Go on, Coady."

I credited everyone's testiness to too much John Barleycorn, and patted Coady's knee. The aftereffects of a drunken dance and Masterson's and Dixon's discoveries left everyone scared—although no one would admit it—and angry.

"It could be Comancheros," Coady went on, sounding much older than his thirteen years. "That's what I meant. They came to the Kwahadi camp twice this year, and the Comanches wanted rifles. Comancheros could have killed those men for guns and hides. Left the arrows to make it look like the Indians did it."

"You've read too many of them five-penny dreadfuls, boy," Butler said, but Jenkins shook his head.

"No, Coady might have a point there," he said as he pulled the makings from his vest pocket. "Or it could be Injuns runnin' with them swine."

The rest of us cursed Comancheros. "Tradin' guns and whisky to Comanches," Jenkins said. "I'd love to get my hands on some lousy Comanchero."

"Their bodies should be buried in the burning sand, their eyelids cut off to bake in the blistering sun, and then honey poured over their heads to attract ants," Coady said, sounding like a boy again, and I had to smile, wondering which half-dime novel had inspired that sentiment.

"Comancheros or Comanch', I suspect things will get hot before summer's over," Barr said. "Glenn, how long does it take you to burn bacon and biscuits?"

"Hold your horses, Capt'n!"

"We've definitely got the Comanches' dander up," Masterson said. "And other Indians, too. Shorty Shadler found Cheyenne sign east of the Walls."

"A mite far off the Cheyenne range," Jenkins said.

"That's what I mean," Masterson said.

We ate breakfast in silence, then moved to more pleasant topics, telling our visitors of Coady's marksmanship and describing our dance. I even gave Captain Grover Barr back his money, explaining Coady's confession. The Texican broke out laughing and tapped a tune on his wooden leg. "Y'all must refresh my groggy memory," Barr said. "Does the boy dance better'n he shoots?"

"Dances better than you do," Moses told his boss. "Ain't that right, Coady?"

The boy grinned. "I didn't mind dancing with you men. Y'all don't stink as bad as our skinners."

Barr guffawed until he coughed and asked for a shot of whisky to settle the dust, but we were fresh out of hooch.

"You ain't exactly no peach yourself, Coady," Trabue said, and we laughed some more.

"We're headin' back to the Walls," Dixon said. "What you boys plan on doin'?"

"We're pushin' north," Jenkins said. "I reckon we ought to take Coady to the Walls since he don't like our smell no more. Pick up some supplies, wait for the buffler to head our way, maybe stick near Adobe Walls just in case Coady's right and them Comanch' is plannin' war."

"You want to ride along with us?" I asked.

"Only if your cook makes better coffee than Mister Marcus," Masterson replied.

"I do," Claybrooke said. "And my fiddling is pretty fair, too."

"His fiddling's better than his coffee," I said. I knew why we kept up this banter, kept cracking jokes. We thought that by making light of everything, we would push the thought of an Indian uprising out of our minds.

"How 'bout you, Capt'n?" Dixon asked.

Barr shook his head. "We got enough hides, and the boys is hankerin' to see civilization. Adobe Walls ain't that civilized, gents."

"And Dodge City is?" Claybrooke asked.

"Well, the whisky's better. An' the dancin'." He winked at Coady.

"Adobe Walls is on the way," Masterson said.

"Maybe so, but if we was to run into a herd of buffs, well, we'd have to share. And I'm a greedy ol' coot. So I reckon this is where we part comp'ny."

"You keep your eyes open, Grover," Jenkins said seriously. "I'd hate to hear some Comanch' braggin' 'bout your scalp."

Grover Barr removed his battered brown slouch hat, revealing a sunburned pate corralled by thinning gray hair on the sides. "Wouldn't be much to brag about," he said, and we laughed again.

Mrs. Elizabeth McIlvain
General Delivery
Dodge City, Kansas
Dear Mrs. McIlvain:

You do not know me, but I bring you joyful news. I am a buffalo runner who is partnering with Cuthbert Jenkins and write this from our camp in the Texas Panhandle. A few weeks ago, a boy wandered into our camp, frightened, dirty, hungry, and sunburned, but generally in good health. This boy is your son, Coady. He had been held captive by the Kwahadi Comanches for about a year but managed to escape and, by luck and God's guidance, found our camp.

You have a fine son, ma'am, and his father would be proud of the way he carries himself. He is a hard worker, a good boy who I am certain will make a fine man. Although we demanded no chores of him—not after the ordeal he has survived—he works hard every day, but longs to see his family again. ~~He reminds me~~

Rest assured, we are sending him back home soon. I send this letter to Dodge City via Captain Grover Barr, another buffalo runner. He and his crew are departing for Dodge City this very morning. I am taking Coady to Adobe Walls farther north in the Panhandle, a trading post along the Canadian River where supply trains run to and from Dodge City. One of these trains will bring your son home as soon as it is safe. He should be in your arms by July.

I will keep you posted if our plans change. You can also look up Captain Grover Barr in Dodge City for more details. He informs me he will be staying at the Dodge House until September.

I know this must come as a great shock to you, but your ordeal, like Coady's, will soon be over, and you will be reunited with your fine boy.

I set pencil aside with hopes that this letter finds you and your daughters in good health.

Your obt. servant,
Dylan Griffith

"So I just give this to the postmaster in Dodge City?" asked Barr, holding the envelope as if it contained poison.

"That's all you have to do, Captain. He'll see that it gets to Coady's mother."

"Never writ nothin'," said Barr, sliding the envelope into his vest pocket. "Never learnt my letters, but I'll see this gets to the boy's maw."

We shook hands, and I noticed blood seeping through Barr's ankle bandage. I feared he might have busted the leg, and a bone had punctured the skin, but Barr shook off my concerns, saying he had likely aggravated it during our fiesta and would have some sawbones examine it in Dodge. With that, Grover Barr led his hide-loaded wagons north. I watched until the dust settled and the runners had disappeared, then walked over to the chuck wagon for some coffee.

"What's that you gave Barr?" J. C. Claybrooke asked while filling my cup.

"A letter to Coady's mother," I answered. "I wrote her that Coady's alive and we'd send him home on a train from Adobe Walls."

"That'll make her happy."

"I suspect so." I blew on the coffee and took a sip.

"Mind if I ask you a question?"

"Go ahead," I said, eying our cook with curiosity.

"Why didn't you just send the boy home with Barr?"

It took a moment for me to answer that one. It would be safer to send Coady with a wagon train. Grover Barr had only four men with him, and, with as many hides as his wagons held, he would make an inviting target for a war party, especially if Comanches and Kiowas were joining forces with Cheyennes and Arapahoes. That's what I told myself, and that's what I started to tell J. C. Claybrooke, but stopped before I even got one word out. Perhaps, although I liked Captain Barr, I couldn't say I cared much for his crew. Moses and Marcus seemed all right, but Hunter and especially Paria made Lillard Butler look like a shoe clerk. Maybe I had grown attached to Coady, and couldn't cut the cord. Or something else troubled me.

"I don't know," I answered at last, emptied the coffee, and walked away.

Chapter Twelve

We found the bodies on the Salt Fork of the Red: a two-man buffalo team staked, spread-eagle, on the ground, horse and mules killed, wagon burned—and any hides along with it. With the toe of his boot, Dixon rubbed a piece of smoldering buffalo hide near the charred wreckage of the wagon and lamented the waste. Apparently the two men had made camp along the muddy stream and had been surprised by Indians and, unfortunately for them, captured alive. Billy Dixon couldn't find any tracks, and, as best as we could tell, the massacre had happened a few days earlier. It easily could have been our camp, or Grover Barr's, I thought, while kneeling over one man's tortured, bloated body. The Big Fifty in my hands felt twice as heavy.

"Why do they prop their heads up like that?" I asked no one in particular.

"So . . . so they can watch themselves die."

I spun around at the sound of Coady's voice. He stood a few feet behind me, face pale, tears welling in his eyes at the horrible sight. "I told you to stay with the wagons," I snapped. I thought he might vomit or pass out, but he simply nodded and turned, head down, and walked back to Claybrooke's chuck wagon.

"Likely rememberin' his pa," Billy Dixon whispered once Coady was out of earshot. "I feel for the boy. I shorely do."

Coady McIlvain hadn't had much of a chance this past year to be a boy, and I had done him no favors by keeping

him with us. J. C. Claybrooke had been right; I should have
sent Coady back to Dodge with Captain Barr, but I was
selfish.

Buffalo wolves kept their distance, watching us suspiciously on the far bank of the Salt Fork. I wanted to draw
my Colt and fire a few rounds to scare them off, but knew
better. Gunshots might bring a war party down on us. I
looked back at the dead men's faces, choking down the bit-
terness in my throat.

"You know them, Dylan?" asked Bat Masterson, twirling
an arrow he had pulled from a dead mule.

"Yeah," I answered wearily. "You?"

He nodded somberly. "Barely recognized them," he said
dryly. "Guess we should say some words over them, give
them a proper burial. What were their names?"

"Wheatley and Pattison," I answered, staring at the rifle
I had won off them in Dodge City. "Guess they found
someone to grubstake them."

"They should have stayed in Dodge. Never had much
luck at cards or shooting contests. No luck out here, either.
I'll go fetch a couple of shovels."

"No Comanche made this arrow," Coady said, and
passed back Masterson's souvenir. We had made camp several miles upstream of the massacre, not daring to discuss
Wheatley and Pattison until Masterson brought out the
arrow and asked Coady for his thoughts. J. C. Claybrooke,
who had always been Coady's biggest protector—much
more than me—started to complain, but Coady told him it
was all right, that he wanted to help.

"It's got two black grooves on one side and red spiral
grooves on the other," Dixon pointed out. "That's Comanche sign."

"Yeah, but it's like I said the other day. Comanches will reuse arrows that killed buffalo, or any kind of animal, but any arrow used to kill a man, enemy or another Indian, stays there. Besides, this is too light and crooked for a Co-manche arrow. Comanches like dogwood or ash, maybe cherry. I don't know what this is."

"Hackberry," Dixon answered.

"Well, they might use hackberry if they had to, I reckon," Coady conceded, "but they'd bend it out more, shape it better, and leave it to dry over a fire. I watched Quanah once, and he'd put warm bear grease on the crooked spot and put the arrow in his mouth and straighten it. This is . . ."—he shook his head—"this just isn't like any Comanche arrow I ever saw. And those feathers. They ain't right, either."

"Go on, Coady," Masterson said.

"Well, Quanah used turkey feathers, mostly. Some of the other braves preferred owl feathers, and Ecabapi liked vulture feathers. That was his medicine. Those feathers came off some other bird."

Cuthbert Jenkins took the arrow and examined the feathers. "Hawk," he said after a moment, and passed the arrow back to Masterson.

"Hawk feathers's what I'd use if I was an Indian," Lillard Butler commented. "You gents listen to this boy like he's been living with the Comanches all his life. He ain't no expert. By jingo, he's barely thirteen. Now, Billy Dixon, he knows what he's talking about."

Dixon tugged on his mustache and asked to see the arrow again. "Hawk feather," he said with a nod at Jenkins, who smiled at himself. "Coady's right. Comanche would never use a hawk feather. Kiowa neither."

"Cheyenne? Arapaho?" Trabue asked.

The buffalo runner didn't answer. "I'm thinkin' Comanchero, like Coady says," Jenkins drawled. "Somebody wants us to think it's Injuns. I ain't scared, boys, but I, for one, will be mighty glad when we get to the Walls."

Civilization lay far from Adobe Walls. Grover Barr had been right about that, but the post looked like St. Louis to buffalo runners who had been on the *Llano Estacado* for months. Four buildings sat in the middle of nowhere, surrounded by crumbling ruins of the Bents' old trading post. Piles of hides, stinking and drawing scores of flies after an afternoon thunderstorm, lay stacked six feet high behind Charles Rath's adobe store. Jim Hanrahan had built his adobe saloon a few yards away, and just north of his place sat Tom O'Keefe's blacksmith shop, a flimsy picket building that would likely be washed away come a good Texas flood. Charlie Myers's store also had picket walls and a sod roof, but seemed much sturdier and was attached to a picket corral with an adobe storehouse resting catty-corner from the store. Not much to look at, and the smell alone would drive away most people, but Adobe Walls must have had a population of around thirty or forty people as we made our way toward the hide wagons parked in front of the Myers's corral. Two bearded men stood by a well, holding Enfield rifles, and several others gathered outside Jim Hanrahan's to watch us. I hoped someone here planned on leaving for Dodge City soon, but was out of luck.

"The Mooar boys lit a shuck for Dodge two weeks back," Jim Hanrahan said while pouring us all, except Coady, rye. "Rath and Myers left, too, the next day, and took a load of hides. Don't know when anybody will be coming down this way, and I surely doubt if you'll find any runners heading back to Kansas before the buffalo come back. Why don't y'all take the boy to Dodge?"

"Buffler," Jenkins answered, and slid his shot glass to Hanrahan for a refill. "That's why."

"Yeah, but there's a reward for this boy. His folks have put up a right smart of money to see him delivered."

"What kind of reward?" asked Lillard Butler, the quickest to recover after the shock to learn of a reward for Coady McIlvain. "How much money?"

"Oh, I don't know," the barman answered. "Shorty Shadler mentioned something about it. Said he met two pilgrims down around the Pease River hoping to ransom the McIlvain boy. Shorty and his brother, Ike, should be back here in a day or so. You can ask him about it. Or Billy Tyler. He rode out yesterday, Bat, looking for you."

"That pard of yours is apt to get himself kilt, Bat," Dixon commented.

"I want to know about this reward," Butler went on. "It might make sense for us to light a shuck for Dodge, sell what hides we got, and collect that money. We could split it, the reward that is. I mean, that makes sense to me. It could be. . . ."

"You talk too much, Butler," Claybrooke said.

"Well, a sodbuster's widow ain't likely to have much cash to offer," Jenkins said.

"I don't know," Hanrahan said. "It got the Shadler brothers' attention. If you do decide to take the boy north, you'd do me a service by taking Missus Olds with you. She's got a bum tooth."

"You got a petticoat here?" Butler exclaimed.

"She ain't a-goin'," a runner down the bar said. "She wouldn't go with the Mooars, and she ain't a-goin' now. 'Sides, she's too good a cook for you to try to run off ag'in,

Hanrahan. An' Ike Shadler said that reward was five hundred dollars."

"Five hunnert?" Jenkins shook his head, saw Coady standing in silence at my side, and smiled. "I reckon the boy's worth more'n that."

They kept on talking, debating the reward, challenging Ike Shadler's memory, carrying on as if Coady McIlvain stood a thousand miles away. I finished my drink, and led the boy outside. It had turned hot, and the buffalo hides stank something awful, but our nostrils had grown immune to the stench. We sat on the back of a wagon near Myers's store and watched thunderheads roll over a butte a mile or so away.

"You all right?" I asked.

"Yeah," he said.

"You want us to take you home?"

"Do you want that reward money?"

"Wouldn't accept it," I said. "I don't think Cuthbert would, either, and we boss this outfit. Don't pay any attention to Butler."

"Somebody's looking for me. Two men. Risking their lives. . . ." He dropped his head and sniffed.

Risking their lives? Yeah, I thought, *but for five hundred dollars, not you, son.* Those two men were probably nothing more than saddle tramps, out of work and looking for easy money, although trading with Comanches would prove far from easy. Coming to Adobe Walls had proved to be a bad choice. We had missed the last supply train to Dodge City, and now I would have to squash Lillard Butler's hankering to take Coady back to Dodge for money. Some of the other runners at the Walls didn't look like they'd be above kidnapping the boy from us and taking him to Kansas. I thought about leaving that night.

* * * * *

In the end, Jenkins and I decided we would take Coady to his mother's farm. That managed to silence Lillard Butler, because we didn't tell him, or anyone else, that we would refuse the reward money. Once the buffalo migrated north, I would take Coady home, leaving Jenkins, Claybrooke, and the skinners at work. If Butler could find a rifle—I had no intention of loaning him mine—he could take over my job as a runner, but he'd also have to help McDonough skin. On top of the $50 he got per month for skinning, we agreed to pay him ten bits for every buffalo he killed. Once I returned, he'd have to go back to skinning only.

"What's to keep him from leaving us behind and taking that reward money for himself?" Butler asked.

"Nothin'," Jenkins said. " 'Ceptin' he can make a lot more money running buffler than sellin' boys back to their maws."

"You'll be gone a month," Dixon told me. "That's a lot of buffalo you'll miss."

"There will be plenty more," I said lightly, although I didn't believe that. In just a few years we had wiped out the Kansas buffalo, and it wouldn't take long for us to make the Texas herd history.

My plans were derailed two nights later.

Ike and Shorty Shadler arrived with their wagons and buffalo dog, and Masterson's friend, Billy Tyler, showed up that afternoon. Several other runners had departed in search of buffalo, leaving twenty-eight men at the Walls, plus Coady and Hannah Olds. We celebrated Tyler's and the Shadlers' return with four or five rounds at Hanrahan's; after that, I broke out my deck of cards.

"You met two men looking for Coady McIlvain?" I asked Shorty Shadler while dealing him, Jenkins, Masterson, Dixon, and Hanrahan a game of five-card stud. "On the Pease River."

"Yeah," he grunted. "Plumb loco they was. Tradin' with Comanch'. I told 'em 'bout them pilgrims I found scalped, told 'em they was fools. But they was the boy's kin. Reckon I can't blame 'em none."

"Kin?" I folded my hand to concentrate on Shadler's story and the deal.

"Yeah." Masterson bet heavily, and Shadler folded. "His pa and a gent named Silas."

"His father was killed," I said, "by Comanches when the boy was kidnapped."

"Well, my memory ain't what it once was, 'specially after them drinks Jim serves. But Silas I'm certain of. That's my dog's name. They was goin' down to The Flat, I think, to re-outfit themselves." I knew of The Flat, the roughshod settlement near Fort Griffin, farther south in Texas. I remembered setting type for the *Dallas Herald* two or three years back that called The Flat the wickedest town since Sodom. It served soldiers, outlaws, tinhorns and, now, buffalo runners. "You should talk to Billy Tyler. He heard the whole story a-fore he left Kansas."

"Where is Billy?" I asked Masterson.

"Sleeping."

"Which is what I'm gonna do," Shadler said. "I ain't killed enough buffs to be losin' my money to you sharps. See you in the morn."

I returned my focus to poker, figuring to interview Billy Tyler and the Shadlers again after breakfast. I would also ask Coady if he knew anyone named Silas. Again, my plans were derailed.

We spent the night in the saloon. Hanrahan offered his dirt

floor, saying Coady might enjoy sleeping with a roof over his head for a change, and we accepted the hospitality just in case it rained that night. Well, that was Jenkins's and Claybrooke's excuse. Our skinners slept by our wagons, to keep an eye on our gear and hides, while Jenkins and Claybrooke sampled Hanrahan's liquor until the wee hours, and Coady and I unrolled our blankets on the far side of the saloon.

"Silas?" Coady said. "I got an uncle named Silas, but he's in North Carolina."

"I don't think so," I told him. "We'll talk to Billy Tyler in the morning, but it seems your uncle is looking for you. Your mother must have asked him to help."

"Who's with him?"

"That I don't know. We'll ask Tyler."

"I had lots of cousins," he said in a faraway voice. "Back in North Carolina. They were older than me mostly. One of Uncle Silas's boys maybe. Sometimes I miss North Carolina. I had this tobacco stick, took it with me. I. . . ."

"I remember," I said, and tousled his hair. "I'm thinking maybe instead of taking you to Dodge, we should ride down to The Flat, see if we can't find your Uncle Silas." I winked. "Maybe shoot some buffalo while we're traveling south."

He smiled, said that sounded like a crackerjack idea, and closed his eyes. My grin widened, too, until I happened to look up and catch J. C. Claybrooke frowning at me. The boy belonged in Dodge City with his mother. Deep down, I knew that as well as our cook, but I had grown attached to Coady McIlvain, enjoyed his company, enjoyed playing a father to him. Or maybe I just liked having a son.

A sharp *crack*, followed by Hanrahan's scream, rescued me from a nightmare. I thought I smelled gunsmoke, but understood I must still be half asleep, trying to escape my nightmare in which I had killed a boy and his mother with my Sharps rifle.

"Clear out!" Hanrahan shouted, kicking Jenkins awake.

By the light of a lantern in his hands, I could see Hanrahan's face, frozen in fear. "The ridgepole's breaking! Clear out, boys, or the roof'll bury us all."

I swept up Coady in my arms and led Hanrahan, Claybrooke, and Jenkins outside. The excitement woke up other runners, including Masterson and Dixon, who had pitched their bedrolls just outside the saloon. Claybrooke and Jenkins debated what to do, while the quick-thinking Hanrahan asked if I could find another pole. I rooted around in the pile of freshly cut timbers beside the saloon, and soon picked up one that would work perfectly, a convenience I didn't think about until later. Over the next few hours, we removed the ridgepole and replaced it. My nightmare faded from my thoughts.

The sky was lightening in the east by the time we finished, and Masterson and the other runners started back for the bedrolls, only to turn around when Jim Hanrahan offered to buy everyone a drink on the house. Knowing the rarity of Hanrahan's generosity when it came to free liquor, we marched into the saloon for a morning whisky. Masterson put a pot of coffee on, and we talked of our good fortunes, how we had saved not only our lives, but Jim Hanrahan's forty-rod.

After whisky and coffee, dawn began to break, so Dixon and Masterson, who planned to take another scout that morning, headed outside to feed and saddle their horses. About fifteen minutes later, the ground started shaking.

"Buffler!" Jenkins shouted excitedly, and grabbed his Sharps.

Masterson dived through the door, followed by a screaming Billy Dixon, and I stepped into the doorway to see the stampede.

It wasn't buffalo. An arrow whistled past me as I slammed and bolted the door.

Chapter Thirteen

As soon as the last bar dropped, the door strained and a horse snorted outside. An Indian had backed his mount to the door and was trying to push it open, but the two thick cottonwood planks held firm. I drew my Colt only to realize the slugs would never penetrate the heavy door, and cried for my rifle. The wood groaned, dirt and grass began falling from the roof and frame, and, if the door opened, Indians would swarm through and we'd all be dead in seconds.

"Get down!" a voice shouted, and I dropped to the floor as a Big Fifty thundered and filled the room with acrid, white smoke. The horse outside screamed and took off running, throwing the brave to the ground with a *thud*. Blinking away tears caused by the smoke—and a fear I had not felt since the Rebellion—I saw young Coady McIlvain sitting on the floor, against the bar, my smoking Big Fifty at his feet. I crawled the few yards, swept up my rifle, and called out fearfully: "You hit?"

He shook his head. "The gun knocked me down."

I told him to stay down, and ran to the wall. Coady had been the first to react, had fired my Sharps through the door, and had likely saved all of our lives. I cried out for .50-90 cartridges, and Coady, ignoring my orders to stay down, brought a box from behind Hanrahan's bar. I didn't scold him, and, when Hanrahan asked for a box of .44 rimfire, Coady took off running. We'd need his help if we were to survive this morning.

"Comancheros, you said!" Dixon yelled at Cuthbert

Jenkins while reloading his .44 Sharps. "Does them look like Comancheros to you?"

I stuck the barrel of my Big Fifty through a gun port in the door and fired. These weren't traders dressed as Indians. Hundreds of warriors rode whooping and firing in the early morning, peppering the saloon's walls with bullets and arrows. The heavy reports of other buffalo rifles echoed our own gunshots, informing us that the raiders had not captured everyone at Rath's and Myers's stores by surprise, yet we had no idea if anyone had been killed. Our skinners could either be in one of the buildings, hiding in our wagons, or dead. All I knew was that nine of us—Masterson, Dixon, Claybrooke, Jenkins, Hanrahan, a pair of runners named Billy Ogg and Mike Welch, Coady, and me—had taken refuge in Hanrahan's saloon.

"Boy was right about one thing," Welch said. "Ain't just Comanch' an' Kioways. I just kilt me a Cheyenne Dog Soldier."

"By jingo," Jenkins said, "if that ridgepole hadn't cracked, them bucks would 'a' been on us before we could 'a' lifted a finger."

We were too busy to comment, knocking out chinks to use as gun ports, reloading, sweating, cursing, praying. A humming in my ears grew more intense, and my mouth turned drier than crumbling adobe. Coady might have had the hardest job, running back and forth, delivering each man bandoleers or boxes of ammunition and reloading Hanrahan's pair of Henry repeaters.

Outside, the cover of one of Coady's beloved half-dime novels sprang to life. Hundreds of painted warriors circled the Walls on horseback, churning up thick dust while hanging over the sides of their mounts and loosening arrows or gunshots. I had never seen such horsemanship. With a scratch shot, I dropped one red- and yellow-painted warrior and watched, amazed, as two other braves galloped by and picked up their dead or dying comrade off the ground and carried him away.

Almost as soon as that had happened, another warrior leaped from his horse and charged the saloon. Billy Ogg had a clear shot but jerked the trigger and missed, then, shrieking, fell to the floor as the Indian stuck a Remington revolver through the makeshift gun port and pulled the trigger six times. The Arapaho sprinted back for his horse, but Masterson and Dixon fired simultaneously, catapulting the brave toward the cistern.

"Anybody hit?" I called out, relieved to see Coady hugging the wall beside Jenkins.

"No," Billy Ogg answered while reloading his single-shot Rolling Block, "but if another buck tries something like that, I'm likely to soil my britches."

The circle the warriors rode had been getting closer to the buildings, but now I noticed the Indians widening the loop, and I knew we must have inflicted heavy casualties. Attacking Adobe Walls had been a gamble, one I probably would have taken had I been an Indian leader. They had expected to find a bunch of sleeping white men at the buffalo outpost only to have been met by some of the best shots on the southern plains.

"You hear that?" Jenkins gasped, leaned his Sharps against the wall, and craned his head to hear better.

"Sounds like a bugle," Billy Dixon said, and Ogg and Welch broke out into cheers.

Over the din of gunshots, whoops, pounding hoofs, and incessant ringing in my ears, I could make out the strains of a horn, although it sounded like nothing I remembered from my Army days. Bat Masterson must have observed the same thing because he said: "That's one lousy trumpeter."

Coady had put his ear near Hanrahan's makeshift gun port but pulled away as a gunshot thudded the wall and showered his hat—for I had bought him one the other day at Rath's store—with dust. "Boy," I said sternly, "you'll get your head blown off."

"It's the cavalry," Welch said. "It's gotta be the cavalry."

Coady, however, shook his head. "It's Naséca," he said. "One of Quanah's friends. The Comancheros gave him a bugle. I recognize his notes."

I hadn't expected the U.S. Army to come charging to the rescue of a bunch of buffalo runners who many believed had broken the Medicine Lodge Treaty, but my heart dropped like an anchor at Coady's words. He looked as disappointed as everyone in the saloon, faces and hands blackened by gunpowder and dirt, sweat streaming down our faces, soaking our clothes, burning our eyes. The day was turning into a scorcher, and it wasn't even eight o'clock.

The Indians pulled back, regrouping, and I took time to run a wet rag down the Sharps barrel while Coady made the rounds again, hauling a bottle of Hanrahan's forty-rod, instead of bullets, and we all gladly took a sip or two. A few minutes later, a voice called out from Myers's store: "Bat! Bat Masterson? You alive?"

"Yeah!" he yelled back, and told us: "It's Fred Leonard."

"Bat, Billy Tyler's been hit bad. He's dying. Are y'all all right?"

Masterson's head dropped, and he tossed his derby to the floor. He sighed, cursed, and called back as he headed for the door: "We're alive! I'm coming over!"

"Don't be a fool!" Hanrahan argued, but Dixon was helping Masterson lift the bars from the door. I leaned my

Sharps in the corner and went to their aid. Tyler was Masterson's partner and bunkie, and I would have done the same. Hanrahan stifled further protests and lifted his Henry rifle. The door cracked open, Masterson winked, and took off. We slammed the door behind him and barred it while Hanrahan, Ogg, and Claybrooke unleashed a withering covering fire that lasted half a minute.

"He made it!" Mike Welch yelled, and the gunshots ceased.

"Just in time, too," Jenkins said, " 'cause here them devils come ag'in."

I barely had enough time to wipe my eyeglasses clean and resume our defense. The miserable strains of the bugle were lost amid the barrage from three buildings. Horses and men screamed, and the attackers soon retreated again.

"I kilt that bugler!" a runner named Harry Armitage cried out from Rath's store. "Maybe that'll make 'em quit."

They didn't. They charged twice more with little effect. I never once questioned the Indians' bravery, but they were outmatched. We had well-fortified positions and long-range rifles. What we didn't have, I learned around mid-morning, was much ammunition.

"It's a wonder we've lasted this long," Claybrooke said while reloading his Spencer. "This is a saloon."

It had been a well-stocked one, however, with more than kegs of cheap whisky and pickle jars. Empty boxes and brass casings littered the sod floor, but this war showed no sign of ending soon. The heat became stifling, and the gunsmoke filling the saloon made breathing difficult. Every five minutes, I had to clean my glasses of soot, dust, and sweat. I had quit running a wet rag down the Sharps barrel to conserve our water.

"Dylan!" Masterson yelled. "How y'all doin'?"

"We're still here," I answered. "How's your friend, Tyler?"

"Dead."

I lowered my head, and Welch yelled the news over to Rath's store, where Harry Armitage reported that Ike and Shorty Shadler had been killed in their wagons. *Wagons?* I wondered if our skinners had survived. J. C. Claybrooke had the same thought for he called out toward Rath's, and Trabue answered: "We're all here. Barely made it inside. Ignacio got an arrow in his left calf. Guess he won't be dancin' a spell."

We were lucky. Only three men dead—ironically, though I wouldn't think about it for days, the three men I planned on asking about Coady's Uncle Silas and the reward offered for his return. The Shadler brothers had been caught outside. Apparently they realized they'd never make it to the buildings, so they hid underneath buffalo robes, their black Lab beside the wagon tongue. During one of the charges, a Kiowa brave killed the barking dog and began to loot the sugar, coffee, and supplies in the wagon. When he lifted the robe, Ike or Shorty blew him apart with a round from a buffalo rifle. The Indians quickly avenged their dead comrade, however, hacking the Shadlers to pieces.

Billy Tyler had been shot through the lungs when he and Fred Leonard ran toward the corral in a futile effort to save our horses. They were quickly driven back to the store, and Tyler fell in the doorway. After Masterson ran from Hanrahan's to be with his friend, Tyler begged for water, and Masterson rushed outside to the well, dodging bullets and arrows, filled a bucket, and hurried inside, miraculously unhurt. He washed Tyler's face, gave him a drink, and watched him die a minute later.

This I learned afterward. All that morning, we had no

way of knowing what was going on in the other buildings. Three deaths, but that might soon change if we didn't get any ammunition.

"Bat!" I yelled. "Our ammo's running short!"

"What'll y'all need?"

I did a mental tally. Welch and I fired .50-90 Sharps rifles, Jenkins had a .52-caliber linen, Billy Dixon shot a .44-105, Claybrooke had a .56-.50 Spencer, Billy Ogg needed a .45-70 Remington, and Hanrahan's Henry rifles used .44 rimfire.

"Fred Zimmermann's storeroom!" I yelled back, and heard Masterson's faint chuckles before I called out our grocery list. Jenkins would be out of luck. I seriously doubted if Myers's store had ammunition for his old rifle, and I wasn't certain Claybrooke's caliber would be stocked. Hanrahan, however, had two Henry rifles, so we'd only be short one rifle, and I had spotted a percussion shotgun behind the bar. It would be ineffective except at close range, but it would make a lot of noise.

"No luck with the linen, and only one box for the Spencer," Masterson said an eternity later. "How you want to handle this?"

"I'll go," Dixon said quietly.

"I'll help," Hanrahan added.

"You're about to have two visitors!" I bellowed, and motioned for Coady to get the door ready.

"Send over a bottle of Jim's best Scotch whisky!" came a voice I didn't recognize. "That'll be a fair trade."

Smiling, Hanrahan grabbed the nearest bottle of tongue-blistering rye—a body wouldn't find any decent Scotch between here and Dodge—and tossed Jenkins one of his rifles.

"How's it look out there?" Dixon asked.

"Looks like they're gettin' ready for another run at us,"

Jenkins said. "Best hurry."

With a nod from Dixon, Coady pulled open the door, and Dixon and Hanrahan bolted into Hades. They had just stepped outside when gunfire erupted from the stacks of hides, and Jenkins cursed, jacking another round into the repeater. I moved around the building, knocked out chinks, stuck the Big Fifty barrel through the opening. I aimed just below the puff of white smoke rising above one of the stacks and fired, reloaded, and heard J. C. Claybrooke's shout: "Coady, come back here!"

The whisky bottle had exploded in Hanrahan's hand, and another bullet clipped his left boot heel, sending him spilling and the Henry rifle sailing toward the well. Billy Dixon turned, fired, and started to help the saloon owner, but found himself caught in an enfilade and had to dive behind O'Keefe's blacksmith shop. Hanrahan, confused and panicked, crawled around on hands and knees, searching for his rifle. That's when Coady rushed outside.

The .50-caliber bullet slipped from my fingers when I heard Claybrooke, and I ran to the door, and started to go after the boy, but big Mike Welch gripped my shoulder and pulled me inside, sending me sprawling on the dirt floor. Gunfire and shouts all around us revealed that the Indians were charging again, and Welch and Ogg slammed the door shut, ignoring Claybrooke's protests and my curses, leaving Dixon, Hanrahan, and Coady locked outside.

What I wanted to do—besides murder Welch and Ogg—was to open the door and run outside, but I knew by the time I got the bars off, if Welch and Ogg didn't kill me, the Indians would be upon Coady. They had closed the door fearing, if they left it open, the Indians would have us dead to rights. The two men and a boy would have to fend for themselves, and the best I could do was provide cover. I grabbed my Sharps, found another bullet, took up position beside a window, fired blindly, and drew my revolver.

Coady had grabbed Hanrahan's rifle, sent three or four rounds in the general direction of the buffalo hides, and helped pull the barman to his feet. Lead and arrows whistled past them, kicking up sand, thumping into the well. A bullet tugged at Hanrahan's collar, and an arrow ripped off Coady's hat. I recalled veterans telling me how they'd been blessed in battles, covered with God's shield it seemed, as bullets flew around them but never struck them. On the other hand, I had seen scores of corpses ripped apart by bullets and canister. Somebody on June 27, 1874, however, truly watched over Billy Dixon, Jim Hanrahan, and Coady McIlvain.

Dixon shot again and raced to the store, yelling for Coady and Hanrahan to follow. Hanrahan took the rifle, grabbed Coady's hand, and ran, practically dragging the boy behind him. A shroud of dust swallowed them.

I wouldn't know Coady's fate for another forty-five minutes.

Chapter Fourteen

The breath exploded from Coady's lungs, and he landed on his side, rolled over, fighting for air. One second he had been stumbling behind Jim Hanrahan, expecting the saloonkeeper to pull his arm from its socket as they ran for Myers's store. An instant later, something slammed into them, launching Hanrahan one way and Coady the other. Half blinded by dust, tasting blood on his lips, Coady smelled the horse that had knocked him down. He also recognized the strong scent of a Comanche brave.

Breathing again, he couldn't get his legs to work so he started crawling backward, away from the store, doing anything possible to escape the figure emerging from the dust.

Battles are not neat affairs. Even when led by the greatest generals, Washington or Lee, Napoléon or Quanah Parker, they rarely go according to plan. They are marked by confusion, chaos, unspeakable violence. Coady had never experienced anything like this, and the half-dime novels he read depicted nothing resembling a massed attack by hundreds of warriors. There was no glory to be achieved, no medals to be won, only primal fear and an animalistic instinct to survive. Coady ground his teeth as Ecabapi, his most vocal Comanche enemy, unleashed a lance.

The bone point nicked the frightened teenager's right earlobe and bounced across the ground. Coady tried to scream, couldn't, and scrambled to his feet, legs working now, but Ecabapi kicked him in the stomach before he could stand, and he fell, moaning, wondering why

Hanrahan, Dixon—or I—did not appear in the last moment to kill his attacker.

Ecabapi had lost a few more teeth since the night of Coady's escape, and blood trickled down his forehead just below the scalp. With his mangled left hand, he drew his knife. His right hand gripped a war axe. He did not come slowly, did not say a word, simply charged and cut loose with a fierce howl. Coady sat up, frozen, until old Ugly Face reached him. Then Coady's hands flared up and unleashed fistfuls of dirt that blinded Ecabapi, who tripped, his momentum carrying him on top of Coady. Coady reacted swiftly, either by instinct or from those penny dreadfuls, lifted his knees, caught the Comanche with his shins, and flipped him over.

Coady was up, trying to find his bearings, made out the picket building, took one step, and dropped in agony. Ecabapi had swung his war axe, catching Coady's left ankle with the blunt side, almost breaking the bone. Clawing at his eyes with his left fist, the brave moved slowly, chasing down Coady with methodical purpose, instead of Comanche rage. Coady bit his lip, blinked back tears, crawling backward again. His hand gripped something, and he stopped, recognizing the feel of Ecabapi's lance. He whipped the weapon around and jabbed it into the Comanche's stomach.

The Indian staggered backward, dropped the axe, and covered his bleeding gut with both hands. He bled like a pig at a slaughterhouse, but the wound was far from fatal, and the ferocity returned. He scooped up his axe and charged.

An arrow stopped him this time. Ecabapi skidded on his knees, crying out in agony while gripping the shaft of the Comanche arrow that had torn through his calf. A horse thundered past and disappeared around the store, but not before Coady recognized the rider. Ecabapi tore out the arrow and stood, axe still in his hand, limping forward to finish the job and lift another scalp.

"Boy!"

Ecabapi turned, sent the axe somersaulting at the voice. A gunshot answered—once, twice, three times—and Ecabapi staggered back, his chest erupting crimson, and dropped to his knees. A fourth shot slammed into the Comanche's forehead and blew out the back of his skull. Ecabapi dropped without a sound, and Jim Hanrahan jacked another shell into the Henry, threw Coady over his shoulder like a sack of grain, and ran inside the store.

Although I never would completely forgive him, Jim Hanrahan deservedly got all the credit at Adobe Walls for saving Coady's life. Coady, however, claimed that Ecabapi would have killed him, for sure, if not for Quanah Parker. It was Quanah, Coady said, who galloped by and put that arrow in Ecabapi's leg. Maybe, we conceded, although silently we harbored strong doubts. Ecabapi's body was never found—Comanches had a way of carrying off their dead—so we never knew if he had been slowed by an arrow or if such deliverance had been the imagination of a terrified thirteen-year-old.

I doubt, however, if anyone who survived the Battle of Adobe Walls ever believed that Quanah Parker wounded Ecabapi intentionally to save the life of a former captive. If Quanah, or some other Indian, shot Ecabapi, it had to be by accident. With all that dust and gunsmoke, Quanah could not have recognized Coady, and perhaps not even Ecabapi. *¿Quién sabe?* Coady swore to it, though, and that's the way Billy Dixon, Bat Masterson, Jim Hanrahan, and myself told the story over the years. In any event, Coady made it inside Myers's alive.

★ ★ ★ ★ ★

The store had the fewest sharpshooters, so Billy Dixon agreed to stay. After the Indians withdrew, never to charge again, Jim Hanrahan insisted that Coady stay put, too—I'll always owe the barkeep that much—and ran back to the saloon with a canvas sack full of various cartridges, a loaf of bread baked by Hannah Olds, and a canteen.

Coady helped reload rifles, hauled a water bucket, and tried not to look at the blood-soaked body of Billy Tyler in the corner of the store. He limped about until Mrs. Olds made him sit down, examined his ankle, and wrapped it up tightly with strips torn from her paisley skirt. He had an easier time now—we all did—because the fight became a siege, and again the attackers found themselves outgunned, if not outmatched. Firing on both sides became sporadic as we kept driving the Indians farther and farther back. I hit one hiding in the grass about four hundred yards away, and Cuthbert Jenkins dropped a horse near the far buttes.

Eventually the warriors could have forced us out, for all three fortifications had little water, but Indians have no patience for sieges. They also care little for seeing their men shot down by long-range rifles. By late that afternoon, they stayed on the top of a butte almost a mile away. That's when Billy Dixon made his greatest shot.

"Spot for me, Coady," said Dixon, gesturing out the window. "See that warrior on the dun horse atop that butte?"

Coady squinted his eyes. "Barely."

"I'm gonna torment him some. You look for dust, if there's any, and tell me how close I come to puttin' a burr under that buck's saddle."

"You're plumb loco," Bill Olds told him. "Save your powder and lead. That buck's a mile away."

"Just about," Dixon told him casually, and tossed a handful of sand into the air to check the wind.

"Uphill to boot," a runner named Henry Lease muttered.

"I'll put my money on Billy," Masterson said, but no one else dared take that wager.

Coady stuffed fingers in both ears and concentrated on the distant target. Dixon's .44-105 roared, and nothing happened. The horse wheeled at last, the rider spilled, dust rose, and the occupants in the store cheered. Over at Hanrahan's, we had no idea what the commotion was about.

"By thunder," Coady said when he found his voice. "Not even The Unknown Scout could 'a' done that!"

"Huh?" Billy Dixon said.

I'd have my work cut out for me if I intended on proving to Coady that I was the greatest shot since his nickel hero, not that I could ever accomplish such a feat. Some brag that Dixon's shot killed that unfortunate brave, while others say the Indian was merely stunned by the spent bullet, but, no matter, it was a once-in-a-lifetime display of marksmanship, or a buffalo runner's luck. I read in a newspaper account some years back that Dixon's shot stretched 4,200 feet, but that's not true. Coady and I stepped off the distance two days later.

Four thousand, six hundred, and fourteen feet.

By four o'clock the firing had ceased and we drifted outside, cautiously at first, and checked the damage. The Indians were gone—Dixon's shot had taken the fight out of them—but we found ourselves stranded with only two horses, the rest killed or stolen, and fear that the raiders might return.

"They won't," Coady told us. "They won't trust Isa-tai's medicine any more."

He was right, of course, but how many grown men are willing to put their lives in a thirteen-year-old boy's faith? We buried the dead, and Bill Olds tied a black shirt to a pole, which he stuck on top of Rath's store, calling it a distress flag. Lease, the best rider of the lot, volunteered to ride to Dodge and bring back help, and took off after sunset. I doubt if anyone slept that night at Adobe Walls, and the tension hadn't eased by dawn.

That's when Bill Olds blew his head off.

The best we could tell is that Olds had climbed a ladder to the top of Rath's store for a look-see, had spotted rising dust, screamed that the Indians were coming back, and hurried down the ladder. He had a Sharps carbine with him, cocked. The hammer struck a rung, the gun discharged, and Bill Olds toppled to the ground, dead. Hannah Olds had been holding the ladder steady for him, and screamed when it happened. Masterson and Dixon rushed her inside Hanrahan's and gave her a couple of drinks to steady her nerves while some of the other boys wrapped Bill Olds's body in a wagon tarp and hauled him to the Walls' ever-growing cemetery.

Coady just stood there, blinking in horror, and I led him to the woodpile beside the saloon.

"His face . . . ," he started.

"Don't think about it," I said, and changed the subject. "As soon as we replace our horses, we'll head on down to Fort Griffin, find your uncle, and get you home." I was talking to hear myself talk, although I told myself I was trying to take Coady's mind off the bloody accident he had just witnessed. I got him to describe Billy Dixon's shot again, and then we talked about our boyhood homes, about fishing, about anything other than buffalo, Indians, and Texas.

"You ever think about going back to North Carolina?" I asked.

"No. I like the West. Would you ever go back to Wisconsin?"

"No," I said sharply, forced a smile, and added: "I'm a Westerner just like you."

He pressed his toe against the ridgepole we had replaced, tried to roll it over, and laughed. "Good thing this cracked," he said.

I figured he would be all right. "Yeah," I said, and found myself staring at the pole. J. C. Claybrooke came over to check on Coady, or lecture me, and I left them alone, saying I had an errand to attend. Five minutes later, I slammed Jim Hanrahan against the side of the privy behind the Myers store.

"What the . . . ?"

He shut up when I slapped him. "That ridgepole isn't cracked, Jim. I thought I smelled gunsmoke that night, figured I was just dreaming, but it was smoke, wasn't it?"

Hanrahan didn't answer. If he had, I might have killed him.

"It all fits," I said. "Now." Hanrahan had tried to get Mrs. Olds to leave with the last wagon train to Dodge. He had suggested we take her and Coady to Dodge. His saloon had been stocked with plenty of ammunition, and not just the .44 rounds for his Henry rifles. He had fired a pistol that night— looking back on it then, I recalled that little pocket Remington stuck in his waistband as he directed our efforts to remove and replace the ridgepole—to wake us, then kept us up replacing the pole and offering us a drink on the house.

"You knew," I said, and spit in his face.

"I had to," he whined, and I stepped back from him,

waiting. "A scout I know named Amos Chapman rode in here two weeks back, said a friendly Penateka Comanch' told him he went to this sun dance, said an attack was coming at the Walls on the morning after the next full moon. That's why the Mooar brothers and Charles Rath left, why they took their hides with them."

"Why did you stay?" I asked.

"Protect my investment. If we lost the Walls, I'd lose everything. That's why I. . . . It worked." He let out a mirthless laugh. "We saved our hides, saved the buffalo trade here. Griffith, I had to do it."

"Tell that to the Shadler boys, Billy Tyler, and Bill Olds. Who else knew?"

"Just me."

I turned to leave, and he grabbed my shoulder. Spinning and ducking, I buried my fist in his gut, and he doubled over. He hadn't been trying to attack me, though; he just wanted to beg for his life. "Griffith," he said hoarsely, his eyes pleading. "Don't tell the boys. They'll. . . ."

This is the first time I've revealed the truth about the "cracked" ridgepole. Hanrahan took the story to his grave. As far as I know, neither Rath nor the Mooars ever set the record straight. Maybe I should have told everyone, but Jim Hanrahan was right. The runners would have lynched him had they known how the saloonkeeper had used them, and I had seen enough men die, had caused the deaths of many, and didn't want to be a party to another death, so I kept Hanrahan's secret. Besides, as much as I hated the yellow swine, he had saved Coady McIlvain's life.

I paid that debt with my silence.

The dust Bill Olds saw belonged not to Comanche raiders, but to a buffalo runner named George Bellfield.

Later that evening, two more runners, brothers Jim and Bob Cator, showed up. None had come across any Indian sign, and slowly we began to relax.

A week or so later, Henry Lease returned with a party of rescuers from Dodge City. They brought food, ammunition, and some livestock. Two days later, more horses and mules arrived, and we traded buffalo hides or went on tick to re-outfit our crews. I didn't fancy doing business with that coward Charles Rath, but it was either that or walk through Indian country. Hanrahan spoke to Rath to make sure he gave our outfit the best deal possible. A bribe? I don't know. I made up my mind, however, that Rath would never get my business again. We'd take our hides to sell at The Flat, or Denison.

"The best market's at Dodge, Dylan," Jenkins said, perturbed when he heard my demands. "It don't make no sense to travel to Fort Griffin to sell them hides. Ain't no railroad there. Now they've laid tracks to Denison, but, criminy, Dodge City's closer."

"You want to do business in Dodge, you're welcome," I said testily. "But I'm taking my share south."

He shook his head and rolled a smoke. "This ain't like you, son."

"Shadler said Coady's uncle was in Fort Griffin." Calmer, I opted to explain with a half truth. "I thought if we went there, we'd leave the boy with his uncle."

"Collect the reward?" Lillard Butler asked.

"Collect the reward," I lied. "We'll see what the market is at The Flat. If it's no good, we'll head over to Denison. What did we get for hides back in Dodge?" When Jenkins told me, I promised to match that offer if we got less in Texas out of my own share.

"Well," Jenkins agreed, "I guess it's best for Coady."

J. C. Claybrooke muttered something underneath his breath, and tossed coffee dregs between my feet before heading back to his chuck wagon.

"There's another thing to consider." As it often did, Coady's voice surprised me. I thought he had been out gathering buffalo chips for our cook fires. We looked at him, all smiles now, and listened. "The Texas herd still hasn't come north yet. We'd likely get first shot at all them buffler . . ."—his grin widened as he paused—"if we head south."

Oh, to be a boy, naïve, always able to block out recent horrors and see a shining future.

Cuthbert Jenkins laughed so hard he shook out the match he had just lit for his cigarette. "By jingo, Coady," he said, "we'll make a buffler runner of you yet."

Chapter Fifteen

Thunderstorms had transformed the streets of The Flat into a moor, our horses, mules, and wagon wheels churning up Front Street's gooey mud. Called The Flat because of its location in a meadow below the military post, the town of Fort Griffin smelled worse than Adobe Walls with its mixture of mud, dung, vomit, blood, gunsmoke, urine, sweat—you name it. We had arrived on pay day for the Army boys and local cowhands, and the rawhide town boomed with people.

Cuthbert Jenkins managed to guide his team to the hitching post in front of the Beehive Saloon and had barely set the brake before Ignacio, Trabue, McDonough, and Butler leaped into the thick mud—McDonough tripping and landing on his knees—and raced through the batwing doors, above which had been nailed a painted wooden sign shaped like a beehive and the words:

> **Within this hive we are alive,**
> **Good whisky makes us funny.**
> **So if you're dry come in and try**
> **The flavor of our honey.**

Down the street, J. C. Claybrooke stopped his chuck wagon in the alley beside a grocer, while I rode my big bay gelding, with Coady hanging on behind me, to the town marshal's office, dismounted, and helped Coady down. We stepped onto the boardwalk, knocked as much mud off my boots and Coady's moccasins as possible, and I tried the door. It was locked.

Behind me, Coady stared up and down the streets bustling with activity. A circus of some kind had been set up at the far end of Front Street near the fort, and men hooted at the caged animal as a barker preached about the wonders of the world he had seen—and everyone else could see tonight for the price of two bits—but the crowd drowned out most of his pitch. Piano music belted out from several saloons with no harmony, and two black troopers got into a row in front of another saloon while six or seven other soldiers placed bets and cheered on the amateur pugilists.

The Flat made Dodge City look like a Sunday social.

"Lookin' for the marshal?" asked a black cavalry sergeant who had no interest in crossing the street to break up the fisticuffs.

"Yeah."

"He's dead." The sergeant laughed. "Got hisself kilt Wednesday night. You missed the funeral."

"Deputies?" I asked.

"Only had one, and he lit a shuck for Albany come first light Thursday. No, sir, no law here no more. Makes it a mighty interestin' town. You a buffalo hunter?"

"We're buffalo *runners*," Coady corrected, and the cavalryman smiled.

"Yes, sir, *runners*. Figgered that by that Big Fifty your daddy carries." He hooked his thumb down the street. "Bunch of other *runners* drinkin' down at Shannsey's saloon, iffen you can stand the smell. No offense."

"None taken, sir," Coady said.

The sergeant straightened. I doubted if he'd ever been sirred before—not in a place like The Flat—and he told me: "You gots a good boy there."

I didn't correct the lineage, simply asked: "Is there a newspaper office here?"

"Nah. Ain't many folks in The Flat can read."

"If I wanted to find someone. . . ."

"John Shannsey's." He looked across the street where his soldiers dragged both fighters, who had beaten each other senseless in the mud, into an alley and left them there before disappearing inside a saloon. "Well, I best check on my boys."

"One more question, Sergeant?"

"Yes, sir?"

"The men I'm looking for were trying to ransom a boy captive back from the Comanches. Maybe you saw them at the fort. It's likely they would have talked to your commanding officer."

He shrugged, repeated that John Shannsey was the man to ask, and crossed the bog to make sure the two troopers dumped in the alley still breathed.

I shot a glance down the boardwalk and started to send Coady to join Claybrooke at the mercantile, but the kid read my mind and said he wanted to stay with me, that he had sneaked into a saloon before at Dodge City, that it would be all right, and he wouldn't get into any trouble or down a whisky shot. So we dodged drunken cowhands and ducked inside John Shannsey's canvas saloon.

The first man I saw looked as stunned as I must have.

"What in tarnation are you doin' here?" Grover Barr asked.

A moment passed before I could reply. Captain Barr should have been in Dodge City, but here he stood on his crutch and peg leg, splashing the contents of a whisky bottle into five tumblers. Sitting at the table were his skinners, Hunter, Paria, Moses, the cook Glenn Marcus, and a few

142

painted ladies. His eyes dropped first to Coady before landing on the Sharps rifle at my side.

Instead of answering, I asked him the same question, and he laughed and handed me the bottle. "Got scared of all that boy's Injun talk. How you been, Coady?"

"Fine," he said, barely audible above the din inside the saloon.

"Have a seat, gents, and have a drink on ol' Grover Barr." He collapsed into a chair while Marcus dragged two empty chairs from a nearby table.

"Good afternoon, ma'am," Coady told the nearest prostitute, and tipped his arrow-ruined hat.

"Ma'am!" Hunter slapped his thighs and pulled the woman closer. "You hear that, Doris, you's a 'ma'am'."

"I'm fine, son," the woman managed to say with a smile. "What's your name?"

"Coady McIlvain, Miss Doris."

Hunter howled some more. "You's a 'miss', too, gal. Ain't that somethin'?"

Barr grunted an oath and sent the loud-mouthed Hunter to fetch two more bottles, and we exchanged stories. Barr's crew had started toward Dodge but turned south after running into too much Indian sign. That had likely saved their lives, I told them, and related the attack at Adobe Walls.

After finishing my story, in salute I lifted the glass of rye Hunter had just poured and glanced at Coady. He sat wide-eyed, taking in the roulette wheels, poker tables, faro layouts, whores, gamblers and ne'er-do-wells. He had lied to me. That boy had never snuck into a saloon. I grinned, downed my drink, and asked Grover Barr: "Did you mail that letter to Coady's mother?"

"Glenn give it to the postmaster here in town," Barr answered. "Boy's maw should have it now or pert near." He picked up Coady's hat and examined the holes in the crown made by the arrow. "You gonna get that boy a new hat?"

"I don't want a new hat," Coady said, and Barr, laughing, pulled the hat, which Coady wore like a medal, down over the boy's eyes. "He's got the makin's, Griffith. He's shorely got the makin's."

I figured it was time to get to business. "You sell your hides here?"

"Yeah. Got a dollar seventy for most of 'em, twelve bits for the rest. Buyer ain't as finicky as the gents in Dodge."

"Not as free with greenbacks either," I said. Jenkins and I sold our lot in Dodge City for two dollars a hide. I'd be paying him out of my own pocket, but, well, I had been the one insisting on coming to The Flat. Jenkins had been right, but I had known that, too. The best prices for buffalo hides were found in Dodge City. Fort Griffin would become the center of the Texas trade, but not for a year or two. I drank another whisky and asked: "You know John Shannsey?"

"He's the mick behind the bar," Glenn Marcus said. "With the wool hat."

Barr, also, turned to business. "You see any buffs 'tween here and the Walls?"

"Not many," I answered, "but the herd will be moving north soon. Has to be." Maybe that's why Grover Barr had turned south. He always called himself a greedy rapscallion, and I supposed he wasn't sick of running buffalo, after all.

I excused myself, telling Barr we had business with John Shannsey and that Cuthbert Jenkins and our boys were drinking at the Beehive. "We'll likely mosey over yonder at some point," Jenkins said. "If not, we'll see you on the trail."

"I hope so," I told him.

"Me, too."

Silas Coady
1839–1874
Rest In Peace

John Shannsey had told us where to find Coady's uncle. The boy pulled off his hat, and shuffled his feet. The sniffles soon began, and I put my hand on his shoulder. We just stood there in boothill, ankle-deep in mud, staring at the chunk of pine and the rough carving that would fade with time.

"It's all my fault," Coady said.

"It's nobody's fault," I told him.

The story John Shannsey heard—for he had been in Weatherford when Silas Coady arrived and died—was that Silas Coady and his partner, a rough-looking gent named McIlvain, had ridden into The Flat three weeks ago, low on supplies and morale after spending months trying to find Coady and barely escaping with their hair on at least three occasions. Silas Coady came down with brain fever, and died two days after reaching Fort Griffin. His partner sold the stock, informed the marshal about the five hundred dollar reward offered for Coady's return, and rode north, to the Nations, maybe, or back home to Ford County, Kansas.

His partner, Coady guessed, would be Uncle Thaddeus, his father's younger brother. Thaddeus McIlvain and Silas Coady, we deduced, had left their farms in North Carolina to try to find their kidnapped nephew. They were Confederate veterans, not afraid of anything, and had doted on Liz McIlvain and her children.

"Come on," I said, and led Coady out of the cemetery. "Let's get you something to eat."

"Ain't hungry."

"You need to eat."

We went inside Mary Louise's café, found an empty table, and quickly ordered ham, eggs, bread, coffee, and water. When the food came, Coady picked at first, but must have soon realized how hungry he was, how long it had been since he had tasted fried eggs and ham, and soon cleared his plate. I looked at his stained buckskins.

"We'll stop at a mercantile next and get you some new duds." Adobe Walls had not been stocked with boys clothes—finding a hat that fit had been a miracle—but The Flat offered more than just saloons.

"What'll we do next?" Coady asked.

I didn't answer because a woman walked past the window, and I tossed coins on the table and hurried outside.

"Sarah!" I called out, and the sandy-haired woman in green dress and high-buttoned boots spun around. I had already formed the apology in my mind. *I'm sorry, ma'am, I mistook you for someone else.* The last person I expected to see in Fort Griffin—including Grover Barr—was Sarah Elizabeth Cabell, yet my poor eyes had not deceived me. We stood blocking the boardwalk, stepped toward the café's walls to avoid being trampled, and stared at each other like a pair of idiots. I thought she'd still be in Denison, but she had moved west, although, by the looks of her clothes and face, she hadn't stopped whoring.

Her green eyes beamed, then turned confused at the sight of a thirteen-year-old boy in Comanche clothes at my side. I hadn't realized Coady had followed me out of the café. After clearing my throat, finding my voice, and introducing them, she said at last: "It's been a while, Dylan."

"Yeah." What a great conversationalist I had become.

"Buy you a dri. . . ." Her eyes fell to Coady, and she wet her lips and tried again. "How long are you in town?"

I answered with a shrug.

"Well, my place is down behind the Beehive. Third crib. Blue drapes. Can I . . . ?"

"I'll see you around seven. I need to buy Coady some proper clothes."

"It's good to see you, Dylan. And nice meeting you, Coady McIlvain."

Coady dropped his head, shuffled his feet, but failed to hide his blush.

It took half a bottle of wine for Sarah Elizabeth Cabell to apologize for the heated words she had fired at me back in Denison and to tell me how she wound up at The Flat, which wasn't much of a story. The bottle was empty by the time I finished telling her of my adventures, and about Coady McIlvain.

"Where's Coady now?" she asked.

"He and J. C. Claybrooke went to check out that circus."

"Your cook's not worried about being arrested for stealing that chuck wagon?"

"Well, his outfit was down around the Frio River, and Fort Griffin's short of law these days."

"And the rest of your friends?"

"Still drinking at the Beehive or passed out on its floor."

We were alone. She fingered the top of her empty glass absently, and I stared at her, wondering why I had left Denison. I guess a lot of men wouldn't have found her beautiful, maybe not even pretty. Ten years of whoring isn't an easy life, but Sarah's eyes had a way of looking into your soul, and she didn't hold back her feelings or her mind. That had led to the scar above her right eye up in Denver when I had been setting type for the *Republican*. I had thrashed the miner who hit her, wound up spending ten days in jail, and losing my job, which was no loss. That had been back in 1867. I had known her seven years, off and on. Denver, Abilene, Dallas, Denison, and now Fort Griffin, and likely would have married her by now if not for our baggage. She was a prostitute, and I had my own skeletons.

"What are you going to do with Coady?" she asked.

I shrugged, and she tossed the wine bottle into the trash, her eyes hot, and I knew my shrug wasn't the answer she wanted.

"He's not your son, Dylan Griffith!" she snapped. Our argument, which had led to my leaving Denison in February of 1873, came roaring back: My past blocked any future we might share.

"I'm aware of that."

"Put him on the stagecoach, Dylan. Send him to his mother. That's where he belongs. Not. . . ." She waved her arms around her crib and laughed mirthlessly. "He's a boy, Dylan. He's been through enough."

"I'll take him home. I'm not some . . . fiend."

"You're a good man, Dylan, but. . . ." I exasperated her. I always had. Her cascading tears shamed me, but then she struck me low. Well, I found it a cheap shot at the time.

"You can't bring him back. Or her back. Bury them. . . ."

But I had stormed outside.

148

Chapter Sixteen

Proprietor of The Extraordinary Traveling Wild Animal Exposition of North America, Commodore Gary Monserud lauded himself and his heroism before the forty or fifty customers who had agreed to pay twenty-five cents each for the once-in-a-lifetime opportunity to view the myriad savage beasts he had personally captured and now displayed in caged wagons parked inside the giant canvas tent that had taken two days to erect.

"You will be shocked and amazed, ladies and gentlemen, boys and girls," he said. "I have traveled far and wide across this great continent to put together an awesome display that is in demand. Why, just the other day I received a wire from New York City asking me to bring my discoveries to Bunnell's dime museum." As he talked, an assistant helped him out of his plaid sack suit, and he rolled up one shirt sleeve to reveal a series of scars and scabs. "I have been bitten by rattlesnakes, and survived," he said. All the while Coady stared at the nickel-size mole beside Monserud's flat nose. "Charged by the great American bison. Jumped by the catamount. You will see these wonders of nature. Don't feed the animals, especially . . ."—he gasped—"especially keep your distance from the last cage. A young ruffian in Jacksboro just two weeks ago was nearly strangled by that savage monster." He held up his arm and pointed to the most recent bite marks and scratches. "The most fierce creature in all of the states and territories almost took off my own arm while trying to save the poor fool."

"What is it?" a cowboy asked. "Badger?"

"One of Lottie's chirpies!" came a rude reply from the crowd.

"You shall see. And after you exit, I will be selling autographs in the back of my wagon, along with a book of my adventures published by Beadle and Adams of New York City. So, step inside, my friends, but only if you are not weak of heart."

Begrudgingly J. C. Claybrooke followed Coady inside the tent, fighting the pushing and shoving, hearing the complaints and heckles as two black men in stable clothes pulled back the curtain so the dupes—Claybrooke and Coady included—could see about a half-dozen living prairie dogs, and two dead ones, sitting, half starved, cooped up like chickens.

"Yup," a cowboy said, "them prairie rats is fierce creatures."

The next cage revealed various antlers, a longhorn hide and, inside a glass box, one annoyed rattlesnake. Wagon Number Three sported a chained, frightened coyote, various animal pelts, leading several customers to call Gary Monserud a gyp, and storm outside. After seeing the broken-winged falcon in the fourth wagon, J. C. Claybrooke had a mind to follow the crowd through the open flap, but Coady suggested they might as well see the rest of the show. Only fourteen customers made it past the bawling buffalo calf, various mounted birds, half dead bobcat and black bear that looked old enough to have been eating berries when Lewis and Clark had been traipsing across the frontier, although Coady did find the pile of horns from bighorn sheep fascinating, if no one else did. What amazed J. C. Claybrooke was to find Commodore Gary Monserud standing in front of the last wagon.

"You're a skunk!" one lady shouted.

"Nah," a jocular cowboy commented, and spit out to-bacco juice. "The skunk skin was in with them other sorry hides."

"Friends, friends, friends," Monserud said, his hands pleading, "surely the most recent addition to my exposition is worth the parsimonious price of two bits. Benson, if you please."

A stable hand drew the curtain, and J. C. Claybrooke found himself taking an involuntary step backward when the beast inside shrieked and rattled the cage's iron bars. The woman who had made the skunk comment passed out, and only a fast-thinking buffalo soldier caught her, saving her dress from being ruined by the mud.

"Surely," Monserud said wickedly, "nothing is more savage than a Comanche crone."

Coady gasped, staring in horror at the young girl in rags, half naked, crying out like a rabid dog, lashing out at the stable hands before they picked up well-used poles, beat the bars, then poked them through the gaps and forced her into a corner, where, tears streaming down her dirty face, she began singing her death song. Coady took off running, and Claybrooke, confused, followed after him, calling out Coady's name, asking what was wrong, pleading with him to stop.

"Tell those who left early," Monserud yelled, "and all your friends that for twenty-five cents they can see this most wicked wonder of the world!"

I downed my fifth rye as Cuthbert Jenkins and a stranger in greasy buckskins and new boots staggered into John Shannsey's saloon. Once Jenkins pointed me out, the two men weaved through the crowd and sat beside me. Grover

Barr and his crew had cleared out of the saloon, and I was glad. I didn't want company, but knew my solitude wouldn't last forever.

Jenkins introduced his new-found friend as Victor Flynn, and, with a shrug, I pushed the bottle toward them. "No thanks," Flynn said, "I'm lightin' out. Tarantula juice and buffalo rifles don't mix." He wore a wide-brimmed hat, carried a Springfield .45-70 at his side, and stuck his buckskin britches inside a pair of fancy brown boots.

"Victor and me's been chewin' the fat," Jenkins said, took a swig from the bottle, and leaned forward. He lowered his voice. "The herd's movin' north. He seed it."

I caught the bottle my partner slid across the table, but no longer wanted whisky. I turned to Flynn, who nodded his confirmation.

"Below the Clear Fork of the Brazos," Flynn said. "I warrant I'll make my first stand at the Double Mountain Fork in three, four days."

"Why tell us?" I asked.

He shrugged. "I don't fancy gettin' my scalp lifted just yet, gents. Like I told Cuthbert here, I ain't lookin' for no partners, but I wouldn't mind knowin' they was some reliable buffler runners nearby, just in case things get prickly."

Jenkins cleared his throat, and I passed the bottle back to him. After he slaked his thirst, he told me he had sent the skinners back to the camp we had set up at the wagon yard. Flynn was pulling out tonight, and Jenkins wanted to leave come first light.

"Did you tell Grover Barr?" I asked.

My partner snorted. "Reckon he'd tell us?" I smiled at that reply, and Jenkins said he saw no point in blabbering the news to everyone. Barr would find out soon enough.

"So I figgered you'd tell Claybrooke, and bring the boy. . . ."

"Coady's not coming," I blurted.

"Huh?" He couldn't hide his disappointment.

"He belongs with his mother and sisters," I said, and all the tension I had felt suddenly lifted. "I'm buying him a ticket home, putting him on the next stage to Kansas."

"Well," Jenkins said with a sigh, "I'll miss the kid. Miss his shootin', too." He winked, and I grinned in spite of my mood.

I stood, unsteadily, and picked up the Sharps resting on the table top, and headed outside—leaving Jenkins and Flynn, or rather just Cuthbert Jenkins, to finish the bottle I left behind.

The next stage would leave Monday morning, but I went ahead and bought the one-way ticket, found my horse, shoved the Big Fifty in the saddle boot, mounted, and rode to camp. I explained that I would stay behind with Coady until Monday, see that he got on the stage to Dodge, and catch up with Jenkins and the crew as soon as possible. For the first time in weeks, J. C. Claybrooke smiled at me, but Coady looked anything but happy.

"I don't want to go!" he wailed in the first tantrum I had seen him throw. "And I gotta do something."

"What?"

He looked away. "Nothing," he said petulantly.

"You're going," I told him.

"But I want to run buffalo. I want to stay with you. There's nothing for me back home. I hate that farm."

He didn't want to face the memory of a dead loved one. I understood that, all too well. "Your mother's worried sick about you," I snapped. "What about her?"

Lillard Butler lashed out at me, too. "What about the reward money, Griffith? You said we'd share that five hunnert dollars. That's a right smart of money, you son-. . . ."

"Finish that sentence," I said, "and you'll never finish another."

Butler couldn't match my stare, and he cursed underneath his breath and started honing a knife blade. I hadn't bothered to unsaddle my horse, so I pulled myself into the saddle and reached over to help Coady up, but he pulled away from me and shouted: "Get away from me!"

"Coady," I said, "if I have to get down off this horse, you're going to become acquainted with my razor strop. You belong with your family."

"Imagine all the stories you'll be telling your sisters," Sarah said, raking bacon and eggs onto his plate. "You'll be the most talked about boy in Kansas, I expect. Your sisters will be jealous. I know I would be."

I don't know why I took him to Sarah's crib, other than I wanted to apologize to Sarah, to tell her she was right, as always, and that I had been a fool. I'm certain Liz McIlvain would not have approved, but it had a roof, and a wooden floor, and it was in town.

Coady didn't even look at his food, didn't say anything. After we ate, Sarah made Coady wash his face and hands, then helped him out of his store-bought duds, and tucked him, reluctantly, in her bed, and I know Liz McIlvain would have had a hissy fit over that.

"Sweet dreams, Coady," Sarah said, and kissed his forehead. The boy still didn't say a word.

"He's upset," she told me once we walked outside.

"He'll get over it." I felt her hand around my waist.

"You'll miss him."

"Yeah."

She laughed, told me I was just like Coady McIlvain, and pulled me closer. We kissed. "Where do we sleep?" I asked.

"On the floor, love," she answered. Thunder rolled in the distance and the wind picked up, but we talked outside for another forty minutes, not about us, or our pasts, or even our future, just talking about nothing, enjoying our voices, giving Coady time to fall asleep. When I opened the door, however, I saw the covers on the floor and back window opened, and I cursed my own stupidity.

Coady held his breath until the two stable hands, mumbling about Gary Monserud's incompetence and miserly ways, headed away from the sprawling tent and toward the plethora of saloons lining Front Street. He listened until satisfied no one remained inside, then opened the pocket knife I had bought for him at the Fort Griffin Mercantile, cut a rope, and crawled underneath the heavy canvas.

The bobcat snarled, and he froze briefly to get his bearings and make sure no one heard the animal. He found he was alone, except for The Extraordinary Traveling Wild Animal Exposition of North America's exhibits and, using the dim yellow light of lanterns hanging from various poles, crept toward the wagon in which the Comanche girl slept.

"Tunequi," he whispered.

Her eyes fluttered, and she leaped to life, growling, ready to scream and slash, and he panicked, fearing Monserud or someone would hear the commotion and investigate. "Please, be quiet." He closed his eyes, remembering, and spoke to her in Comanche, then repeated his name again and again. "It's me, Soyáque. Soyáque. Soyáque."

Recognition came quickly, and she fell silent and

crawled toward him, stuck her hands through the bars, and touched his face. Tears drew lines down her dirty cheeks, and Coady found himself crying, unashamed. "Soyáque," she said. "Soyáque. Soyáque. Soyáque. Soyáque."

"I'm gonna get you out of here, Tunequi," he said, but found himself speaking English, so again tried Comanche. She nodded enthusiastically, and Coady walked to the door in the back of the wagon. He cursed at the sight of the padlock.

"The keys?" he asked urgently, but she stared at him blankly. There was no Comanche word for keys. What would a Comanche know about a padlock? One of the stable hands likely had the key, he reasoned, seeing the plate of mush and slop bucket in one corner. Someone had to feed her, clean her cage, empty her slop bucket. He'd never find those men, however, wouldn't even know where to begin looking for them. That left Commodore Gary Monserud. Surely he had a key, but where would he be? Saloon? Hotel? The wagon parked outside that seemed to serve as the circus's office?

"I'll be back," he told her in Comanche, and sprinted toward the exit, pulled open the flap, and felt rough hands lift him off his feet, and toss him back inside. He landed with a *thud*.

"You thieving little swine," Monserud hissed in a whisky-soaked breath. "You want to see my show, you pay two bits like everyone else in this flophouse." The drunken commodore kicked at Coady's face, missed, and almost lost his balance. "You torment my animals, wake me up. I'll leave welts on your hide, boy."

Monserud's boot shot forward again, but this time Coady caught it with both hands and twisted savagely. Monserud grunted, screamed, and fell sideways into the mud, striking his head against a trash barrel with a sickening *thud*. The scalawag lifted his bleeding head out of the mud, vomited, and collapsed.

"Oh my gosh!" Coady blurted out, and crawled through the sludge, rolled Monserud over, and placed his head on the man's chest. Coady lifted his head, sighed, and thanked God. He started pulling Monserud's pockets inside out, leaving coin, cash, a .31-caliber Ells hide-away gun, and a brothel token in the mud. No keys of any kind.

Outside, a horse snorted, and Coady fell silent, frozen over the supine, unconscious body of Gary Monserud. Cautiously he crawled through the mud and peeked through the canvas flap. Mules and horses had been picketed near the exhibit's other wagons. One of the horses snorted again, and Coady, relieved, returned to Monserud, grabbed the little Ells, and ran to Tunequi's prison.

"Get down," he told her, aiming the barrel at the padlock. It had worked for Buffalo Bill in THE PEARL OF THE PRAIRIES. He hoped it wouldn't fail him. The little pistol popped, the bullet whined as it ricocheted, and Coady opened his eyes, beaming with satisfaction at the sight of the broken lock. He tossed it aside, swung open the heavy door, and grabbed Tunequi's hand.

"Come on," he said, suddenly aware that while no one probably heard the report of the tiny gun, every animal in this horrible zoo had awakened and now howled, roared, or pounded the cages with hoofs. "We gotta hurry."

Chapter Seventeen

"What happened?" Sarah asked.

After shoving my Big Fifty into the saddle boot, I stuffed my saddlebags with food, oats, and cartridges while explaining to her all that I had learned over the past couple of hours. I hadn't slept all night, and neither had Sarah. We had looked up and down The Flat for Coady McIlvain, but it never occurred to us to check the circus tent at the edge of town. In fact, no one ventured inside The Extraordinary Traveling Wild Animal Exposition of North America's big top until shortly after dawn when the two stable hands came in to feed the animals. They had found Commodore Gary Monserud unconscious, covered with blood, his supper, and mud, the Comanche girl missing and two horses stolen.

Once they finally revived Gary Monserud, he demanded to speak to the town marshal or county sheriff, but The Flat had neither. He said he wanted to file a formal complaint with the commanding officer at Fort Griffin, but a young lieutenant, who had paid twenty-five cents to see Monserud's sorry act, informed him that this was a civilian matter so the military had no jurisdiction. John Shannsey, head of the town's vigilante committee, conceded the seriousness of horse stealing but wasn't about to send his men chasing a kidnapped Comanche girl and snot-nosed boy. He added, however, that he might be persuaded to run a certain brigand who had arrived with a miserable circus act out of town on a rail.

What I should have done was head to our camp, enlisted Claybrooke, Jenkins, and some of the skinners to help, but I didn't think of that—too scared, I guess, too worried sick about Coady—until well past daybreak, long after Jenkins and the boys had followed Victor Flynn in search of buffalo.

"Why would he free that girl?" Sarah asked. "I mean, I'm glad he did, and I wish they would run that scoundrel out of town on a rail, or tar and feather him, but. . . ."

"I'm not sure," I said, and swung aboard the big bay. "But I've got a notion."

"What will you do after you find them?"

I found Sarah a bit optimistic. Coady had an eight-hour start on me, and tracking had never been one of my skills, but I thought the young fool would be trying to send the girl back to her people, so they'd be riding toward Comanche country, the *Llano Estacado*. Well, I hoped Coady had sense enough not to try to deliver the girl to the Comanches personally.

"I'll get Coady back to his mother, Sarah," I said. "I promise you that."

"I know." Her fingers touched my thigh, and her eyes pleaded with me to take care of myself, and to come back. I had ignored those eyes, those begs, for years, had never been able to bring myself to commit to a relationship. I had told myself it was because Sarah was a whore, but that had been a lie.

"Don't leave town?" I said. It came out as a question.

"I'll be here," she said, and I touched the bay with my spurs and loped down the alley, turned right at Front Street, and galloped out of Fort Griffin.

The bay had a comfortable loping gait, and didn't tire easily, so I pushed him hard at first, riding northwest. Comanches were practically born on horseback, but Coady didn't have the knack. He'd slow the Comanche girl, or so I hoped. Still, I had to find their trail. I reined up, let the bay cool down, and moved into an easy walk, staring at the wet ground, following hoof prints that I hoped belonged to Coady and the girl. I splashed across what would pass for a river in that part of Texas, and let the gelding drink while I pried off my eyeglasses to wipe the lenses.

That's when I spotted the piece of cloth stuck on a branch. I guided my horse to the tree, freed the bit of cotton, and examined it closely. It was a piece from Coady's yellow calico shirt. I was certain of that, for I had just paid hard money for it at the town mercantile. Tracks led out of the riverbed, but pointed northeast, which I found odd. Coady's trail had led northwest, as I had expected. I studied the tracks again, shook my head, and chuckled at the boy's ingenuity. Or naïveté.

"Too many Buffalo Bill novels, Master McIlvain," I said, tossing the cotton into the river.

He had cut a piece off his shirt sleeve with the pocket knife I had given him, speared it with the branch, ridden out of the river a few yards, then backed his horse into the water again. He wanted his trackers to think he had turned north, for Indian Territory perhaps, and had actually come close to tricking me. I don't think he would have fooled a Tonkawa scout, though, or anyone with decent eyesight. Kicking the bay into a walk, I rode in the middle of the stream about a quarter of a mile before I saw the tracks emerging on the west bank.

"How did you get away?" Coady asked Tunequi. "That night after . . . after I escaped?" He had started to say "after Piarabo was murdered" but remembered that Comanches considered speaking the dead's name taboo.

They sat on the banks of the Double Mountain Fork of the Brazos. His horse had worn out, and hers wasn't in much better shape. Coady's backside had played out, as well. He hadn't thought to steal a saddle, or he had lacked the time to do so, nor had he realized the need to bring grain for the animals. A horse could live on cheap grass, but a mount fed just a little oats or grain would go much farther.

Nor had they stolen any food for themselves. For the past three days, all they had eaten were a few roots and berries Tunequi had managed to find. He suggested he might try to pull a catfish from the river, if they could fashion a pole, hook, and line, but Tunequi said she'd rather die than eat fish. *Nice going,* Coady thought. *We'll likely both starve to death out here.* He hoped talking to Tunequi would take his mind off his hunger, his weary bones, his chaffed butt and thighs.

Tunequi never reached the top of the cañon, she told him. She had stopped at a switchback, leaped off, sliced the pony's rump with her knife, and hidden in the rocks. Her horse screamed and bolted, leading Comanches and Comancheros away. She had waited until the guards galloped past, and then Coady, before walking back down the trail, mounting another horse, and leaving the Kwahadi camp for good. Her plan had been to ride to the Indian Nations, to find the peaceful Comanches who lived at the reservation near the place the white men called Anadarko. She rode to the Medicine Mounds far to the east, but her horse tripped in a gopher hole and broke its leg, so she had wandered on foot for days, luckily reaching the big river known as the Red. She swam across the river, and walked northeast, thinking she might be delivered. The following day, she had been captured by Spotted Face—Commodore Monserud, Coady understood, with his ugly mole.

"I hoped to die," she said, "but now I know why I could not die. The spirit knew you would come to deliver me."

"Guess we're even," Coady said, falling back on his half-dime dialogue that The Unknown Scout had told Buffalo Bill at least twice in that cherished old novel.

Trace chains jingled in the distance, and Coady's heart skipped. He recovered, slowly slithered up the bank like a rattlesnake, and spied through the clumps of grass, amazed to see what looked like an entire army moving through the country, heading toward the *Llano*. He turned, placed a finger on his lips, and shook his head. A useless signal, he realized. Tunequi was smart enough to keep quiet, and she had covered her mount's muzzle with her hands. Coady's horse, half dead, looked too exhausted to make any noise. He looked again at the blue-coated soldiers driving wagon after wagon, guarded by cavalry troopers and Indian scouts. Coady slid down the embankment and told Tunequi, who bit her lower lip.

"You stay here," he said, and headed back up the embankment. The soldiers churned up more dust than buffalo, and his eyes stung. They hadn't spotted them, didn't have any interest in the river, just kept plodding along north, drifting farther and farther away. He smiled as the distance between them increased, thinking Tunequi safe, then heard her scream.

Coady tumbled down the embankment, saw a pock-marked Indian gripping Tunequi's waist. The Tonkawa scout looked just as surprised to see Coady, mumbled something, then cursed in English when Tunequi slammed her heel against his foot. Both fell backward into the river, and Coady dived in after them, forgetting that he had never learned to swim.

Although the water was shallow, Coady splashed about in a panic, swallowed almost a half gallon of the iron-tasting liquid, reached out, and pulled the Tonkawa's hair. Or maybe it was Tunequi's. He wasn't sure of anything until the Indian scout lifted him over his head and slammed him to the ground.

"Fool boy!" the Tonk roared. "Fool white boy!"

Coady opened his eyes, coughed, groaned, and suddenly laughed. The Tonkawa cursed as Tunequi flew into the Indian's saddle, kicked the horse, and took off in a lope down the opposite bank.

"Run!" Coady coughed, cleared his throat, and shouted. "Run, Tunequi, run! Don't look back. Just keep riding!" The Tonkawa unfastened the flap of his military-issue holster, drew a Remington, and aimed. Coady found his feet and charged, but the Indian whacked the barrel against the boy's head, and he dropped like a stone, conscious but stunned. The hammer fell with a loud *snap*. The Tonk cursed, cocked the pistol again, and tried again with the same effect. Wet powder! Coady smiled as the Indian shoved the gun into the holster and Tunequi disappeared. The Tonkawa turned to Coady and said angrily: "Fool boy. Fool white boy!" He added a few more English curses.

Despite pain, hunger, and exhaustion, Coady McIlvain somehow managed to smile.

Chapter Eighteen

A dozen or more Tonkawa scouts kept looking up over the simmering kettle, pointing at the prisoners, laughing among themselves, and commenting about Coady's bony features while adding ingredients to the boiling stew. Tonkawas were cannibals, Tunequi told him, the Comanche's most hated enemy—even more than the *tejanos*.

Tunequi hadn't made it far before two Indians and a white civilian scout rode her down, killing her stolen horse, and marching her back to the column of soldiers. A few cavalrymen had stared at Coady, and others made lewd gestures at Tunequi, but no one even tried talking to the prisoners. The harder Coady tugged at the rawhide bindings, the deeper the bonds dug into his wrists. Tunequi didn't even try to escape, just sat there, despondent, head down, singing her death chant, resigned to the fact that she'd soon become supper for those horrible Tonks.

"Comanchero?"

"I don't know, sir, but I doubt it."

"Renegade?"

"Little young for that, sir."

"I don't like surprises, Mister Wallace."

"I understand, sir."

Coady stopped struggling at the sound of the voices and concentrated on the footsteps heading toward him. Two men in field uniforms rounded the corner of the wagon, and the Tonkawas fell silent. Coady looked up at two pairs of hard eyes bearing down on him, and swallowed. The only sound came from Tunequi's soft, sad hum.

"What's the girl doing, Lieutenant?"

"Death song, sir, or so Mister Ammons tells me. Likely expects to be killed and put in some Tonk' stew."

The shorter man grunted and formed what might have been a smile. His face had been shaved, and he smelled of soap, suggesting a recent bath, but dust and dried mud caked his uniform, and his hat had seen better days. A man of medium build, he had straight brown hair, long side-burns, and the coldest gray eyes Coady had ever seen. Coady couldn't help but stare at the scarred right hand, which was missing two fingers. The second man, a sandy-headed lieutenant in need of bath and razor, removed his weathered black slouch hat and knelt in front of Coady.

"You speak English," the lieutenant said. It wasn't a question.

Coady tried to say something, but he found himself too scared, so he simply nodded.

"Good," the officer said. "I'm Percival J. Wallace, second lieutenant, Fourth United States Cavalry. This is Colonel Ranald Mackenzie, commanding. Where are your parents, son?"

He swallowed before answering. "My pa's dead. Was killed in Kansas. Indians."

"And your mother?"

"She still lives outside Dodge City, I reckon. I got took a long time ago. More than a year ago."

Mackenzie muttered an oath—Coady first thought the colonel was cursing him—and kicked sand at Tunequi. "Mister Wallace, can't you shut up this little witch?" He pressed fingers on both temples and closed his eyes.

Coady feared the colonel might have her killed, so he called out Tunequi's name and asked her to be quiet. She looked at him, and he pleaded with her in his best Comanche, telling her everything would be all right, to trust him. She glared at the two officers briefly, then closed her eyes and moved her lips silently.

"You speak Comanche?" Lieutenant Wallace said in surprise.

"Just a little."

"Did you escape with this girl?"

He started to tell the truth, but stopped, fearing the Army would return them to Fort Griffin to face the wrath of Commodore Gary Monserud. They hanged horse thieves in Texas, or so he had heard. "Yes, sir," he lied. "We've been on the run for days now. Weeks."

"Ask him if he could guide us to the hostile encampment," Mackenzie said as though Coady didn't understand English.

"Could you?" Wallace asked.

Coady shook his head. "I don't have any idea where it was, or where we are. This country all looks alike."

"That's the God-honest truth," Mackenzie said. "What about the girl?"

He considered this a moment. Tunequi wouldn't cooperate with the soldiers, ever, but if Coady told them that, this Colonel Mackenzie might hand her to the Tonks. "She doesn't remember, either," he tried. "That's why we're lost."

"He's lying," Mackenzie stated.

"Sir?" Wallace asked.

"Those horses the Tonk found with them, Mister Wallace. Use your brain, Lieutenant. Shod horses."

"Could have been stolen in a raid, sir."

"A raid these two vermin led. The Tonk said those tracks came from the south. They were riding to the Comanches, not from them. And if this boy has been living with the savages for more than á year, he's kept care of his clothes. Those are store-bought, Mister Wallace. Dirty and torn, but he hasn't been wearing them for a year. Don't they teach common sense at the Point?"

Wallace lowered his gaze to Coady. "Is that true?"

Coady didn't answer. His mother had been right. Adults can always see through a child's lie.

"What's your name, boy?" Mackenzie asked sharply. When Coady didn't answer immediately, the colonel kicked sand at him, cursed, and fired off the question again, reaching for the flapped holster on his left hip. Coady didn't think the colonel would shoot him, but. . . .

"Soyáque," he answered.

"Little savage," Mackenzie said, and spat.

"What do you want to do with him, Colonel?" Wallace asked.

"I'd like to hang him by his thumbs, and might just do that. We'll let him and his friend sweat it out for a few days, or as long as it takes. If he leads me to the Comanche camp, we'll reconsider his status as a traitor to his country."

"With all due respect, sir. . . ."

Mackenzie cut him off. "Put them on half rations, Mister Wallace. Keep the Tonks away from them, though. When the ungrateful little brigand tells me what I want to hear. . . ."

"Sir, we're not far from Fort Griffin. We can send them back now. I'm sure. . . ."

"You have your orders, Lieutenant," Mackenzie snapped, whirled, and stormed away.

Sighing, Percival Wallace followed his commanding officer.

★ ★ ★ ★ ★

It took thirty-one hours before I lost Coady's trail for good, and, since I had not packed enough supplies for a long journey, I headed back to The Flat, told Sarah what had happened, mailed a letter to Kansas, and rode to the mercantile to stock up for what I knew might become a lengthy expedition. As the clerk recited my list, a consistent thumping on the wooden floor told me I had company. I recognized the sound of Grover Barr's peg leg and crutch before I heard his voice.

"Your pard leave you?" Captain Barr asked. "Or did y'all part comp'ny?"

Barr didn't look happy, and I couldn't blame him. We had elected not to tell him the buffalo herd had begun its move north. The hide business was competitive. Everyone understood that, but Barr had considered us friends, although I seriously doubted if he would have tipped us off had Victor Flynn confided in him, instead of Cuthbert Jenkins.

"I've got a chore to do first," I said. "Then I'll catch up with Cuthbert. I'm surprised you're still in town. Figured you'd be out chasing the buffalo by now."

"I'll get them hides directly," he said. "No rush. Where's your sharpshootin' shadow?"

I slowly exhaled, and came clean, telling Barr that Coady had freed the Indian girl from Monserud's circus and took off for Indian country. I informed him of the reward Coady's mother had offered, about his dead uncle, about how, if the boy wound up getting killed, I'd never forgive myself. I said I had written Coady's mother that morning, told her I'd let her and her brother-in-law, Thaddeus, know by telegraph as soon as I found him, and said I had no interest in the $500 offered. That scalawag,

168

Gary Monserud, had lit a shuck yesterday morn for parts unknown, so I planned to bring Coady back to The Flat and put him on another stagecoach to Dodge City—if I could find him.

He snorted, wished me luck, and hobbled outside.

"You payin' cash for all this?" the clerk asked. He had to repeat the question, and I nodded, staring through the open door as Barr tried to outwit the wobbly planks laid across the muddy street. I had hoped Grover Barr would have volunteered assistance, maybe send Paria and Hunter, although I disliked them, to help me pick up Coady's trail. He was a buffalo runner, though, and had no interest in Coady McIlvain, not even the $500. A runner could make much more than that with one good hunt.

The clerk gave me the final tally, and I reached into my carpetbag and peeled off several greenbacks.

It sounded as if the 4th Cavalry had captured a grizzly bear.

Coady heard roars and curses answered with shouts, grunts, and the awful sound of wood and metal striking flesh. The cries and beatings ceased, making way for more cussing and excited chatter. Coady, tied to a wagon wheel again, craned his neck but couldn't see anything but the setting sun. Three soldiers rounded the bend, dragging a big man in Mexican pants who they dumped, face down, beside Coady and Tunequi. A red-headed sergeant, sporting a busted nosed and missing part of his left earlobe, bent over and shackled the unconscious man's hands behind his back with irons, spit on the new prisoner's back, and said hoarsely: "Go fetch the colonel."

When Mackenzie and Lieutenant Wallace arrived, the sergeant ordered two troopers to prop up the prisoner. A

169

private dumped a bucket of water on the captive, who roared and pulled at the manacles with no effect. The sergeant stopped the struggles by planting the toe of his boot in the man's ribs, and stepped back as two troopers pulled the man to a sitting position. One tossed a sombrero in the prisoner's lap, and he lifted his face and spat.

Coady gasped at the sight of José Piedad Tafoya.

The dirty Comanchero spoke in Spanish, malevolent eyes moving from the sergeant to his guards to Mackenzie, Wallace, and passing over Tunequi and Coady without much interest. Coady licked his lips and thanked God for deliverance. Tafoya apparently did not recognize either Tunequi or Coady. The burly Mexican locked his stare on Mackenzie, who spoke instead to Wallace.

"Comanchero?" the colonel asked.

"Likely. Corporal Sandoval says he claims to be a simple trader. Sandoval's patrol found him alone, driving a cart loaded down with trinkets, bolts of cotton, some pots and pans. Nothing much, although he had a Morgan with a fancy saddle tethered to the cart."

"No guns or whisky?"

"No, sir."

"Where's Corporal Sandoval now?"

"With the surgeon. This *hombre* broke his jaw."

Mackenzie's gray eyes focused on Tafoya. "Do you speak English?" he asked.

"*No sabe.*" Tafoya shrugged, feigning confusion.

"Who are you and what are you doing here?"

"*No sabe.*"

Mackenzie kicked sand at the Comanchero's face. That's what the colonel always did when he lost his temper, which happened often. Coady had lost track of the times Mackenzie had peppered his clothes with dirt. "Do we have anyone who speaks Mexican other than Corporal Sandoval?"

"I don't think it matters, Colonel. *No sabe* was all he would tell the corporal, too."

"All right." The colonel crouched, lifted Tafoya's chin, and whispered: "Mister No Sabe, I think you're a Comanchero. I think you know where we can find the hostiles, and you'll tell me. You . . . or them." He tilted his head toward Coady and Tunequi, and Coady held his breath when Tafoya's gaze stopped on him. The Comanchero, however, still showed no signs of recognition, looked at Mackenzie again, and spit in his face.

Mackenzie's slaps sounded like gunshots, and he was kicking Tafoya savagely when Lieutenant Wallace pulled him off.

Coady woke with a start, tried to scream only he couldn't breathe, and he tasted and smelled the hand of José Piedad Tafoya that almost crushed his jaw. *"Gringo,"* the Comanchero whispered harshly, and removed his hand. "You think José did not remember you, no? Well, José Piedad Tafoya never forgets. The only good that came from being caught by these *soldados* is that they have given me you, Soyáque, and that little Comanche crone. By the time I am through with you, you'll be begging to die. I will make you pay for what you did to me at the Palo Duro."

"What happened to your manacles?" It was the only thing he could think to say.

"I am a coyote, Soyáque. I chewed off my hand to take my vengeance on you," Tafoya said, although the Comanchero's hand was neither bloody nor missing. He must have picked the lock, or bribed his freedom. Coady chanced a glance. Where were those guards? Mackenzie

171

would have a royal conniption, but then he saw two forms on the ground near the wagon tongue, unconscious or dead. José Piedad Tafoya had learned much from the Comanches. Suddenly Coady felt a cold knife blade against his throat, which pricked his skin when Tafoya slapped Tunequi after she started to cry out. "Silence," he said first in English, then Spanish.

The Comanchero moved the blade and cut the rawhide biting into Coady's wrists. Before he freed Tunequi, he whispered: "One word from either of you, and you will die like this *puta's* old guardian. Remember?"

Coady couldn't get that vision out of his head: Piarabo lying dead in a pool of blood in her teepee.

Tafoya cut Tunequi free and shoved her toward the picketed horses, then gripped Coady's sore right wrist and pulled him along. *"Vamanos,"* he said.

Chapter Nineteen

"I've spent the better part of a month looking for that boy," I told Colonel Mackenzie, shouting to be heard over the wind. Mackenzie pinched the brim of his hat with his left hand to keep it from blowing away, and I demanded to know what had happened.

We stood in front of his Sibley tent, a brutal afternoon wind buffeting the dirty canvas and peppering us with sand. I could tell the officer had little use for civilians, especially a buffalo runner challenging his competence, but, reluctantly, he invited Lieutenant Wallace and me inside so we wouldn't swallow a mouthful of sand trying to carry on a conversation in the dust storm. He poured each of us three fingers of bourbon. After we washed down Panhandle sand, he and Percival Wallace explained everything.

I cursed my timing. I had come across the trail left by the 4th Cavalry command—finally—and had caught up with the expedition near the badly misnamed Running Water. I hadn't expected to find Coady and the Comanche girl traveling with the Army, had merely hoped to trade information, but Coady and Tunequi had been with Mackenzie all along—until escaping with a Mexican prisoner last night or early that morning. Wallace had described Coady to a T, and I swore at Ranald S. Mackenzie under my breath. Any decent officer would have sent the kids to Fort Griffin six weeks ago.

"Isn't there a reward posted for this McIlvain kid?" Mackenzie asked no one in particular.

"Yes, sir," Wallace answered.

"He should have told us his name in the beginning," the colonel grunted, blaming the absent Coady for everything. "Would have saved us all headaches." He sighed and changed the subject, eying me carefully. "What's your relationship with this boy? Are you his father?"

I stared at Mackenzie, wondering if he were testing me, knowing Brent McIlvain had been killed fifteen months earlier.

"Friend of the family," I said, which was partly true.

"I suppose five hundred dollars buys a lot of friends," he said caustically, and were I not pressed to rescue Coady, I would have thrashed Mackenzie then and there. "As soon as this dust storm breaks, we will pursue that Comanchero and those kids," the colonel said calmly. He seemed able to switch off his anger and rudeness with a spigot, a professional soldier once more. "You are welcome to accompany us as civilian scout, without pay, of course." He addressed Wallace. "Send Captain Mercedes my compliments and inform him that you, myself, and a dozen troopers from C Troop will track down this Comanchero. No one brains two of my men and gets away with it. Tell the captain he is to continue in a northwesterly course in search of the hostiles, but is not to engage until our return. I will dictate written orders to that effect. Understand?"

"Yes, sir."

José Piedad Tafoya cursed and kicked like Colonel Mackenzie. The cavalry patrol that had captured him had brought the Morgan and two oxen back to camp but had left the giant cart on the Staked Plains. Coady figured the wind had scattered many of the beads, blankets, and cloth across the countryside, but the Mexican blamed the Comanches, who he cursed as loafers and thieves. Looking closer, Coady spotted horse droppings, and guessed that Tafoya was right. That meant the Comanches had been close, but were now likely fifty miles or more from the cart.

Tafoya had retrieved his Morgan and stolen an Army mount, forcing Tunequi and Coady to ride double. They had waited out the howling dust storm in an arroyo before pushing hard to the cart. The wagon sat at a slight incline, and Tafoya crawled inside, tossing out the few remaining cotton bolts and coffee sacks, then prying loose floorboards with his bare hands. When he had removed a couple, he laughed, looked around, and spotted a shovel the Comanches had left behind. He slid down the cart, landed in the dirt, and hurried to the tool, lifted it off the ground, and tossed it at Coady's feet.

"Dig," he ordered.

Coady hesitated, and Tafoya smiled. "Do not fear me yet, boy," Tafoya said. "If José Piedad Tafoya wanted to kill you and your friend, he would have slit your throats at the bluecoat camp. You have value to me, little *gringo*. So does the Comanche. *Sí*, you shall both bring José Piedad Tafoya many *pesos* once I sell you to the silver mines in Zacatecas. That shall be my revenge. Now dig. I cannot carry these with me, so I will bury them and return later. Stupid *soldados norte americanos*." He went back to removing the false floor, grunting, cursing as the wood bit into his calloused hands, breaking off the planks with brute strength. "Hurry," Tafoya ordered. "That finger-missing colonel will not tarry."

Coady picked up the shovel and pushed the blade into the hard ground. Tunequi simply watched the Comanchero's back. Coady considered the Comanche girl, but she didn't notice him, so intent was her glare, and it suddenly dawned upon Coady that Tunequi was telling him what to do. He whirled, gripped the shovel's handle tightly, and took a tentative step forward. Tafoya only swore, concentrating on his task. A board popped like a gunshot, and Coady almost wet himself, but the Mexican hurled a piece of wood over the cart's side and never bothered to look up. Slowly Coady crept forward. Tafoya had stolen a trooper's Remington revolver and Springfield carbine, plus he had that sharp knife. If Coady made a mistake, Tafoya would kill him easily. Coady prayed for the courage—and strength—it would take for him to slam the shovel against Tafoya's skull.

Just a few more yards, he told himself, and began raising the shovel.

"Little *gringo.*" Tafoya's voice turned Coady's stomach. "Do you not know that José Piedad Tafoya has eyes in the back of his head? Dig, or it will not only be rifles I bury after all."

Coady sighed, turned around, and heard the Comanchero's laugh. Defeated, Coady lowered the shovel, but Tafoya's cynical laughter angered him, and without thinking he pivoted, charged, raising the shovel, howling with rage. The shovel swung savagely. Tafoya had turned, sliding down the cart, the jagged ends of the wooden planks tearing his expensive trousers, and had the Remington .44 halfway out of his waistband when the back of the shovel smashed his face.

The violent vibration ripped the tool from Coady's grasp, and he lost his balance and landed hard. Roaring in pain, Tafoya dropped the revolver and buried his bloody, bearded face in his hands, tumbled out of the cart, and fell to the ground, spitting out teeth and blood.

"Soyáque!" cried Tunequi, pointing at Tafoya's faster,

stronger Morgan, while she climbed atop the stolen cavalry gelding. Coady was on his feet, sprinting, yelling for Tunequi to ride, but she wouldn't leave until Coady was mounted. He tried to find the high stirrup, then heard a bullet whip past his ear. The slug burned the Morgan's rump, and the stallion reared, screaming, sending Coady to the ground. The horse bolted toward the sun, and Coady stood, trying to find Tunequi. A second bullet burned his thigh and dropped him into the dust. He rolled over, hearing Tafoya's curses and hoof beats. Tunequi still refused to abandon him. She had ridden over, was reaching down. Coady gripped her hand.

Tafoya fired again, killing the horse instantly, and Tunequi went over the side before the gelding collapsed. A fourth shot slammed into the dead mount's belly, and Coady and Tunequi dived behind the horse. Two more bullets buzzed over their heads. Then the Remington clicked on an empty chamber.

The Comanchero cursed, tossing the .44 aside, half blinded from pain and rage. "No one does this to José Piedad Tafoya." His voice was barely recognizable, as was his face. He wiped away blood with a dirty shirt sleeve, and spit as he returned to the cart. Coady's eyes darted every which way, searching for some sort of cover, but this spartan land offered no reprieve, and he sank lower behind the foul-smelling carcass. He thought he saw dust, but couldn't tell, and ducked lower at the sound of Tafoya's cursing. Tunequi once again began her death song.

"Shut up!" he snapped, and cursed her, immediately regretting his harsh words. He bit his lip, looking for some weapon, anything. Nothing. Tafoya had rounded the cart, angling cartridges into the side of a Winchester rifle.

The cart's wheel suddenly splintered, and Tafoya staggered back, confused, swinging the Winchester barrel away from Tunequi and Coady. He heard the report of the rifle at last and dived into the cart.

"Missed!" Ranald Mackenzie's sharp comment was absolutely useless to me. I knew I missed the moment I pulled the trigger.

"Three feet wide right," said Wallace, using a spyglass to spot for me. As I slid another .50-100 cartridge into the Sharps, Tafoya jumped into the cart. The Comanchero answered my shot with his own, but the slug kicked up dust well in front of us.

"We're out of his range," Mackenzie said.

"Those kids aren't," I snapped back, and adjusted the tang sight and my shooting sticks. Still sitting, I moved around a little on my butt for a better position, aimed, and waited. Tafoya stood in the cart, fighting for balance against the incline, and fired blindly. I aimed at the smoke a second before I heard his shot. He ducked out of sight, and the wind carried his curse away from us as I fingered another cartridge.

"You must have shot high," Wallace said.

"Shouldn't we ride closer, surround him?" Mackenzie asked. "He's outnumbered, and we must be six hundred yards away."

"Nearer seven," I said, and fired again. The colonel had a point. I had dismounted and shot first simply because of the lack of time. Now I feared that if we charged him, he would kill the two kids for spite. I hoped I could persuade him to surrender from a distance of seven hundred yards.

"Hit the cart," Wallace said. "Sent up a bunch of splinters."

Mackenzie also lifted his field glasses. "The boy and the

Indian are all right," he said.

Tafoya fired another shot, and I answered it.

"Perfect," said both officers. "Hit the cart again."

The cart was made with thick lumber but, even at this range, wouldn't stop a Big Fifty slug, so I reloaded and shot again, and again, forcing myself to ignore the intense heat from the barrel. Ordinarily I would space my shots and cool the barrel with a wet rag, but I couldn't afford such a luxury with two young lives at stake.

Two rounds later, Mackenzie ordered me to stop. "He's waving a white scarf," the colonel said. "I dare say he has had enough."

So had my shoulder. I let Lieutenant Wallace help me to my feet.

A sergeant bandaged José Piedad Tafoya's face while two troopers ran down the Morgan. Mackenzie and Wallace examined the two dozen Winchesters in the cart's hidden compartment, and I gave Coady McIlvain my fiercest scowl.

"You got some explaining, young man," I told him.

"I know," he said, and mumbled an—"I'm sorry."— lifted his head, and his words shot out like canister. "I had to, Dylan, I just had to. I didn't mean to be gone this long, just wanted to get Tunequi back to her people. I couldn't let her live with that Monserud fella, I just couldn't. It ain't right, I mean. Nobody should have to live like that. And this is Tunequi, the girl I told you about, the one who helped me all that time I was with the Comanches. I'm sorry I run off like that, and I'm sorry I made you mad. I'll go home now, if you want me to. I promise."

I lifted his dirty, arrow-ruined hat, tousled his hair, and handed him the Sharps rifle. "Hold this for me, Coady," I said, and approached Mackenzie and Wallace, now busy interrogating the Comanchero.

"Running rifles to the Comanches, mister, is serious business," Mackenzie said, brandishing a Winchester in the bandit's face. "Assaulting two United States soldiers, stealing government property, kidnapping. . . . I should hang you and be done with you."

Kidnapping? I likely could prefer similar charges against Ranald S. Mackenzie, but I held my tongue.

"Start talking," the colonel ordered.

Tafoya shrugged and said mockingly: *"No sabe."*

Mackenzie cursed, and Tafoya, giving the best bewildered expression his mangled face could manage, said: *"¿No sabe? Yo no comprendo. ¿Habla usted español?"*

"He speaks English," Coady said, and Mackenzie focused on the thirteen-year-old weighted down with my Big Fifty. "His name is José Piedad Tafoya. He was planning on selling these rifles to Quanah."

"Well?" Wallace jabbed a rifle barrel in the Mexican's belly. "Speak up. Where's the Comanche camp?"

Tafoya shrugged. *"Yo no comprendo,"* he said. *"¡Caramba! No sabe. Yo soy Roberto Gómez. Soy de Meoqui."* He looked at me, grinning, and said: *"Usted dispara muy bien, hombre."*

"Gracias," I answered, and asked him, in Spanish, where was the Comanche encampment.

"Se me olvidó," he said, and shrugged again. The defiant attitude returned to his voice. *"No sabe."*

"Es una lástima," I said casually, and asked a nearby trooper to fetch a rope.

Two cavalrymen propped up the cart's tongue, which I used as a makeshift gallows. With Mackenzie's reluctant blessing, we hung José Piedad Tafoya three times—a little harsh for a boy and girl to see, but I don't think Tunequi or Coady minded. After we lowered Tafoya the third time, he remembered his English and the location of the Comanche camp, promising to lead Mackenzie's forces to the Palo Duro if the colonel promised to spare his life. A sergeant and two troopers escorted the prisoner away, and Mackenzie turned his attention to us.

"The boy's free to go with you, sir," Mackenzie told me, "and the United States Army thanks you for your help in this matter." He was dismissing me, but one glance at Coady and I realized the colonel's terms were not satisfactory.

"What about Tunequi?" I asked.

"Who?"

"The Comanche girl."

"She's a ward of the government, sir, a prisoner of war. She stays with us."

"She actually belongs to Commodore Gary Monserud," I said, and, hoping I wouldn't butcher the name of the circus, added: "and The Fabulous Traveling Wild Beast Exposition of America." Mackenzie thought me to be a bounty man of a sort, considered me a savage after how I had refreshed Tafoya's memory, so I went on. "Monserud's put up a fifty dollar reward for her return, Colonel."

Mackenzie looked to Wallace for help, and the lieutenant said: "There was a troupe at Fort Griffin led by this Monserud, and I understand he did have an Indian girl in his show. That would explain a lot, sir."

Placing his fingers on his temples, Mackenzie shut his eyes and relented. "Very well. Give them the Mexican's horse. And get them out of my sight, Mister Wallace. Carry on."

★ ★ ★ ★ ★

The following morning, I filled the saddlebags on the Morgan with hardtack and jerky, then stepped back to my bay, and watched as Coady led Tunequi to the horse.

"I reckon this is good bye, Tunequi," he said. "You be careful now." He placed the Morgan's reins in her slender hands and stepped back, sniffling a bit.

She quickly brushed away a tear, placed her right hand on Coady's cheek, and stared at him. She said something in Comanche, swung into the saddle, and galloped away, toward the Indian Nations, or so I hoped. I never asked Coady what she told him, considering it none of my business, and he never offered. We didn't talk much the rest of the day as we headed south, Coady's arms tightly around my chest, pack mule pulled behind us.

We rode southeast, not pushing the bay. I had given Lieutenant Wallace a letter, asking if he would send it along with any dispatches the next courier took to one of the Army posts, and he had agreed, saying it was the least the 4th Cavalry could do for us. The letter was to Liz McIlvain, saying I had found her son, again, and would have him back at Fort Griffin as soon as possible. This time I would make sure Coady McIlvain took that stagecoach to Dodge City if I had to ride up there with him.

Three days later, we saw the great Texas herd.

Bulls, cows, and calves covered the broken plains like the wine-dark sea, flanked by cautious buffalo wolves, moving slowly toward us. I had never realized just how magnificent these bulky, powerful creatures were, and the sight of so many thousands of them filled me with awe and wonder. Faint echoes in the distance told us that the herd had more company than just wolves and ravens.

"You reckon it's Mister Jenkins?" Coady asked.

"Could be," I said. "Wouldn't do us any harm to be sociable. Might even let you shoot one more buffalo before riding on to The Flat."

I couldn't see Coady's face, but knew he had to be smiling.

Chapter Twenty

Having figured our scalps hung in some Comanche lodge by now, Cuthbert Jenkins gave me a bear hug that almost squeezed the life out of me, then moved over to crush Coady. J. C. Claybrooke promised to open a can of peaches he had been hording and fix up a cobbler. Everyone seemed happy to see us, but one person was missing.

"Where's Butler?" I asked.

"Fired him," Jenkins said. "Sent him packin' off to The Flat."

Claybrooke handed me a cup of coffee, and I squatted beside a wagon tongue and listened as Jenkins explained. While he talked, we heard the echoes of other buffalo runners making their stands. Using Claybrooke's Spencer, Butler had tried his hand at shooting buffalo, Jenkins told us.

"He just didn't have the knack," Jenkins said, winked at Coady, and added, "like our little marksman here." He sucked in some air, reached for his sack of Bull Durham, and continued. "I tried Butler for a week, but he'd use three or four shots on one cow, hardly ever hit the leader first. I kept tellin' him runnin' buffler is mighty diff'rent than shootin' antelope, but you couldn't tell that oaf nothin'. Stampeded the herd practically ever' day, and powder and lead cost too much to be wasteful. I told him he was through shootin', could go back to skinnin', but he wouldn't have none of that. So I persuaded him to get out of my sight. Good riddance, says me. And now that I got you back. . . ."

"How long are you and the boy staying?" Claybrooke interrupted. His face looked as bitter as his coffee tasted.

"I'd like to rest my horse for a day or two," I said, "give Coady a chance at making a stand, maybe." I also winked at the boy. "Then we're going to Fort Griffin, and Coady's going home."

Claybrooke nodded in satisfaction, and began opening the drawers of his chuck wagon, trying to find that airtight of peaches.

"I got somethin' to show you, pard," Jenkins said after finishing his smoke. "You too, Coady." We followed him to the skins laid out to dry, and he rolled another cigarette and nodded at a robe the color of snow, well, dirty snow. Coady drew in a sharp breath, and his eyes widened.

"Son-of-a-gun, Cuthbert," I said, "you killed an albino."

"Albino nothin'. I got me a white buffler." He struck the match to life and lit his smoke. After taking a couple of deep drags, he flicked an ash, caught his breath, and said: "I was hopin' you might take this hide in to The Flat when you leave. Ask Albert Mason, he's a saloon tender there at the Beehive, to keep it for me. Don't want to lose this white buffler hide iffen them Injuns act up ag'in."

"You've seen Comanches?"

"Ain't seen nothin' but buffler for the past month, Dylan, but them savages kilt poor ol' Victor Flynn three weeks back." He swore and finished his smoke before continuing. "Never had a notion he was in trouble, Dylan, till J.C. saw the smoke one morn, and we rode to his camp. Them bucks scalped him, cut him up, shot him to pieces, burned his wagon, killed his skinners, even taken his boots." He put a hand on Coady's shoulder. "That's why I feared them Comanches had sent y'all to glory."

"Poor Victor," I said, just to say something.

"Well, he was lucky in one regard. He bit the bite. Poison killed him quick, so he wasn't tortured none."

Coady wet his lips and looked up at Jenkins in confusion. He didn't say anything, but I asked him if anything was wrong. He took a while before talking.

"You said that man was scalped?" he asked at last.

"I did, and I know where you're goin'. Victor bit the bite so he was dead, and Comanches ain't supposed to scalp no one who done that. That what you're thinkin', Coady?"

"Yes, sir."

"That's what I thought, too. Maybe them bucks isn't as particular as they used to be. My uncle got hisself kilt in Arizona Territory back durin' the late War for Southern Independence. Apaches. Apaches ain't supposed to take scalps, but Uncle Zeb's hair was surely lifted. Reckon the Apaches learned other ways, like these Comanch' done. Injuns is like white folks, Coady. They pick up all sorts of new bad habits just when you think you got 'em figgered out."

That was the most I ever heard Cuthbert Jenkins say in one stretch. He squatted beside his trophy robe and began rolling yet another smoke.

"You got a lot of hides already," I commented.

"Been a good run," Jenkins said. "Wagons almost loaded down." He flicked his match toward the drying hides. "Your gallavantin' across Texas made you miss one of the best runs ever, pard, but I reckon it was worth it since you found Coady. Reckon you can shoot a mite of buffler oncet you get back from The Flat."

"Well. . . ." I paused, forming my words carefully. "I won't be coming back, Cuthbert." He crushed out his new cigarette, let Coady help pull him to his feet. He looked ashen. Coady looked simply surprised. "I guess . . . well, I'm a tramp printer, pard. It's time for me to move along."

★ ★ ★ ★ ★

Not only did J. C. Claybrooke break out his fiddle that evening, he also read Mark Twain's "The Celebrated Jumping Frog of Calaveras County". The peach cobbler he served for dessert was pretty good, too. We told our stories, did a lot of catching up, and turned in early. Coady unrolled his blankets next to mine, and we just stared at the flickering stars for several minutes before he asked why I was quitting with buffalo.

"It's just time," I said.

"You gonna marry that Sarah woman?"

"I. . . ." How could I explain to a thirteen-year-old that some women aren't the marrying kind? Did I truly believe that? No, Sarah probably would have accepted my proposal, and other men had wedded whores. As much as I traveled, we could have gone somewhere where nobody knew of her former occupation. I felt the past creeping up on me again, the strong urge to run. "Get some sleep," I told him. "We've got a busy day tomorrow."

"I ain't never gonna see you again," he blurted out. "You'll be just like Tunequi, just like my pa. Once you put me on that stagecoach. . . ."

He was crying, and I let him cry. Had I tried to comfort him, I probably would have bawled myself.

Bloating, skinned buffalo carcasses dotted the countryside like juniper. The rancid air, coupled with the brutal Texas heat, became suffocating, and our eyes watered, our throats turned sore, and we choked down the bile climbing up our throats. If I had not already decided to end my career as a buffalo runner, that morning would have persuaded me to return to setting type. Ink, I'd always found, had a pleasant aroma. Rotting buffalo didn't.

Coady and I pushed through the gruesome forest, followed by Ignacio and Trabue in their hide wagon, and turned north, leaving the dead animals to wolves, coyotes, ravens, and turkey vultures that had watched our passing with suspicion. An hour later we crept up on the far side of the buffalo, hobbled my horse in a dry wash, and, using the wash for cover, moved closer, leaving the two skinners waiting in the wagon.

I pulled up less than two hundred yards from the herd, set up my shooting sticks, and tossed canteen, rag, cleaning stick, and bandoleer of .50-100 cartridges at my side.

"All right," I told Coady, "which one's the leader?"

Chewing on a piece of jerky, he stretched out beside my Sharps and concentrated on the buffalo. I set my hat down, pushed back my sweaty bangs, and waited for his pick while studying the herd myself.

"That one," he said, and I followed the line of his finger.

"Why?"

"He's standing a bit away from the others," Coady said, "like them other buffs want to give him plenty of ground, and I don't know. He just looks mean. I wouldn't tangle with him none."

"Her," I corrected, and slid down to the rifle. I sighted down the barrel and waited.

"Am I right?"

"It's as good a guess as any," I told him, thought of something, lowered the stock of the Sharps to the ground, and backed away. I had promised him the chance to make a stand.

"You try her, Coady," I said, and grinned as he eagerly crawled to the rifle, struggled with it despite the rest sticks, and trained the barrel at the old cow. A minute passed before he squeezed the set trigger.

"Take your time," I coached him. "The herd isn't going anywhere anytime soon."

He took my advice, for a minute, two, three . . . and I realized he was shaking. I whispered his name and moved beside him, put my arm around him.

"It's all right," I said softly. "Take your finger out of the guard." He couldn't move, and I had to ease his hand away from the trigger gently. Coady sat there frozen, and I gripped the Sharps and lowered the hammer. He lay there sobbing for a minute or two, then backed into the wash. I followed him.

He took a seat on the dirt and pulled his hat down tight. He wasn't crying any more, but wrapped his arms around his legs and rocked, apologizing for acting like his sisters.

"Buck fever," I said. "It happens to the best, Coady, even The Unknown Scout, I guess."

"It ain't that, Dylan," he said, and I squatted beside him.

"It's just. . . ." He sighed. "I can't . . . it's . . . well, Tunequi and Quanah . . . they . . . well, I don't want to go back living with the Comanches or nothing like that, but . . . I guess it just ain't like I thought it was going to be."

The journey through the buffalo killing ground that morning hadn't only troubled me. It had haunted Coady, but I maintained my façade.

"It's a business, Coady," I said. "I told you before it wasn't hunting."

"I know. But the Comanches depend on buffalo. . . ."

They'd label him an Indian lover for such sentiments.

"It's also a war," I said.

"It ain't right."

I couldn't argue with him, so I told him to wait. I paused when he called out my name and said: "I wish. . . ."

189

He couldn't finish. "Coady," I said, "Cuthbert and the others. . . ." I nodded toward our skinners. "They depend on buffalo, too. They have a right to make a living."

"Couldn't we . . . ?" he began, but stopped as I shook my head.

"We can't let them down, Coady. Those hides fetch a lot of money." I thought about lecturing to him about the way of the world—progress, civilization—but these rang hollow to me, so I simply asked: "You understand?" His head bobbed slightly, but tears welled in his eyes again. I left him there, however, and simply climbed up the side of the wash, prepped the Big Fifty, and aimed. Suddenly I had a case of buck fever, or could it be something else? The Sharps boomed at last, and the ground began shaking. Two minutes later, I crawled down the wash beside Coady, bandoleer and canteen over my shoulder, rag in my vest pocket, shooting and cleaning sticks in one hand, Big Fifty in the other, a cloud of dust rising behind me, blocking out the sun.

"What happened?" Trabue yelled.

"Missed!" I yelled over the thundering hoofs. "Stampeded them."

"Stampeded 'em pretty good," Trabue said in disgust, while Ignacio laughed good-naturedly and commented: "You lost your touch, señor. You shoot as bad as Butler."

"Yeah," I said. "Sorry, boys. Y'all might as well head back to camp, get ready to move out. I don't think we'll be running any buffalo this day."

I've played that shot ten thousand times through my mind. Did I miss on purpose, or did I just botch a shot? Honestly I don't really know. Coady thought I bowed to his wishes, and I let him think that. The skinners turned their wagon around, and I shoved the Sharps into the scabbard, draped the canteen over the saddle horn, rammed my shooting possibles and hobbles into a saddlebag, and swung into the saddle. I moved the bay closer to Coady, kicked my boot free of the stirrup, and leaned forward to help him up.

He just looked up at me, eyes dancing, unable to stop that spreading smile.

"What are you grinning at, boy?" I snapped.

Coady McIlvain just laughed.

We didn't go straight to camp, just drifted across that miserable expanse of country full of buffalo wallows, buffalo dung, enjoying our company, although I kept a watchful eye on the threatening skies. Laughing, Coady said that he had never seen such a display of poor marksmanship and that Cuthbert Jenkins would surely tan my hide for scaring off the buffalo.

"You want to walk back to camp?" I asked in jest.

We ate cold bacon and biscuits by a shallow stream, washing down J. C. Claybrooke's leftovers from breakfast with the iron-tasting water.

Coady started needling me again, and I knew I'd hear a lot worse once we got back to camp. I swallowed the last bit of biscuit, rinsed out my mouth with the stream's unpalatable water, and Coady, as talkative as he had been in ages, began talking about his sisters. That was a good sign. He was homesick, maybe ready to face his father's grave.

I brushed away a tear, my own mind racing back to a cemetery in Baytown, Wisconsin.

"You've been like a pa to me, Dylan," Coady suddenly blurted out, and I washed my face in the stream. "I mean it. I don't know how I. . . ."

"Coady," I said, turning around, "I've been a louse."

"Huh?"

"If anyone's been like family to you, son, it's J. C. Claybrooke." I had started my confession, couldn't hide my tears or pain any longer. "Any decent man would have sent you home a long time ago, but I wanted you with me. I felt. . . ." I shook my head, trying to collect my thoughts.

"I had a wife, Coady, and a son. He would have been about your age now had he. . . ."

"He died?"

"Yeah." I pried off my glasses and wiped my eyes with an end of my bandanna. "I went off to war in 'Sixty-One, to preserve the Union. He was just a baby then. Anyway, when I came home four years later, I learned Elwyn had died. Diphtheria. Back in 'Sixty-Three."

"Didn't your wife write you?"

"She died, too."

"Diphtheria?"

I nodded in a lie. Margaret had become inconsolable after Elwyn's death, had walked one night to the St. Croix River and waded in. They found her body two miles downstream, but Coady didn't need to hear all of that. "My father wrote, four or five times," I said, "but I never got the letters. So I got home, saw the graves. . . . That's why I've been roaming all these years, trying to forget. That's why I've never asked Sarah to marry me. I guess when you showed up, I saw . . . it was like another chance. I thought I might get back a little. . . . I was wrong, and I'm sorry."

Coady reached out to place a hand on my shoulder. "It's all right, Dylan," he said. "You can stay with us if you want, till you're back on your feet. My ma won't mind."

I thanked him for the gesture, and washed my face again. I actually felt good, relieved, as if someone had pulled an anvil off my chest. Maybe I was finally accepting their deaths. Elwyn would have died had I been in Baytown, instead of fighting with Berdan. Margaret might have killed herself, as well.

Attempting to cheer me up, Coady suddenly asked if I had ever heard the song "Goober Peas"?

"No," I lied, and he launched into it. I tried to enjoy this as much as he did, although I dreaded putting him on that stagecoach, but I had been putting that off too long. In the distance, I detected the pops of gunfire.

"Quiet!" I snapped, and he looked at me in confusion, then also heard the faraway reports.

"I guess you didn't run off all the buffalo," he said, trying to reassure himself, and me, that everything was normal, but I knew better. Those shots weren't spaced like a buffalo rifle; they came from several repeaters—fired in the direction of our camp.

Chapter Twenty-One

Thick, black smoke snaked higher in the darkening sky. Sweating, nauseated from fear, I reined in the lathered bay, and let Coady dismount. I didn't bother with the hobbles, simply slung the bandoleer over my shoulder, handed the reins to Coady, and pulled the Sharps from the scabbard. "Stay here!" I said urgently, "and I mean it this time. If I'm not back in thirty minutes, mount up and ride. Head to Fort Griffin, but take it easy. That horse is tuckered out."

He stood there, nodded grimly, and, crouching, using scrub for cover, I crossed the hundred yards of broken country for camp.

Voices. I scaled a mound of rock and prickly pear, waited for my breathing to relax, and peered over. Several bodies lay scattered over camp, unmoving, while a handful of men scurried about like bees. One of the wagons had been turned on its side, while flames engulfed J. C. Claybrooke's Studebaker, and a man in buckskins splashed coal oil from a can against the other hide hauler—only, most of the hides had been transferred into another big wagon. These weren't Indians. They were white men in moccasins.

"You rakes hurry!" a voice boomed. "Marcus, get that wagon a-movin'! Rest of y'all finish up. You know what to do!"

I ducked below, fighting the urge to throw up. The voice made me sick.

Captain Grover Barr.

Coady had been right all this time. Indians hadn't killed Wheatley and Pattison, Victor Flynn, and how many more—well, Indians hadn't killed all of the buffalo runners that year. Barr's crew had paid a visit, perhaps gotten friendly, then murdered the unsuspecting runners, left behind arrows and the like, and stolen the hides, leaving a few in the burning wagons to make it appear that all of the hides had been torched. How many times? I wiped my sweaty hands on my trouser legs before chancing another glance.

Barr stood in the driver's boot of his wagon, now filled with our hides, including Cuthbert Jenkins's prized white one. Glenn Marcus had climbed aboard another wagon loaded with stolen hides, while the skinner named Hunter moved about camp, brushing away sign with a juniper branch. I didn't see the black man, Moses, and that troubled me, but not as much as what the half-breed, Paria, was doing.

He fetched an arrow from a quiver, notched it in his bow, and shot it into the lifeless body of Ignacio, a gentle man who had never hurt anyone. I had never even heard Ignacio raise his voice in anger. Paria shot twice more, then squatted and lifted the dead man's scalp. My eyes swept across the camp. Trabue's body looked like a pincushion. Chet McDonough had been staked to one of the burning chuck wagon's wheels. The smell of burning flesh overwhelmed me, and I slid down the rocks and vomited, hoping no one would hear my gags above the increasingly tumultuous wind. Claybrooke and Jenkins hadn't been filled with arrows . . . yet.

One man. Against Barr, Paria, Marcus, Hunter, and Moses, if he were lurking about somewhere. What could I do? I had killed scores of men during the war, but I had never seen their faces. I had cheated death in that regard, using a brass telescopic sight affixed to a Sharps rifle so that I could take human lives without witnessing the blood. This was different. I could see these men clearly, and they could easily kill me.

Suddenly Grover Barr cursed. "That belly-cheater's movin', 'Breed!" Barr shouted. "You best finish him now. We'll meet y'all back at camp."

I froze just a moment, then found determination and climbed up the embankment. Claybrooke was dragging himself away from camp, followed by a laughing Paria, who fingered another arrow and drew the bowstring tight. I slammed the stock against my shoulder, aimed, and pulled the two triggers almost simultaneously.

"What the . . . ?" Barr began, and the rest of his words were drowned out by the loud ringing in my ears. Already I had reloaded, swung the barrel around, and fired. The slug must have torn into Barr's wooden leg and sent him toppling over the wagon's side. Paria lay spread-eagled, blood pooling underneath his body, and Claybrooke stopped crawling. That was smart on his part. Had he continued trying to drag himself to safety, one of those demons would likely have shot him. "Stay put," I whispered, though the cook couldn't hear me. On the other hand, I had to move. Those renegades would have spotted my smoke by now, so I scurried down the rocks, reloading as I moved, while bullets began clipping cacti and whining off rocks.

"Stop shootin' till you see what you're shootin' at!" Barr snapped.

The wind, carrying the threat of thunderstorm or cyclone, had shifted direction, and I used the thick smoke for cover. One bullet buzzed past my ear, but I dived behind our second hide wagon, which the killers had overturned.

My eyes stung from sweat and smoke, and I quickly wiped my eyeglasses before peering around the side. Jenkins lay on his side, eyes open, chest covered with blood, right hand gripping the handle of my carpetbag. His Old Reliable lay a few yards away, and I guessed he had shot once, then tried to find another weapon before those bloody butchers cut him down.

Wood splintered above me, and I ducked back.

"He's behind the wagon!" Hunter shouted, and I was moving again.

Too far. I rounded the wagon, and slid, swinging my rifle, firing blindly at the figure hovering above me. It was a scratch shot; there's absolutely no way I should have hit Glenn Marcus, but I did. He was flying backward off his wagon as I scrambled back to cover. Bullets peppered the wagon above me, showering my back and hat with splinters. I opened the breech, reloaded, set the trigger, tried to breathe. The cannonade ceased, replaced by rolling thunder, and I heard Grover Barr's voice.

"Griffith? Is that you, *amigo?*"

I didn't answer, just crawled on my belly toward the wagon tongue, and slowly sat up, holding the Sharps close.

"Dylan Griffith, as I live and breathe. I reckon that is your carpetbag, friend, lying there beside Jenkins. Didn't place it till you started shootin'. Son, you knocked my wooden leg off. What are you doin' back in these parts, friend? I thought you was out chasin' down your shadow." Then nothing.

"Maybe he's dead," Hunter said an eternity later.

"Stick your head around that wagon and find out," Barr fired back, and Hunter swore.

My mouth had turned to sand. My heart raced, and my lungs burned. I had plenty of cartridges for the Sharps, plus the open-top Colt remained holstered on my right hip, but I had little experience with a short gun. I kept only five rounds in the Colt's cylinder, leaving the chamber underneath the hammer empty so I didn't accidentally blow off my foot, but, now, shooting my toes was the least of my worries, so I leaned the Big Fifty against the wagon, drew the revolver, set the hammer at half cock, rotated the cylinder, and filled the empty hole with a cartridge from my shell belt. I lowered the hammer and slid the gun back into the holster.

The wind had changed direction again, and I was grateful because it lessened the stench of burning flesh. I wet my lips and tried to think of some strategy, some way I could flank both Barr and Hunter.

A bullet tore through the wooden bottom and ricocheted off the wheel above me, and I rolled away, dropped to my belly, pulling the Sharps down with me. Another torrent of bullets slammed into the wagon before stopping abruptly, and I heard Hunter refilling the magazine of his repeater. I had chosen poorly. The wagon on its side had kept me alive, so far, but my luck wouldn't hold out. (I didn't know it at the time, but one bullet had scratched my neck.) I found myself trapped. When I lifted my head off the dirt to scout out a new location, Glenn Marcus was wobbling toward me. His left arm, soaked crimson, dangled uselessly at his side. In fact, blood ran down his entire side all the way to the tops of his moccasins, and his lips quivered, but he kept walking, slowly, painfully, lifting a Whitney Navy revolver in his right hand.

I jumped to my knees, braced the rifle stock against my hip, and shot Marcus in the chest. The cook went flying backward, crashed hard against the burning chuck wagon, sending a shower of sparks skyward. Marcus stayed like that briefly, as if nailed to the flames, before collapsing, his clothes smoldering.

"Get him!" Barr bellowed. "Before he reloads!"

Footsteps drew closer, and I tossed the Sharps to the ground and drew the Colt. The running stopped, though, and Hunter called out: "Maybe he's got a pistol!"

"He ain't got no pistol!"

"I don't know, Capt'n. I recollect he did have one."

I aimed the Colt at Hunter's voice and fired through the wood. Hunter screamed and tripped, accidentally pulling the trigger on his Henry rifle. To the surprise of both of us, he fell forward, and I had a clear shot at him. He was scrambling, trying to jack another .44 round into the rifle when I shot him twice in the face. Hunter shuddered and lay still. Trying to ignore the gory sight, I gripped the hot barrel of his rifle and pulled it to me, then reloaded both revolver and Sharps. Barr didn't fire back, and I began to believe maybe I had hurt him. Perhaps I had crippled him so that he couldn't do much more than direct Hunter's assault.

Barr cursed and laughed. "Guess you do have a pistol, Griffith. My mind's a-failin' me."

Now, *I* felt like talking.

"Barr!"

"Yeah!"

"It's over Barr. Give yourself up." For some reason I laughed.

"What's so funny, Griffith?"

I had felt as though I had been reciting dialogue from one of those half-dime novels Coady so admired, but I didn't answer the murderer's question. Instead, I asked: "You were going to kill us in camp that morning, weren't you? Until Billy Dixon and Bat Masterson showed up. Shoot us in our sleep."

"Would 'a' been less painful for you that way, son. See how messy things got here. We just rode up, said howdy, and started shootin'. But I reckon we got us a Mexican stand-off, ol' friend. Tell you what, Griffith. Why don't we call a truce? I let you ride out of here. You do the same for me. 'Course, I might need some help. Don't move as fast as I used to."

I was backing away, using the overturned wagon for cover, dragging Hunter's Henry in my left hand and the Sharps in my right. I figured if I could reach this arroyo about fifty yards away, I'd swing around behind Barr and force him to surrender, or kill him. Barr kept talking, which is what I wanted. When he mentioned Coady's name, I froze.

"The one thing we gotta figger out is who rides off with Coady," Barr was saying. "You recollect your shadow, don't you? You want to leave him with me?"

He was bluffing, and yet. . . . I cursed.

"Dylan!" It was Coady. "Don't listen to 'em, Dylan. Get out of here. They'll kill you."

A new voice yelled: "What'll it be, *hombre?* You step from behind that wagon, or I'll see if Coady still dances a fine jig."

Moses! He was still with Barr.

"You got thirty seconds to show your ugly face."

I crawled back to the wagon, and stood. "Let the boy go!" I yelled.

"Soon as you step so we can see you," Barr answered. "But first, pitch that Big Fifty over here where we can see it."

I looked at the rifle, saw where I had carved the stock to commemorate Coady's first buffalo kill, and sighing, feeling sick again, I pitched the heavy rifle into the clear. It landed just beyond Hunter's feet.

"Hunter's rifle and your six-gun, too!" Barr yelled.

I obeyed. What choice did I have?

"Now, let's get a good look at you, Dylan," Barr said. "It's been far, far too long."

I hoped another buffalo camp had seen the smoke from Claybrooke's chuck wagon and were off to investigate, but I had stampeded the herd that morning, and any neighboring runners were likely too busy trying to catch up with the buffalo. Someone would come eventually, but I doubted if they would arrive in time. Not in two minutes or so, which was about all the time I had left to live.

"Time's up!" Moses shouted, and, hands over my head, I stepped over Hunter's body and into the clear.

Cuthbert Jenkins's lifeless body rested perhaps ten yards from me, beside my carpetbag. Paria was still alive, but not moving except for rapid blinking. I had hit him square in the chest, an ugly, gaping, through-and-through wound that probably nicked his spine and paralyzed him. Claybrooke no longer moved. I couldn't tell if he were alive. Moses held Coady in front of him, and trained an old Dragoon pistol at my gut, while Captain Grover Barr sat beside his hide wagon, resting his back against the front wheel. His hat lay a dozen feet from him, and blood trickled down his bald head, cheek, and chin. My Sharps round had, indeed, knocked off his wooden leg, and he had broken his already injured left leg falling off the wagon.

"You crippled me good, Griffith," he said, brandishing a Colt.

I remembered back to when we first met, when he had said he had broken or sprained his ankle in a prairie dog hole, remembered seeing the blood stain around his bandage. Prairie dog hole? No, I guessed, it had been a bullet hole when one of his victims fought back. "I'd kill you myself," Barr said, "but I ain't much a hand with no pistol, and can't reach my Remington."

"You kill us," I said, "and you'll have a lot of explaining to do. Other runners will be here soon. They'll be checking out that smoke."

Barr nodded. "I thought of that while I been sittin' here. Reckon Glenn did set that wagon afire too soon, then you went and bollixed things up, but ain't no runners here yet, and, iffen they do come, well, I'll just say that you attacked us. You was the one killin' off all them good ol' boys, makin' it look like Injuns done it. I mean, Coady, yonder, lived with the Comanch' for a year. Turned him into a renegade, I guess."

While he talked, I tried to figure out how I could kill Barr and Moses, save Coady, and not get killed myself. Staring blankly at Cuthbert Jenkins's body, Coady wasn't fighting any, and Moses had relaxed just a bit. Only I soon understood that Coady wasn't looking at Jenkins at all. He was trying to tell me something, and I remembered.

"Flies, Dylan, flies," Coady suddenly said.

Grover Barr, bewildered, shot a glance at the boy, but I understood, and jumped as thunder and lightning cracked. Moses got off one round before I landed beside Cuthbert Jenkins. His second shot hit my dead partner's body, and I reached into the open carpetbag, my right hand finding the butt of the Navy .36 nestled beside my Mark Twain book. Barr emptied his pistol, but he had been right. He was a pitiful shot with a handgun, although one bullet cut a furrow across my thigh and another knocked off a boot heel. Moses could have killed me, but Coady kept clawing his face. The skinner cursed, pushed Coady to the ground, and leveled his pistol. I shot him through the carpetbag. The bullet struck him in the groin, and he staggered back, still clutching the Dragoon. I pulled the Navy from the bag for a better shot and hit him again. My aim wasn't much better. The bullet ripped into his groin again, and he groaned and fell to his side, although he still held the old horse pistol.

Thinking fast, Coady scurried over on his knees, and jerked the heavy gun from Moses's grip, while I turned to face Barr, crawling toward the Remington Rolling Block. I aimed and fired, and, although the bullet kicked up dust far from either the rifle or Barr, the miserable swine stopped.

An hour later, Billy Dixon, Bat Masterson, and a half dozen other buffalo runners rode into camp.

"What kept y'all?" Coady asked.

Chapter Twenty-Two

The thunderhead passed over us without shedding a drop of rain, typical of Texas, and Paria died two hours later without ever moving anything other than his eyelids. We buried our boys separately, including the burned corpse of Chet McDonough. Billy Dixon removed his hat, and we took the cue and bowed our heads. "Lord," he said, "here lie some pretty good men. You'll know what to do with them, and forgive us if we have some other business to attend that you might not like. Ashes to ashes and dust to dust." Afterward, the adults among us dumped Paria, Hunter, and Marcus in a shallow grave. The buffalo runners working shovels and picks didn't cover that grave just yet.

Coady and a skinner named Astor stayed beside Claybrooke all that time. Astor had worked in the Confederate medical corps during the War Between the States, so he knew a few things about bullet wounds. Claybrooke had four bullets in him, but somehow wouldn't give up the ghost, and we loaded him into the back of a wagon to get him to The Flat, trying to make him as comfortable as possible. Astor offered to ride along with us, while Masterson promised to sort things out and deliver the hides to The Flat as soon as possible.

"What about them?" I asked, eying Grover Barr and Moses.

"We'll take care of 'em," Dixon said grimly, "as soon as you get the boy out of here."

I didn't object. Truth is, I didn't care. The town of Fort Griffin had no law, and putting Barr and Moses on trial would have been a waste of time. The Flat being The Flat, those two probably wouldn't have survived a day in town before vigilantes, buffalo men, or both hauled them out of jail and strung them up.

Coady, Astor, and I reached town three days later. I kept expecting Claybrooke to die, but he never did, despite losing a lot of blood. Astor rode back to the buffalo herd shortly after we found a doctor, an old sawbones named William Kuykendall, who also conceded that our cook wouldn't last out the evening. Nonetheless, Kuykendall dug out the two bullets in Claybrooke's back, one in his shoulder, and one in his buttocks, and gave him a tumbler of brandy when Claybrooke woke up. The doctor also told the undertaker to get a coffin ready.

Two days later, J. C. Claybrooke asked for a cup of coffee and a bowl of grits. Coady and I brought him his breakfast, and Coady spoon-fed him.

"I'm sorry you got shot," Coady said, "and I'm sorry they burned your wagon and all." He eagerly shoved the tasteless mash into Claybrooke's mouth.

"Easy, son," the cook said, almost choking. Coady mumbled an apology and reined in his alacrity. "Let me have some of that coffee."

"It ain't coffee," Coady admitted. "The doc says you don't need coffee just yet, but it's chicken broth. Smells good." After wiping off the spoon with a napkin, he dipped the utensil into the mug of broth.

"All these months on the range, my nose can't smell anything but buffalo," Claybrooke said. "Can't taste anything, either." He swallowed and looked at me. "Cuthbert?"

I shook my head.

"Anyone get out other than me?"

My answer remained the same.

"We captured the colored man and Captain Barr," Coady said.

Feeling the need to lie, I quickly said that Billy Dixon was taking the two men to Fort Worth, but Coady shook his head and gave his patient another taste of broth. "That's what they want me to believe, Mister Claybrooke, but I ain't no idiot. Billy Dixon and his friends hung them two."

"Well," Claybrooke said, "don't make a point of telling anyone else that, Coady . . . especially your mama."

"I won't."

Claybrooke's eyes trained on me in a hard stare I had grown used to. "Stage leaves Monday," I said. "Coady's going on it. Bat should have the hides in today, tomorrow at the latest, and I'll sell them. You don't know if Cuthbert had any family, do you?"

"That rapscallion? No one that would claim him." He forced a smile.

"Ignacio? Trabue? McDonough?" The cook shook his head at each name, and I sighed. "Then I guess I'll sell the hides, if that's all right with you, and you keep it all."

"You deserve a share," he argued.

"I didn't kill any buffalo." He knew that. I had been chasing down Coady while Cuthbert Jenkins claimed his hides, and I had already taken my split from the few hides we sold or traded at Adobe Walls and during our first trip to The Flat. Claybrooke said all of those hides didn't belong to Jenkins, so we agreed to cut out a portion and leave it with John Shannsey to pay relatives of Pattison, Wheatley, Flynn, or anyone else Grover Barr had murdered, if anyone ever filed a claim. "And Coady gets a share."

"Uhn-uh," Coady argued. "I didn't kill any buffalo, except that one. So maybe I'll take one hide home with me. But you keep your money, Mister Claybrooke. You need to buy another chuck wagon."

Coady fed Claybrooke for the next ten minutes, then the cook grew tired and said he had eaten enough. The boy carried the tray outside, and I was about to follow when Claybrooke asked me to stay a minute longer.

"What day is it?" he asked.

"Friday. Don't worry, J.C., I won't let Coady get away from me this time."

"Where you staying?"

"With . . . a friend. Stop fretting. Get some rest. And will you trust me, just this once? I know I've been a fool, and one day I'll explain it all to you."

He shook his head weakly. "I know you'll do the boy right," he said. "Just want to get one more thing straight. I hired on for seventy-five a month. You pay me what I'm owed, no more. Take the rest and make sure it goes straight to Coady's mother. Didn't want the boy to hear that because he'd put up a fight. He's a good kid."

"He is."

"Be a . . . an anonymous donation, something like that."

"I'll do it."

"Watch the boy," Claybrooke said as I closed the door behind me.

I sold the hides on Saturday morning, made a deposit in the newly opened town bank, and drank a couple of beers at the Beehive with Billy Dixon and Bat Masterson before they mounted up and rode off to run buffalo. I had left Coady at Sarah's crib, the two of them playing checkers, while I attended business. By dusk, The Flat started howling again, its streets, saloons, and gambling parlors filled with tin-horns, soldiers, cowboys, and more than a few buffalo men. The town seemed well on its way to becoming the buffalo capital of Texas, and businessmen and entrepreneurs had realized this. Less than two months had passed since I went searching for Coady and Tunequi, but already several frame buildings were being built up and down Front Street, and the makeshift hide yard began towering with stacks of buffalo skins. What the town needed, I found myself thinking as I made my way to John Shannsey's saloon, was a newspaper.

After I opened my carpetbag and pulled out Shannsey's cut of the profits, he poured me a drink, stuffed the greenbacks into a safe behind the bar, and said in an Irish brogue: "I'm glad you dropped in, Griffith, and not just for the money . . . if anyone ever claims it. Been meanin' to speak to you." He closed the safe and turned back to face me. "McIlvain is in town, looking for the kid. Came ridin' in two hours ago. I sent him to the Beehive, but I guess you missed him."

"McIlvain?" I set down the shot glass. "Are you sure?"

"No mistaking him. You can. . . ."

"Dylan!" I whirled at the sound of Sarah's voice. The chatter in the saloon, the piano music, the gambling all stopped as she crashed against a table, and wobbled toward me. Blood poured from her nose, and her eyes were wide. I ran to her, barely managing to catch her before she collapsed.

"He took him," she gasped, her eyes fluttering. I scooped her into my arms, and a half dozen poker players immediately vacated their table, which I gladly used as a bed, laying Sarah down gently. Shannsey had hurdled the bar to help, and he quickly filled a shot glass with brandy. I lifted Sarah's head and gave her a sip.

"Who?" I asked.

"He took Coady!"

"Who did?"

"That man . . . that skinner you had . . . the Yankee with the bad whine."

I cursed Lillard Butler's name. He had to know I was in town with Coady, had likely seen me in the hide yard, bank, or saloons, and wanted that $500 reward. Maybe he knew McIlvain had arrived this afternoon, or maybe not. "He took your rifle, too," Sarah said, "your Sharps. Oh, Dylan."

"It's all right," I told her, but I was already headed outside, asking Shannsey to take care of Sarah. In the gloaming, I looked up and down the crowded streets, trying to think. Butler had my Big Fifty, but I still wore the Colt on my hip, and the Navy in my carpetbag, which I had been carrying around with me all day. I dodged a couple of soldiers, crossed Front Street, and made my way toward the livery stable.

Finding no luck there, I hurried to the wagon yard, where I was met with the same bad fortune. The town wasn't that big, but Butler could have already ridden for Kansas, or parts unknown. Somehow, I didn't think he had left. He had just attacked Sarah and kidnapped the boy, so I guessed he had seen McIlvain, knew Coady's uncle was in town, and wanted to set up a trade. He would have gotten word to McIlvain and arranged a meeting place, only where? I didn't even know what Coady's uncle looked like. John Shannsey had said you couldn't mistake him, but before he could describe him, Sarah had staggered in. I ruled out going back to Shannsey's. I didn't have time to waste. Besides, maybe Lillard Butler had stolen my Sharps rifle for a reason. Sure, he couldn't drop a buffalo cleanly, but he had proved his accuracy by killing antelope and claimed to have served in the Union Army. He might be planning to ambush McIlvain, take the reward money for himself . . . and then what? Kill Coady? A gunshot blasted down an alley, and I jumped, spun around, but a group of laughing waddies emerged, fired another round into the air, and wandered into a gambling den. I could spend all night guessing Butler's plans and jumping at pistols fired drunkenly.

"The hide yard," I said out loud, and ran down Front Street to the edge of town. It seemed the most likely, the least populated spot.

The stacks reached seven feet high—nothing like the towers in Dodge City, but an impressive collection of buffalo hides, nonetheless. Empty wagons and an old corral surrounded the stinking hides, creating a maze now illuminated only by a smattering of lanterns nailed to posts. Two months ago, the hide yard had been a quarter this size; now it had expanded over the grounds where Commodore Gary Monserud once staged his sorry flim-flam circus.

I drew the open-top Colt, stepped over a wagon tongue, placed my carpetbag on the ground, leaned against the nearest hides, and listened, hearing only the buzzing of flies over the stacks and the hubbub of activity back in The Flat's heart. After shoving the spare Navy Colt in my waistband, I stuck my head from behind the cover of buffalo hides, but saw only creeping darkness. I stepped back to the wagon and lifted a lantern off a nail in a post. This wasn't good either, because Lillard Butler would spot me long before I ever got a glimpse of him, but I couldn't think of anything else. I had to see.

Slowly, carefully, I moved down one aisle, holding the

lantern in my left hand, cocked Colt in my right, shining the light at the stacks of hides and shadows. I had broken into a sweat, and my own sour stench almost overpowered the pungent buffalo hides surrounding me.

This could be a waste of time, I thought. *Butler could be miles from here.*

I remember those thoughts clearly, the last crystal memories of that evening.

The rifle shot I never heard.

The next thing I knew I was lying face up, staring at the blackness of night, tasting blood. Maybe I heard running footsteps, or it could have been my head and heart pounding. My head throbbed and burned, and I felt a warm stickiness over my right eye and in my hair. There was light, and smoke. I was sure of the smoke; the light could have been an illusion. I had dropped the lantern when the bullet struck me and could feel the flames from the broken lantern licking at the dry grass. What I couldn't feel were my eyeglasses. Those wire pieces generally pinched the back of my ears fiercely so that the glasses almost never slipped off the bridge of my nose. The impact of the .50-100 slug had knocked off my glasses, I learned later, and had the bullet been an inch more to the left it would have also knocked out my brains.

A face appeared, blurry, frowning. His voice sounded faraway. He moved closer to me, and I tried to place him. He looked familiar, but . . . I blinked.

"Are you The Unknown Scout?" I asked, or at least I tried to. I'm not sure he heard me.

The face vanished. I heard more footsteps, then neither heard nor saw anything.

Chapter Twenty-Three

The flickering glow of a lantern hanging on a pole twenty yards away gave off enough light, and Butler sighted down on the approaching fool wielding another lantern. He had sent word to the man named McIlvain to bring the reward money to the hide yard—and come alone. Coady lay uncomfortably on his back, his mouth gagged with a bandanna and his hands bound tightly behind his back—watching in horror as Lillard Butler brought the stock of the Big Fifty to his shoulder, braced the barrel against the mass of hides, and squeezed the set trigger. Ignoring his hostage, Butler shifted his finger to fire the Sharps. Coady drew up his legs and kicked, knocking Butler aside as he pulled the trigger. The rifle roared, and Coady tried to scramble to his feet, hoping to disappear into the deep recesses of the hide yard, but Butler was too quick, slamming the stock into the small of the boy's back.

"Do that again and I'll kill you, you little runt," snapped Butler, turning his attention to reloading the Sharps. Coady bit his lip to keep from crying out in pain. He refused to give Butler the satisfaction of knowing he had hurt him. Butler turned rapidly, rifle at the ready, and looked down the walkway, where I lay fifty yards away, half dead beside the burning coal oil from the shattered lantern.

"Got him," Butler said with satisfaction. "I'll take that money, then me and you gonna ride up to Kansas, boy, see how much more money your ma's willing to pay." He cradled the Sharps, but footfalls replaced his grin with worry.

That wasn't Coady's uncle bringing the reward, or rather ransom, money. I had beaten McIlvain to the hide yard, had caught a bullet—which wasn't my intention—in his stead. Butler squinted his eyes and swore underneath his breath when he saw a man kneeling over me. The man looked up, and Butler ducked behind the hides, sweating, wetting his lips, trying to think of his next move. He brought up the rifle and peered cautiously around the corner again, but the shadowy figure in the darkness had disappeared. The flames near me had been beaten out, leaving only the eerie light from the haphazardly placed lanterns surrounding the yard.

"On your feet, kid," Butler said hoarsely. "Make a noise and I'll kill you." Coady obeyed, feeling the Sharps barrel against his shoulder blade. "Move, but be quiet, and stop when I tell you to."

Coady's eyes had grown accustomed to the darkness, but patches of the yard turned blacker than midnight, and he had to grope his way along the side, touching the stiff hides for guidance. A faint wind carried the strains of music and laughter from the saloons. That's all Coady heard except for Butler's ragged, nervous breathing.

It grew lighter as they neared the southern end of the stacks, closer to the parked wagons, and, when they came to a place where the pathways intersected, Butler whispered for Coady to stop. With the Sharps digging into his skin, Coady didn't chance running—not yet, at least. Butler stepped around him, and, still hugging the side of the wall reeking of buffalo, he looked around the corner. Satisfied, he stepped aside and told Coady to be quick. With Butler right behind him, Coady hurried across the footpath to another hide shelter. After catching his breath, Butler prodded Coady with the rifle. They moved on.

A pebble skidded across the top of the hides and dropped into the path. Butler, already backing away in a panic, lifted the Sharps in a hurry, and fired blindly into the blackness. Flames from the gunshot blinded both Coady and Butler, and the blast caused Coady's ears to ring. Cursing, Butler flattened himself against the stockpile beside Coady and began fumbling for another cartridge.

He carried no handgun, and Coady realized he should have made a run for it before Butler could reload, which was taking a while. Next time, Coady promised himself. Another pebble skipped over the hide wall closest to Coady and Butler, dropped over the side, and bounced off Coady's hat brim. Butler screamed this time, retreating, lifting the rifle, aiming at some invisible phantom. Coady heard the set trigger *click,* and braced himself to take off running down the pathway as soon as Butler fired.

Only Lillard Butler didn't pull the trigger. Not this time.

The skinner closed in on Coady and shoved him. "Move," he whispered. "We're getting out of here."

They half ran down the path, and the noise from town grew louder. Coady wondered why nobody in The Flat came to the hide yard to investigate, but this was Saturday night in the wickedest town since Sodom, where gunshots occurred frequently, and even ones with murderous intent were seldom investigated until morning.

He could see the exit, lined by two wagons, with a lantern hanging on a pole near the closest one. Butler looked down the pathway, shoved Coady into the clear, and followed. "Run!" he yelled, and Coady did, but tripped over a wagon tongue, landing hard on his shoulder. Butler stopped, tried lifting him by his shirt, but the buttons popped off, and Coady's weight pulled him down. Snorting, Butler gripped harder and jerked. A bullet splintered the side of the wagon, and Butler wheeled, fired, and dived behind the wagon, leaving Coady on his side.

Running footsteps. Coady saw a blurry silhouette emerge from the darkness. A rifle blasted again, and Coady squeezed his eyes shut after the blinding flash. The Big Fifty Butler had stolen answered with a deafening roar. When Coady looked up, and the spots hindering his vision disappeared, the silhouette had vanished.

Lillard Butler reloaded and dashed for Coady. "Come on," he said, and gripped the torn shirt front again with his left hand, awkwardly balancing the cumbersome buffalo rifle in his right. Coady became dead weight, and Butler swore vehemently. Something whistled through the air, Butler looked up, and a loud *whack* followed. "My eye! My eye!" Butler screamed, and Coady felt the flying weapon drop on his chest, bounce, and land at his side. Butler released his grip, fell on his backside, brought the Sharps up, and fired. He scrambled to his feet, forgot all about Coady, and took off running.

Opening his eyes, Coady watched the heavy frame of a man, still only a shadow, step into the light. Mostly he saw colorful spots but could made out the outline of the figure, his hat, and a rifle. His Uncle Thaddeus? There was no way of telling, not in the darkness, not with his eyes rebelling from all the muzzle flashes. Besides, he had not seen his uncle in something like six years. The man ran forward, leaped over Coady, and vanished in the shadows.

Coady shifted to a seated position, and began tugging on the ropes binding his wrists behind his back. The bandanna in his mouth gagged him, and he fought for breath. Suddenly his eyes fell on the chunk that struck Lillard Butler in the face: a piece of hardened wood with a ragged edge where it had been broken. Coady blinked, looked closer.

His vision had cleared, but was his mind playing tricks? It looked like—no, it was—a busted tobacco stick.

The shadowy figure emerged from the shadows alone, and knelt by Coady, cradling a Spencer carbine in his lap while his rough fingers freed Coady from the gag. Coady filled his lungs and stared in disbelief, shock, as the man opened a pocket knife and cut through the hemp rope biting Coady's wrists. A latigo string held the man's hat on his back, revealing a gruesome bald spot on the top of his head. Coady tried to find his voice, but he couldn't be sure. Maybe this was some dream.

"Hello, Coady," the voice said in a soothing Southern accent.

Coady burst into tears and wrapped his arms around his father's neck. "You were dead!" Coady cried. "I saw you killed and scalped."

"I'm alive, son," Brent McIlvain said calmly. "Now be strong, Coady. There's a man back yonder bad hurt. We gotta fetch him a doc."

Brent McIlvain undoubtedly would have been killed if his son had not smashed Ecabapi's face with the tobacco stick that May afternoon of 1873. As it was, Ecabapi and the rest of the war party forgot all about the scalped plow-man and concentrated on capturing the white boy and stealing livestock. McIlvain wasn't the only man to survive a scalping, for I had read newspaper accounts of dozens more and set type myself from one interview in 1871.

Nursed back to health by his wife and children, McIlvain began plans to find his son and ransom him back. Silas Coady arrived in Kansas that winter, and the two began their search in early spring—with little luck because of the uprising and the fact that Coady soon had escaped captivity. After Silas Coady died, McIlvain drifted back toward Indian Territory and didn't learn about my letter to his wife, and the fate of his son, until a letter from her caught up with him at Fort Sill. That's when he rode back to The Flat. I learned all this, along with Coady's version of the events I have described above, while my head wound mended.

As I lay in a bunk next to J. C. Claybrooke, I remembered all the pieces, all the clues I had overlooked. Up at Adobe Walls, when Shorty Shadler had told me that Coady's "pa and a gent named Silas" were trading with the Comanches, looking for the boy, I had corrected him, saying Coady's father was dead and his uncles were leading the search. Colonel Mackenzie had asked if I were Coady's father, and I had thought him trying to catch me in a lie. Others had said similar things, but I hadn't listened—or perhaps I merely hadn't wanted to hear what they said.

The rest could be chalked up to luck. The Shadlers and Billy Tyler had the misfortune to be killed by Indians before I could interview them thoroughly. Kansans gave the attack the misnomer The McIlvain Massacre, even though nary a McIlvain had been killed. That troubled me for a while, festering like a bad wound, until it dawned on me that Westerners always misnamed things, like Running Water, Texas, where I met Mackenzie. These days, I live on Dutch Creek, a place that has never seen any Dutch settlers and even in the wettest of years seldom resembles a creek.

There were more mistakes. Other than talking to John Shannsey, who had been out of town when Coady's uncle died, I hadn't bothered questioning anyone much about Silas Coady and his companion. Had I spent more time in town, making more inquiries, I would have learned the truth. Then again, had I done what I should have done in the first place, had I listened to J. C. Claybrooke, I would have quit running buffalo and brought Coady home right after he wandered into our camp on the *Llano Estacado*.

Doc Kuykendall said the vision in my right eye might always be blurry, and I probably would have trouble hearing out of that ear, but, otherwise, I would heal. Sarah took over, nursing both Claybrooke and myself, while Coady and his father caught up and prepared to leave for home. Lillard Butler had escaped in the dark that night, and Brent McIlvain didn't pursue him. Butler stole a horse and lit a shuck for parts unknown, taking my rifle with him. That troubled me, too. I had planned on giving Coady the Big Fifty. That's why I carved the sentiment in the stock after he shot his first, and only, buffalo.

But Coady didn't care about any rifle. His father was alive.

Sarah was changing my bandage when the McIlvains walked in more than a week after Butler had shot me. They waited until she finished, then she stood, and Coady raced to the chair, sat down, and grasped my hand.

"Sorry about your rifle, Dylan. But the vigilantes have posted Butler for all sorts of crimes. Maybe they'll catch him."

"Maybe." I doubted it, however, and never heard of Lillard Butler again.

"Well, maybe I'll find it for you. Maybe he'll sell it. He's on the run, and he'll need money. 'Sides, he can't shoot as good as you or me with it."

"I'm glad of that," Sarah said.

We talked a bit more, but he soon fell silent, not wanting to say good bye, and I failed to come up with some witty remark. When Brent McIlvain checked his timepiece, Coady blurted out: "Guess it's time to say good bye. Stage leaves in a few minutes." He squeezed tighter. I squeezed back. "Actually, it ain't one stagecoach. We go to Albany, then Fort Worth. Then we take another to Dallas, and then another up to Denison. Did you know that?"

"Nope."

"Then we take a train to Dodge City, though we could 'a' gone on by stagecoach to Dodge City, but that's a lot of traveling." He turned in the chair, and reached across to J. C. Claybrooke, gripping one of his big hands. "I just wanted to tell both of you that you're my best friends, and always will be. I wouldn't be alive if not for y'all."

Claybrooke snorted. I think he might have been crying. "Well, Coady," he said, "we'd be six feet under if not for you."

"Will y'all come visit me?"

"We'll try," we both answered.

"You, too," Coady said, smiling at Sarah. "You're the only person I can beat at checkers."

"I'd be delighted," she said, dabbing her eyes with the hem of her skirt.

"This is for you, Dylan." He reached down and gave me the broken tobacco stick. "I know it ain't much, and I'm sorry I ain't got nothing for you, Mister Claybrooke, or you, Miss Sarah, but, well, I don't know. I thought it might remind you of me, about all our adventures. You might write about 'em someday, put 'em in a book like Mark Twain did."

"Thanks." My vision blurred, not from the gunshot wound, but tears. "But you should keep this. Use it to hunt buffalo when you should be doing chores."

"No," he said, staring at his father. "I got all I need."

He released his grip, and stood. "Well, y'all take care,"

he shot out, voice cracking, and hurried outside.

Sarah had the sniffles, the only sound in the room until Brent McIlvain cleared his throat.

"I posted five hundred dollars for Coady's return," he said, reaching into his vest pocket. "I'm payin' you two."

"No you ain't," answered Claybrooke, his voice surprisingly strong. "You put that money back, or you'll have to fight me."

"Me, too," I added.

The traces of a smile formed at the corners of McIlvain's mouth, and he shoved the money inside. It wouldn't have been much of a fight. In fact, even on our best days, I don't think Brent McIlvain could have worked up a sweat thrashing J. C. Claybrooke and myself.

"Fact is," Claybrooke said, "we planned on giving Coady a share of our buffalo profits. Ain't that right, Dylan?"

I nodded.

"I don't think so," McIlvain answered. "Coady said y'all might try something like that. Coady's taking one robe home, and only one. If any money arrives at my house mysterious-like, it goes in the stove. I appreciate the gesture, gentlemen, but. . . ." He walked forward to shake our weak hands, before tipping his hat at Sarah and heading for the door. "I reckon I'm a lot like my son," he finished. "I've also got all I need."

With that he was gone. The door shut, and a sudden loneliness enveloped me until Sarah sat back down and placed my hand in hers. I had everything I needed, too.

Epilogue

I am old. I thought I was bordering ancient when I ran buffalo with Cuthbert Jenkins, J. C. Claybrooke, and Coady McIlvain, and it's hard to fathom that Coady is now older than I was during our brief spring and summer together.

Reluctantly J. C. Claybrooke and I split the profits from the hides, and the cook left The Flat in September, the month Ranald Mackenzie's forces attacked the Comanche encampment in Palo Duro Cañon, crushing the resistance and, for all intents and purposes, ending the Red River War. I never saw Claybrooke again, but heard that he hired on for some outfit in New Mexico Territory as a cook a few years later. I suppose he's dead and buried by now, or just a crippled, half blind, practically deaf old man like me. John Shannsey departed Fort Griffin before the town began to go bust, and I believe he pocketed the money we agreed would go to any relative of the murdered buffalo runners, although, to be fair, no one ever put in a claim for the cash. Anyway, I lost track of Shannsey, Hanrahan, and most of the buffalo runners I met in 1873 and 1874. Mackenzie went loco, was forced to retire from the Army, and died in 1889. I don't know what became of Lieutenant Percival Wallace, or José Piedad Tafoya for that matter. I read that Billy Dixon got elected sheriff of the newly formed Hutchison County a few years back, but resigned in a huff. Bat Masterson, as you know, became a national hero as a lawman, but he quit the West and moved to New York City in 1902, or thereabouts. Sometimes I miss old Bat and Billy.

More often, I miss the buffalo. They're all but gone, and I regret the part I played in bringing about this tragedy. Of course, my cut of the profits allowed me to open up the first newspaper in Fort Griffin, and the hide business helped the town, and my newspaper circulation and advertising rates grow—at least for a few years. I had spent most of my career setting type for other people's stories, but as the editor and publisher of the *Echo*, I typeset my own articles, including the wedding announcement of one Dylan Griffith and Sarah Elizabeth Cabell. Marrying an ex-prostitute didn't hurt my circulation at all, for Fort Griffin, still known as The Flat, remained the wickedest town since Sodom, but at least its wicked residents loved to read newspapers.

We had a quiet wedding, and Coady chastised me in a letter for not writing him first. He said that he gladly would have given up his chores to stand up for us. He missed us, he wrote, and asked when I would get up to Ford County. I wrote back that we'd see him sometime, but it never came to be. We corresponded for a few years, always threatening a visit, but you know how those things go.

When the hide business began going south, Sarah and I moved to Albany and produced a newspaper there for six more years. I expect The Flat has withered away like old buffalo bones, though I can't say in all certainty as I haven't set foot in Texas in years. Wanderlust sent us farther West. I ran a newspaper in Socorro, New Mexico Territory, from 1885 to 1889, and almost fired a tramp printer there when he used that broken tobacco stick as kindling, but Sarah calmed me down, and he stayed with us till I sold out. We tried Arizona and California, where I set my last type in 1897 and sold the *Murphys Enterprise* and retired. We headed east by train and stopped in Dodge City, where I hoped to find Coady, or someone who knew where he lived.

Although our correspondence had stopped, I had read about Coady on occasion. Quanah and the last free band of Kwahadi Comanches surrendered to Mackenzie in 1875 at Fort Sill in Indian Territory, and five years later Coady began working on the reservation as an assistant to the Indian agent. He lived at Anadarko for a while, then dropped out of the newspapers, not that he was written about much.

Dodge City had not died. The wooden façades and tent saloons that once lined Front Street had been replaced by tall buildings made of brilliant red brick. Few people remembered The McIlvain Massacre, or the McIlvains, but I learned from the *Globe*'s affable *emeritus* editor that Brent McIlvain had died during the blizzard of '88, and his wife followed him the next spring of influenza. The McIlvain daughters, I was told, had married off long before then, and the farm had been sold, the profits split among the heirs. Coady had received his third, but the newspaperman had no idea where any of the three had settled.

While in Dodge, I checked the gun shops, something I did in every town I visited, or lived in, searching for that Sharps rifle with the sentiment carved into the stock. Zimmermann's was gone—Fred had died back in 1888—and none of the new places carried old buffalo rifles. Whenever I asked some gunsmith, broker, collector, or antiquary, I was met with bewildered stares. I finally quit looking for both the Sharps and Coady McIlvain.

So Sarah and I settled here along Dutch Creek, near her old home. Visitors are few, except on the holidays, which is how we like it, which brings me to the end of my story.

It was the day before Thanksgiving last when a package arrived, a heavy, long box, which Mr. Ferguson, who delivered it from town, carried inside since I was of little use because of my arthritic hands. After Mr. Ferguson cut away the box, Sarah unwrapped the crinkling paper, stepped back, and said: "Oh, my."

Well, I knew what it was before she looked up at me, her eyes welling with tears. I hurried over, peered inside at a rusted old Sharps rifle, and leaned forward, squinting at the faded carving in the weathered, broken stock.

Coady M.
Killed His First Buffalo
With This Rifle
Texas, 1874

Wagon traces jingled outside. Sarah said—"They're here."—found her cane, and she and Mr. Ferguson left me alone with the rifle. I heard children's laughter, and Sarah's voice, and more talk. They were giving me time to myself, which was nice of them. Underneath the rifle I spotted an envelope, which I grabbed, sending flakes of rust everywhere. Limping over to my chair, I cut open the envelope with a fingernail, pulled out the paper, and began reading, trying to block out the laughter, the singsong chatter, the slamming of our screen door, and small footsteps racing up and down the hallway, a woman's intonation to quit running inside, and Sarah's jovial reply.

5 November 1904
Dear Dylan:

I know you will be surprised to hear from me, as it has been far too many years. But you see I finally did find your Big Fifty. It seems like only yesterday that we were out chasing the great herds. Well, I'm not much for writing, but I will say that I had a devil of a

time tracking you down. But I'm happy to have suc-
ceeded, and trust this finds you in good health.

You may know that I worked at the Anadarko
agency with Quanah and the Comanches, but I bet
you didn't know that I married Tunequi. If that shock
doesn't send you to Glory, this one might. You'll
never guess what I'm doing.

Give up? . . . Well, I'm a farmer. Try to figure that
one out, huh. We live just outside Kearney, Nebraska, and we had a great alfalfa crop this year, two
years running in fact. I won't bore you with farming
stories. Anyway, I went to Cody, Wyoming, this year
for my grandson's christening. That's right. I'm a
grandfather at 43. My daughter works at the Irma
Hotel, and you should see that place, Dylan. It's fabulous. What's more, when I was there I met William
F. Cody, the one and true Buffalo Bill, in the bar.
When he heard my name, he bought me a drink. I
told him all about our adventures, but I doubt if he
believed one word because he said, after three more
rounds, that I spin better yarns than he ever dreamed
of telling.

I also found this rifle in Cody. Don't ask me how it
got there. The man I bought it from didn't know, said
it had been in his shop for years and there wasn't
much demand for worthless rifles in Wyoming, or
anywhere else for that matter. It's a pity no one took
better care of her. You'll see that the tang sight was
broken off, the silver sight's gone, and the whole
thing's rusted out and ruined. I'm not ashamed to tell
you how I cried when I got it back to my room in the
hotel. So I started looking for you. It's your rifle. I'm
sure this old gun will bring back a flood of memories,

some sad, bittersweet, but many of them fond. Well, it did for me.

So let's not be strangers now that we've found each other again. One of these days, I'll be knocking on your door. Meanwhile, you can write, too, can't you?

Your best friend always,
Coady McIlvain

"What's this?"

I looked up to find a rather handsome man, if I do say so myself, hefting the old Sharps, trying to read the carving in the stock. After fetching a hanky and blowing my nose, I folded the letter, pried myself out of the chair, and hobbled over. The children had stopped running down the hall, and women's voices came from the kitchen. I smelled coffee brewing.

"That's the Big Fifty I ran buffalo with," I said, "many years ago. You've heard me talk about those days. I want you to have it. I mean, it's useless, can't be shot any more, but . . ."

"Where did you get it?"

"It came from an old friend," I told my son. "The man you're named after."

Author's Note

I'm a fair hand with a rifle, but don't sign me up for any sharpshooting competitions. So, while researching THE BIG FIFTY, I sought out 21st Century Old West marksmen for information on Sharps rifles. George Glenn of the National Congress of Old West Shootists and Bruce H. Thorstad, who won the Single Action Shooting Society's End of Trail's Top Gun title in 1989 and 1990, were kind enough to teach me a little about Sharps and long-distance shooting. Of course, George Glenn actually prefers the Remington Rolling Block, but, as I explained to him, REMINGTON ROLLING BLOCK just doesn't have the kick of THE BIG FIFTY, title-wise. They're responsible for any strengths in the firearms department this novel has. Blame me for the errors and weaknesses.

The use of Buffalo Bill Cody's dime novels is literary license. The first bits of fiction written under Cody's name actually appeared a couple of years after this novel opens. DEADLY EYE; OR, THE UNKNOWN SCOUT, the third Cody novel, was originally published in 1875 by the *Saturday Journal* and did not appear as one of Beadle's Half-Dime Library titles until August 13, 1878. I'm not even sure as to the plot of that five-penny dreadful, so I made that up to fit in with my own novel's narrative. Cody's other titles mentioned in this novel, also, are used fictitiously, and many were not published by Beadle's.

Quanah Parker existed in history, of course, as did Fred Zimmermann, Jim Hanrahan, Bat Masterson, Billy Dixon, and many characters mentioned in the Adobe Walls attack. Likewise, Ranald Mackenzie and José Piedad Tafoya were real people. All main characters, however, are figments of my imagination.

For readers interested in learning the truth about the buffalo runners and the Indian uprising, my recommendations include: IN SEARCH OF THE BUFFALO: THE STORY OF J. WRIGHT MOOAR by Charles G. Anderson (Pioneer Press, 1996); THE BORDER AND THE BUFFALO by John R. Cook (State House Press, 1989); THE BUFFALO WAR by James L. Haley (University of Oklahoma Press, 1976); THE BUFFALO HUNTERS by Charles M. Robinson III (State House Press, 1995); SHARPS RIFLE: THE GUN THAT SHAPED AMERICAN DESTINY by Martin Rywell (Pioneer Press, 1979); and THE BUFFALO HUNTERS by Mari Sandoz (University of Nebraska Press, 1954). All were invaluable resources for this novel. The award-winning THE BUFFALO RUNNERS by Fred Grove, colleague, mentor, and friend, is one of the best novels ever penned on the subject, and I highly recommend it.

My sources for Dodge City were QUEEN OF THE COWTOWNS: DODGE CITY by Stanley Vestal (Dutton, 1928), DODGE CITY: UP THROUGH A CENTURY IN STORY AND PICTURES by Fredric R. Young (Boot Hill Museum, 1972), and assorted trips over the years to "The Wickedest Little City in America". Comanche life and language can be examined in THE COMANCHES: LORDS OF THE SOUTH PLAINS by Ernest Wallace and E. Adamson Hoebel (University of Oklahoma Press, 1986) and COMANCHE VOCABULARY: TRILINGUAL EDITION, compiled by Manuel García Rejón and translated and edited by Daniel J. Gelo (University of Texas

Press, 1985). I have read several biographies of Quanah Parker; among the best are THE LAST COMANCHE CHIEF: THE LIFE AND TIMES OF QUANAH PARKER by Bill Neely (John Wiley & Sons, 1995), QUANAH PARKER, COMANCHE CHIEF by William T. Hagan (University of Oklahoma Press, 1993), and QUANAH, THE EAGLE OF THE COMANCHES by Zoe A. Tilghman (Harlow Publishing, 1938).

Lastly, I would be remiss if I did not thank Dean and Tate Wilkinson of Austin, Texas—ages twelve and eight when I started this novel. Many thanks also to their parents, David and Bonnie, for letting me use Dean and Tate as models for Coady McIlvain and allowing me to transport them to the 1870s.

Johnny D. Boggs
Santa Fé, New Mexico

About the Author

In addition to writing Western novels, *Johnny D. Boggs* has covered all aspects of the American West for newspapers and magazines on topics ranging from travel to book and movie reviews, to celebrity and historical profiles, to the apparel industry and environmental issues. Born in South Carolina in 1962, he published his first Western short story in 1983 in the University of South Carolina student literary magazine. Since then, he has had more than twenty short stories published in magazines and anthologies, including *Louis L'Amour Western Magazine*. After graduating from the University of South Carolina College of Journalism in 1984, Boggs moved to Texas to begin a newspaper career. He started as a sportswriter for the *Dallas Time Herald* in 1984 and was assistant sports editor when the newspaper folded in 1991. From 1992 to 1998, he worked for the *Fort Worth Star-Telegram*, leaving the newspaper as assistant sports editor to become a full-time writer and photographer. Boggs's first novel was HANNAH AND THE HORSEMAN (1997). His first non-fiction book was THAT TERRIBLE TEXAS WEATHER (2000), a history of some of the worst natural disasters in the state from the 1800s to the present. He is a frequent contributor to *Boys' Life*, *Wild West*, *True West*, and other publications. His photos have often accompanied his newspaper and magazine articles, as well as appearing on the covers of many Five Star, Thorndike, and G.K. Hall titles. He won a Spur Award from Western Writers of America for his short story,

"A Piano at Dead Man's Crossing" in 2002. Subsequent novels have included THE LONESOME CHISHOLM TRAIL (Five Star Westerns, 2000), a trail drive story, and LONELY TRUMPET (Five Star Westerns, 2002), an historical novel about Lieutenant Henry O. Flipper, the first black graduate of West Point. Boggs lives in Santa Fe, New Mexico, with his wife, Lisa Smith, and son, Jack. His next Five Star Western will be PURGATOIRE.